Anne Allen lives in I
daughter and grandchildren
number of moves, the lo
fourteen years after falling
people. She contrived to l
valid reason for frequent i   ....u in
London, ideal for her city b.....s. A retired psychotherapist,
Anne has now published nine novels. Find her website at
www.anneallen.co.uk

Praise for Anne Allen

Dangerous Waters - 'A wonderfully crafted story with a perfect balance of intrigue and romance.' *The Wishing Shelf Awards, 22 July 2013 – Dangerous Waters*

Finding Mother - 'A sensitive, heart-felt novel about family relationships, identity, adoption, second chances at love… With romance, weddings, boat trips, lovely gardens and more, Finding Mother is a dazzle of a book, a perfect holiday read.' *Lindsay Townsend, author of The Snow Bride*

Guernsey Retreat- 'I enjoyed the descriptive tour while following the lives of strangers as their worlds collide, when the discovery of a body and the death of a relative draw them into links with the past. A most pleasurable, intriguing read.' *Glynis Smy, author of Maggie's Child.*

The Family Divided -'A poignant and heart-warming love story.' *Gilli Allan, author of Fly or Fall*

Echoes of Time - 'Not only is the plot packed full of twists and turns, but the setting – and the characters – are lovingly described.' *Wishing Shelf Review*

The Betrayal – 'All in all, totally unputdownable!' *thewsa.co.uk*

The Inheritance -'A gorgeously intriguing story set in a beautiful location. I completely identified with contemporary heroine Tess and Victorian heroine Eugénie.' *Margaret James, author of The Final Reckoning.*

Her Previous Self - The haunting tale of two women divided by time, yet with the power to set each other free. A gripping read. *Nicola Pryce, author of A Cornish Betrothal*

Also by Anne Allen

Dangerous Waters

Finding Mother

Guernsey Retreat

The Family Divided

Echoes of Time

The Betrayal

The Inheritance

Her Previous Self

The Ghost of Seagull Cottage

Anne Allen

The Guernsey Novels – Book 9

Sarnia Press
London

In memory of my mother, Janet Williams, with love

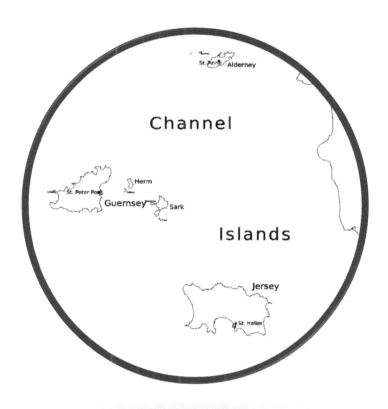

Chapter 1

Guernsey, Spring 2015

Annabel stood by the rickety gate, gazing across the road to the bay, a languid scene of soft waves curling on the shore and colourful little boats bobbing on the water. She took a deep breath of the salt-laden air and smiled. Yes, she had been right to come back to Guernsey and hopefully this cottage would be the haven she had been seeking since…

'Mrs Easton? Are you ready to view inside?' The agent's voice broke into her thoughts and she turned to him and smiled.

'Sorry, admiring the view. Please, lead the way.'

The detached granite cottage was of a traditional Guernsey design, with a central front door and porch and matching windows upstairs and downstairs and with the addition of a small bay window in the attic.

'It's a little tired, which is reflected in the rent, but it does possess a modern kitchen, bathroom and central heating,' the agent, Jon, continued, stepping into the hall. He led the way to the back, presumably keen to show her how wonderful the kitchen was compared to the tired rooms. Although not a great cook, Annabel was pleased to see the gleaming cupboards and appliances, some still bearing manufacturers' labels. Catching her eye, Jon grinned. 'Yes, brand new. The cottage has been in the same family since it was built by the original owner in 1925. It's been inherited by a relative who lives in Australia. He sees it as a long-term investment and took our advice with regard to some improvements.' After giving her time to inspect the kitchen he led the way to the room opposite set out as a dining room with old-fashioned dark, furniture.

'If the furniture's a problem we can have it removed.'

He waved his arm.

Annabel heard a whooshing noise as if someone brushed past her but there was only her and Jon, who by his startled expression had also heard something.

'It's okay, I could live with it. A nice, colourful tablecloth would brighten up the room.' It was a good size with a window overlooking the rear garden and she could perk it up with her paintings on the walls. 'Shall we carry on?'

The young man almost ran down the hall to a room on the right, overlooking the front garden with a glimpse of the sea beyond. Furnished with a sagging sofa and armchairs, it was at least inoffensive and more modern in style and Annabel could see it would be a cosy sitting room.

'And now we have a room which can be either a sitting room or a bedroom, depending on the size of your family.' It was similar in size to the room opposite but contained a single bed, wardrobe and set of drawers. All heavy Edwardian.

'Ah, I wouldn't need it as a bedroom as I believe there are two upstairs. There's only myself and my daughter. She could have it as a playroom. Without the furniture, of course.' Again Annabel was aware of a whoosh of air and she felt the hair on the back of her neck stand on end.

'What's that whooshing I keep hearing?'

Jon shifted his feet. 'I've no idea, Mrs Easton. Perhaps a bird's got in and trying to escape.' Annabel didn't believe him but shrugged her shoulders. She really liked the cottage and, more importantly, it was about the only one she could afford for the size and location.

'Let's go upstairs, shall we?'

She followed him up the stairs, admiring the workmanship of the mahogany handrail and spindles. Someone had spent more time and money on them than was usual for a relatively humble cottage. Upstairs, at the back Annabel smiled as the agent threw open the door to a fully tiled and well equipped bathroom with a shower cubicle and a bath.

And then the two bedrooms, both at the front.

'This is the master bedroom, and as you can see it's a good size and with sea views.' The agent waved his arm towards the window in emphasis. Annabel's eyes, however, were drawn towards a large oil painting hanging on the wall opposite the iron framed bed. It was of a sailor in a Guernsey woollen jumper and serge jacket and offering a glimpse of his dark curls under a jaunty cap. He was sporting the ubiquitous dark beard and smoking a pipe. The arresting features were his eyes. A piercing blue, they seemed to follow her as she moved around the room.

'Whoever is this chap? It's been badly painted and not something you want in a bedroom.' This time the whoosh was louder and she thought she heard a voice shout, 'Get out of my house, woman!' She blinked and turned towards Jon who had grown pale.

'I… I believe he's Captain Daniel Gallienne, the original owner who… who built the cottage.'

Something clicked in her head. Could it be? Surely not! This was the twenty-first century not something out of a Victorian novel.

'Is it possible this captain haunts the place? Is that why the rent is so low?' She risked a quick look at the painting, before turning to face the poor agent.

'Well, there have been rumours, but nobody admits to actually seeing him. Until now all those who've lived here were descended from his sister, there's never been any… any strangers.'

'I see. And when did this captain die? Must have been some time ago, surely?'

'Yes, not long after the Second World War. In his forties, I think. Look, Mrs Easton,' he said, fiddling with his folder, 'I'm sorry if you've been upset and I quite understand if you don't wish to see anymore and leave—'

'Oh, I'm not upset though I'm not sure what I feel. Shocked and… strange. But I don't want to be put off by someone who's been dead nearly seventy years.' She glanced around the spacious room with the enticing sea view. 'I really like the cottage and I'm sure we could be very happy here. Can you show me the rest, please?' Annabel gave him her warmest smile as he nodded and hurried out of the room, closing the door behind them. The other bedroom was slightly smaller but would be fine for Emilia though the furniture would not suit a ten-year-old, which thought she kept to herself. The window framed a similar view, with a window seat ideal for Emilia to sit and read. Perfect.

They then went upstairs to what appeared to have been used as a lookout, the light pouring into a room furnished with a table and armchair and with a splendid brass telescope taking pride of place in the bay window.

'Oh, how wonderful! This would make a great studio for my painting.' She moved towards the telescope. 'May I take a look?' Jon nodded, looking as if he'd rather be outside. After adjusting the lens, Annabel had a clear view over to Herm and close-ups of the little boats she had seen earlier. The captain must have spent many pleasant hours up here gazing out to sea, she thought.

A voice hissed in her ear, 'Be careful with my telescope!' She looked around but she was alone, the agent had left and was clattering down the stairs.

'I'll be careful, don't worry,' she whispered back.

And then she saw him.

Standing inches away, dressed in the seaman's jersey, jacket and trousers as in the portrait and with his blue eyes locked on hers.

'Oh my God, are you real?' she asked, her heart thumping and her mouth suddenly dry. She had to hold onto the telescope as her legs wobbled.

'As real as any ghost can be, I reckon. I come and go as I please. This is still my home, you know, and I don't want a stranger living in it.' His eyes blazed and she stepped back, forcing herself to remain calm. How on earth could she be talking to a ghost? Was she mad? The sound of the front door opening and closing told her Jon had gone outside and she was left alone with someone who appeared perfectly normal, if a little old-fashioned in his outfit, with dark hair and the most startling blue eyes she had ever seen. Except he was apparently dead.

A ghost.

'Well, woman? Cat got your tongue has it? Or are you too scared to say anything?' He stood, relaxed, with his arms crossed and a smile hovering around his mouth.

'No, I'm not… scared. Surprised, yes. I've not seen a ghost before, let alone talked to one. In fact, to be honest, I've never believed in them.' She took a deep breath. Perhaps she was actually mad. Or she was dreaming and would wake up and all would be as it was. Normal.

'And I'd like you to know I plan to move in with my daughter as I think your cottage is lovely and it's just what I need right now. Life's been a… bit difficult lately and to be honest, I can't afford anything else. Except a small flat, and we would hate that.' To her horror, Annabel felt tears prick her eyes and she hastily brushed them away.

'My dear woman, no need for tears. Can't abide a woman crying. And of course a flat wouldn't do for a child. Children need to run around outside.' He stroked his beard, looking thoughtful. 'To be frank, I was hoping I'd scare you away as I have the others, leaving me in peace. But perhaps we could rub along if we have to. Reach some sort of agreement. What d'ya say?'

Annabel gazed at him open-mouthed. It was all so surreal. She nodded, giving herself time to think.

'I don't want you scaring Emilia, she's only ten, so if you could agree to stay away from downstairs and her room it might work. Where and when do you normally… er, show up?'

'I've never been restricted before, seeing as how family lived here. But I suppose I could make do with only coming in the evenings and to this room and my bedroom. Not much at all, considering.'

'Ah, but your bedroom will be my bedroom and I'm not sure I'd like the idea of you popping in when I'm getting ready for bed.' She felt herself flush at the thought.

'Don't be silly, woman, there's no need to get all coy with me! I've no physical body, you're only seeing me because I chose to let you, wanting to scare you. I haven't the ability or the usual desires a man might have in that direction.' He glared at her. 'I suppose we should introduce ourselves. Daniel Gallienne.'

'Mrs Annabel Easton.'

He bowed his head. 'Pleased to meet you. Are you a widow? No mention of a husband.'

'I am a widow, yes—'Annabel was interrupted by the agent shouting up the stairs.

'Are you all right, Mrs Easton? I've been waiting for you in the garden.'

She moved to the door.

'Yes, I'm fine. Coming now.'

When she turned round the room was empty.

Chapter 2

By the time Annabel joined Jon in the garden she had managed to regain some of her usual appearance of calm but inside she was rattled. Rattled by the unwanted intrusion into what she perceived as her new beginning with Emilia; one which excluded interference by well-meaning but overbearing relatives of her late husband and any others who might want to invade the peace she craved. And which most definitely included a ghost. A ghost who could take on his human form at will and tantalise her with those piercing blue eyes which she could have sworn could see into her soul. Or worse.

'Mrs Easton, what took you so long? At one point I thought I heard voices, were you on the phone?' Jon was hopping up and down on the grassed area at the back of the cottage, running his hand through his hair as he avoided her eyes.

'I wasn't on the phone as you well know. That... ghost turned up trying to scare me off. But I've decided to take the cottage in spite of him, and I'd like some of the heavy furniture removed and I'll buy new.' Taking a deep breath, she went on, 'I want to move in by the end of the month, if that's possible.' Annabel fixed her own wide blue eyes on him and he stood still.

'I'm sorry I wasn't completely honest with you, but my boss insisted. We've had the cottage on our books for months now and it doesn't look good in a small place like Guernsey not to be able to shift properties quickly. Under... normal circumstances Seagull Cottage would have been let within the first day.' He appeared to summon up some of his lost credibility. 'But are you really sure you want to move in? We'd happily arrange about the furniture, but you're a woman on your own and, well...' He shrugged his shoulders, as if to say he thought she was mad.

'Don't worry, I won't come to any harm, if that's what bothers you. Now, I'd like to see more of this garden before we return to your office for the paperwork. I'm happy for you to lock up and wait in your car if you'd rather. Won't be long.' She smiled as he shot off to lock the doors as she walked to the bottom of the garden, admiring the shrubs and spring flowers making a colourful display next to what had been a neat vegetable patch. Not much of a gardener herself, she could still appreciate the work of others and would try to keep the garden in good order during her tenancy as it was as lovely as the cottage itself and offering a safe place for Emilia to play.

As she walked round to the front garden she couldn't help look up and thought she caught a glimpse of a bearded face in the lookout. It was only a second and then it disappeared. Annabel whispered, 'Well, Captain Daniel Gallienne, I do hope you'll stick to our agreement as I think I'm going to love living in your cottage.' A deep laugh by her ear was her answer.

Later that day Annabel boarded the flight for Manchester having signed the tenancy agreement for Seagull Cottage and paid a hefty deposit. Settling into her seat she knew she had made the right decision to move back to her birthplace, even though she had left when she was not much older than Emilia. Her parents, growers of the De La Mare Nurseries in La Moye in the Vale, had upped sticks when the growing business was declining. She had been heartbroken at the time, but her father had taken up the offer of a well-paid job as manager of a large nursery in Kent. It hadn't been too bad, she reflected now, and she had always held onto her memories of what had been an idyllic childhood with many hours spent on the beach at L'Ancresse, particularly during the holidays. It was what she wanted for her daughter, who had only known the suburbs of Manchester thanks to her husband Clive's job as a sales manager for a catering company in the north. Miles away from their first home in Devon near the sea.

'Do you really have to take it, Clive? Surely something will turn up near here if we hang on a bit longer.' Annabel, five months pregnant and coping with upsurges of hormones, had pleaded with Clive for hours to change his mind, but he kept saying he couldn't afford not to take it and as her art wasn't bringing in much money back then, his salary was all important. She had stifled the thought he was keen to take the job because it meant moving near to his family, who idolised him as the only son. Her own parents had retired to Australia to join her mother's brother and his family and she missed them more than ever now she was about to become a mother.

Well, now she was free to make her own decisions and she couldn't wait to come back with Emilia and move into the lovely cottage near the sea. Closing her eyes she drifted into a light sleep and found herself dreaming of a dashing sailor with the brightest of blue eyes...

Chapter 3

The end of the month saw Annabel and an excited, though somewhat nervous, Emilia, arrive at Seagull Cottage with all their worldly goods following close behind in a van.

'Well, Emilia, what do you think?' Annabel put her arm around her daughter as they stood at the gate and took in the front of the cottage, looking prettier than ever with pink clematis curling around the front door. She risked a glance upstairs, but no face appeared. Yet.

'It looks lovely, Mummy, and I can't wait to go on the beach.' Emilia's face was lit with excitement and her dark blue eyes shone. She had always been a happy child but even before her father's death a year ago had become withdrawn. Annabel's heart lifted at the sight of her obvious joy.

'The beach will have to wait for the moment, sweetheart, as we have to get the cottage shipshape to live in.' She caught her breath. Where did that come from? "Shipshape" wasn't something she would normally say. Glancing again at the upstairs windows, she held her breath. Nothing. With a sigh she grabbed Emilia's hand, saying, 'Race you to the front door.' Laughing, her daughter let go and sped off down the path. As Annabel unlocked the door the removal van arrived and the all-consuming task of moving in began. Emilia ran around exploring all the rooms before waiting impatiently for her belongings and new furniture to be unloaded and carried up to her room, clapping her hands in excitement when she spotted them. Annabel showed the men where everything went before going downstairs to concentrate on the boxes piling up in the kitchen. Fortunately there wasn't a great deal of furniture; she had ordered herself a new bed and matching wardrobe and chest of drawers and new furniture for Emilia's room. Otherwise it was only her easel and sundry items to be scattered around the cottage. She had brought few memories of the past.

The removal men left after making sure the bedroom furniture was set up in the right place and, leaving Emilia to unpack her clothes, Annabel went across to her own bedroom. It looked very different with modern furniture though cluttered with cases and boxes. It was a moment before she spotted him. Peeking out behind a stack of boxes, the blue-eyed stare was unmistakeable. Her stomach clenched and she was about to tell Daniel to go away when she realised it was the painting she could see. She had meant to ask the men to remove it – the frame was large and heavy – but in the flurry of activity had forgotten. As a temporary measure she pulled out a large shawl from her suitcase and draped it over the painting.

'There, that's better. I'll have you moved later,' she said to herself.

A whoosh of air causing the shawl to flutter was her answer. Then a whisper in her ear, 'That's not very friendly, but I'll let you settle in, m'dear. Bye for now.' A low laugh then silence.

Her immediate reaction was did Emilia hear anything? Going to the door she stood listening as her daughter could be heard singing to herself as she unpacked. Good. But she was annoyed with Daniel for hanging around, invisible but making his presence felt. All she could do was focus on making her bed and packing away as many clothes as possible to avoid bumping into boxes. As the room slowly became her own she calmed down and began to enjoy the thought of living there. Even though it might mean sharing with a bossy ghost. It still felt surreal and something out of a book, rather than her own life. Annabel consoled herself with the thought that if the ghost proved too much to handle, she could call in a priest to exorcise him, or whatever they did with ghosts.

It wasn't long before Emilia announced she was bored

with unpacking and could they go to the beach. Annabel was glad of the break and they grabbed the brand new bucket and spade and a rug and left. The cottage was near a bend on the Rue de Bordeaux, quite a popular road in the north of the island and Annabel held her daughter's hand tightly as they crossed the road to the beach. The tide was out and Emilia rushed down to the wet sand, laughing and waving the bucket and spade, and Annabel's spirits soared as she took off her shoes ready for a paddle. It had been so long since she had seen her daughter so relaxed and happy and the mood was catching. After a quick paddle – the water was freezing – they settled down to build a sandcastle with a moat. There were few others on the beach even though it was the Easter holidays and it seemed almost as if this was their own private beach.

'Mummy, there's a little kiosk at the end of the car park. Do you think they sell ice cream?' Emilia waved her spade in emphasis and Annabel laughed.

'I'm pretty sure they do but once we've eaten our ice creams it'll be time to go back home. I've a lot of unpacking to do, young lady, even if you haven't.'

Once they were back in the cottage, Annabel let Emilia watch the television the removal men had connected for them while she unpacked more boxes in the kitchen. She was down to the last couple when she noticed it was gone six o'clock and her daughter's tea time. Deciding pasta would be a quick solution she boiled a kettle of water and poured it on the pasta in the saucepan. When she went to switch on the hob nothing happened. After fiddling for a few moments she muttered 'damn' under her breath and a voice in her ear said, 'There's a switch in the cupboard next to the cooker. You might need to switch it on, first.'

She jumped and looked around. No-one.

'Daniel! Is that you?' she hissed. 'We agreed you'd keep out of the rooms downstairs so as not to scare Emilia.'

'Yes, but I'm not visible, am I? And I noticed when the men fitted the cooker they wired it to some sort of switch down here.' The cupboard opened as if on its own and Annabel peered in and, lo and behold there was a switch in the off position. After switching it on, she tried the hob again and it worked. She didn't know whether to be relieved or angry.

'Have you been in here watching me since we got back?'

'Not exactly. I was minding my own business in my lookout when I saw you return and then I heard clattering and banging in the kitchen and thought I should see if you were all right.' She heard a deep chuckle. 'I can't help feeling a bit responsible for you, y'know, as your landlord.'

Annabel went to check Emilia was still engrossed in the television before coming back and closing the kitchen door.

'Look, Daniel, I know you think of this cottage as your own, but it isn't. Some relative of yours in Australia owns it and can sell it tomorrow if he wishes. Or perhaps not now I have a lease for at least a year.' She took a deep breath. It wasn't easy talking to someone you couldn't see and was, by their own admission, a ghost who had been dead seventy years. 'I... I came here to make a new start for my daughter and me after a bad few years and it's going to be almost impossible to relax and enjoy our new home if I'm wondering if you're following me around, unseen, and can pop up at any time. And you did promise—'

For a moment she saw a hazy outline of him leaning against the fridge, his arms crossed, as if he hadn't a care in the world. Which, of course, he hadn't.

'I'm sorry if I've upset you, m'dear, but I've been used to coming and going as I've wished for so long it's difficult to break the habit. I will try to keep out of your way and let you enjoy my – your home.' She saw him rub his beard as he continued to stare at her. 'Had a bad time, eh? Something to do with your late husband, I'll be bound. Unfaithful was he? Though why any man in his right mind would cheat on a woman with your looks, I can't imagine. If you'd been my wife—'

'He did not cheat on me! Not that it's any of your

business and as I understand it, you never married. One of those sailors with a girl in every port, I expect.' Flushed, she turned her attention to the pasta bubbling away on the hob and strained it ready to stir in the ready-made sauce. 'Excuse me, I need to get something,' she indicated the fridge and he moved away. Only a few inches and she was aware of his eyes following her every move as she reached for the sauce.

'This is ridiculous! Please leave me alone to make my child's supper.'

'All right, I'll go. And, for the record, I didn't have a girl in every port; there were only ever two or three at any time.' With that his image faded and there was a rush of air going out the open window. Annabel took deep breaths as she dished up the pasta, adding grated cheese before taking it on a tray into the sitting room.

'Pasta's ready and for a treat I'll let you eat it in here while I do some more unpacking. Watch you don't get any sauce on the sofa, mind, as it's not ours.'

Emilia nodded her thanks, eyes glued to the latest episode of *Horrible Histories*. Annabel returned to the kitchen to unpack the last two boxes, all the while alert for any sound or sight of Daniel. But he seemed to have left and she began to relax and when she unpacked a small portable radio she tuned it into GuernseyFM for some lively pop music. After checking on Emilia, she went upstairs to her bedroom to tackle more boxes. This time she was undisturbed and after an hour or so she went downstairs to announce it was bedtime. After an initial 'must I?' Emilia gave in, admitting she was tired after what had been a long and exciting day. It didn't take long for her to wash and change and was soon snuggled in her new bed, too tired to read as she usually did. A hug and goodnight kiss and then Annabel left to prepare her own supper. She struggled to keep her eyes open after the meal, washed down with a hearty red wine, and it was not much after nine when she made her own way upstairs to bed.

The room looked pretty and more spacious with the new cream painted furniture, even with a few boxes still unpacked. Before she undressed, Annabel switched off the light and went over to the window to take a look at the night-time view. One or two boats had their lights showing as they prepared to go out fishing and she could just make out some lights on Herm. It was a beautiful and peaceful scene and she felt lucky it was to be her view for at least the next year. Yawning, she closed the curtains and switched on the lights.

'Good God, woman, you've turned my room into a tart's boudoir! And why have you covered up m'portrait?' Daniel, looking as solid as herself, stood in the middle of the room, arms outstretched and eyes blazing.

Annabel exploded. '*My* bedroom is furnished for a lady of good taste and not some floozy you bedded when in port. And the dark, old furniture which was here was well past its use-by date. We're living in the twenty-first century now not the early twentieth.' She paused. 'Your portrait will be coming down as soon as I find someone to give me a hand. No disrespect to yourself, but it's not what I want looking down at me when I'm in bed. I'll hang one of my own paintings instead.' She took a calming breath. 'And why are you here? I asked you to give me some space and I'm tired and want to go to bed.' Suddenly exhaustion washed over her and she slumped onto the bed, desperate for sleep and closed her eyes.

'You've had a long day, which explains you getting upset so easily,' Daniel said, in the sort of tone she would use to sooth Emilia, 'so I'll let you get to bed and promise not to come back this evening. Goodnight, Mrs Easton.' She felt a slight touch on her hand and when she opened her eyes she was alone. Pulling off her clothes, she crawled under the duvet and was soon asleep.

Chapter 4

'Mummy, Mummy! Come on, it's time to get up and the sun is shining. Can we go to the beach, please?'

Annabel rolled over and groaned. Every muscle ached from all the unpacking and running up and down the stairs of the previous day. Opening her eyes she was greeted by a pyjama-clad Emilia trying to pull the duvet off the bed. The light in the room was dim and she had to squint to read the time on her watch on the bedside cabinet 6.45. So much for the anticipated lie-in of the school holiday.

'Morning, young lady. I don't suppose you checked the time before rushing in to wake me up, did you? The golden rule on non-school days is Mummy has a lie-in until at least eight o'clock. A quarter to seven doesn't come close, does it?' She sat up and ruffled Emilia's long dark hair.

'Sorry, Mummy, I thought it was later. Do you want me to go back to bed?' She looked so crestfallen with her lower lip wobbling that Annabel had to smile.

'No, run along and get dressed while I have a shower. But the beach will have to wait until I've unpacked some more boxes which will be quicker if you help me.' Emilia agreed and left her to get up and head to the bathroom.

They had finished breakfast and started on the boxes when the doorbell rang. Glancing at her watch she noted it was not quite nine. Who on earth? Opening the door Annabel was greeted by a short, smiling woman who she guessed to be in her early thirties.

'Hi, I know it's early but I've just dropped my daughter off at nursery and saw you move in yesterday and couldn't wait to introduce myself. Colette Simon, and I live two doors away,' she waved to her right, 'and I've brought you this to welcome you.' She pushed a casserole dish towards her and Annabel was almost too overcome to speak.

'That's so kind of you, Colette. I'm Annabel Easton and this is Emilia,' nodding towards her daughter. 'Please, come on in and I'll make some coffee.'

'Thank you.'

Colette followed her into the kitchen as she put the casserole on the worktop before putting the kettle on.

'It's a vegetarian casserole to be on the safe side and don't worry, I'm a chef with my own restaurant so no fear of food poisoning!'

Annabel found herself warming to her.

'Although we do eat meat, we also love vegetarian, don't we, Emilia?' She looked at her daughter who nodded. 'And fancy you owning a restaurant! You've done well for someone so young, particularly in Guernsey.' Annabel put coffee in two mugs and added hot water. 'Milk, sugar?'

'Milk, please. I was lucky as my brother helped me financially with property so expensive here.' Colette smiled as she took her mug. 'I assume you must be local or are you here on licence?'

'I was born here but left as a child to move to the mainland with my parents. I was shocked at how much things cost here now and I was lucky to find this place at such a reasonable rent.' She glanced at Emilia who was looking bored. 'Why don't you go and watch some television while Colette and I chat? We'll go the beach soon, I promise.'

Emilia brightened. 'Thank you, Mummy,' she replied and went off to the sitting room.

Annabel pushed her hair behind her ear and sighed.

'I have to be careful what I say in front of her as it's been difficult these past two years. My husband died unexpectedly and coming here is meant to be a fresh start for us both, away from his overbearing family who tried to control our lives.'

Colette reached out and squeezed her hand.

'I'm sorry for your loss, that's a tough one. It's brave of you to come back but I'm sure you'll love it here and I for one would love us to be friends. I only work part-time in my restaurant at the Bridge while Rosie's in nursery and it would be good to have a neighbour to chat to.'

'I'd love that, too. I found it hard to make friends in Manchester where I lived with my husband, Clive. My memories of Guernsey are of smiling faces of my friends at Vale school and beautiful beaches. I want my daughter to have similar memories in time.'

'Ooh, you went to the Vale school, so did I. Where did you live?'

'My parents owned the De La Mare vinery near Beaucette so this part of the island is special to me.'

'I grew up down the road from here so we have something in common. Where are your parents now? In the UK?'

'No, they emigrated to Australia some years ago and I don't have any other family here.' She sipped her coffee, trying hard not to feel maudlin in the presence of such a bubbly person as Colette. 'What about your family?'

'Sadly my parents died years ago and my brother Nick looked after me for a while. He's now married to Jeanne with two children and lives at Perelle. I'll introduce you sometime and I'm sure you'll all get on. My husband, Jonathan, is a GP at the practice in St Sampsons, which is the local one. Once you feel more settled you must come round for dinner.' She hesitated then went on, 'I knew the old lady who lived here, used to pop into see how she was occasionally as she became more housebound. Doris used to tell me tales about her uncle who built this place, a sea captain—'

'Called Daniel Gallienne who haunts the cottage. We've met.' Annabel grinned at Colette's shocked expression.

'Did you know it was haunted before you moved in? There was a rumour that he was trying to scare people off taking it.'

'Yes, he tried to scare me off as well but I fell in love

with the cottage and decided to take a chance after we came to an agreement.' She half expected some sign from him to show he was listening in, but there was nothing. Good, he had to keep to what they agreed if she were to stay.

Colette's eyes widened. 'Blimey, I admire your guts, Annabel, I'm not sure I could take on a ghost. Mind you, some of my friends here have had some experience of haunting and one even had to call in a vicar.' She glanced at her watch. 'Sorry, but I should be on my way to work though I'd love to spend more time chatting. Let's swap numbers and I'll call you later.'

Once they had sent the texts Colette made for the front door, turning to give her a big hug as she reached it. Annabel couldn't remember the last time she had been hugged and felt a lump in her throat. Don't get maudlin, now! She smiled at Colette and thanked her again for the casserole. After closing the door she checked to see what was in it and was delighted to see roasted summer vegetables, including new potatoes, courgettes and aubergine. It gave off a delicious herby smell and would be wonderful with crusty bread, she thought. Supper sorted.

Emilia remained patient a little longer and helped with the unpacking. Annabel had never been a big collector of 'stuff', not having had the money to spare after all the bills were paid and there were few ornaments to unpack along with her favourite books. Her biggest extravagance, although strictly a necessity for her work, had been her art materials. The boxes were waiting to be unpacked in the lookout and she planned to leave them until Emilia was in bed. Painting was not a big priority at the moment.

'Right, beach time,' she said, as the final box downstairs was emptied.

Emilia jumped up and hugged her. 'Love you, Mummy. You're the bestest.' Laughing, she kissed her daughter, telling her to look for the Frisbee among her toys for a game on the beach. They had an hour or so before lunchtime and then she planned to do a grocery shop.

The April sun shone weakly through light cloud and they needed to keep moving to avoid feeling chilled and throwing the Frisbee on the beach certainly warmed them up. Annabel realised she was laughing more than she had done for a long time and Emilia's eyes sparkled.

The wonderful clean air and the intoxicating smell of the sea provided the tonic they needed and they both had flushed cheeks by the time they returned to the cottage.

After a quick lunch followed by the trip to the supermarket, Annabel suggested they spend the rest of the afternoon going for a drive around the island; so far all Emilia had seen was a glimpse of St Peter Port from the ferry as they landed and then the road out to Bordeaux.

'I'd like to see where you grew up, Mummy, if it's not far.'

Annabel laughed.

'Nothing is far on this island, sweetheart, as it's only seven miles by five, much smaller than Manchester. My family home's not far from here and then I'll show you your new school. Of course, it's closed now but we have an appointment next week to pop in and see the head teacher. Although I went to Vale school too, the present school's moved to a new site which I'm keen to see.' She waved a copy of a small book of maps, 'This is *Perry's Guide to Guernsey* and shows all the roads and the most important places and I'm going to need it as I left when I was your age and I'm sure lots have changed. It may be small, but there are loads of small unmarked lanes to get lost in. Right, let's go.'

She turned left out of the drive, heading north and to the area of La Moye and her old home. Along the way Annabel pointed out places she remembered and described the fun she had had with her friends, particularly when they were old enough to go off on their own on bikes.

'Ooh, can I have a bike, please? These roads look much quieter than in Manchester.'

'Let's see after we've got to know the roads better, eh? Oh, and here's where I used to live.' She pulled up in a lane near a row of derelict greenhouses, with a cottage just visible behind a granite wall. Switching off the engine she allowed herself to drift back to the day her parents announced they were selling up and would move to England.

'Please can't we stay here? I'll miss all my friends and... and school and the beaches and everything.' Tears poured down her face as she pleaded with her parents. Her mother hugged her and made soothing noises as she saw her father looking the saddest she'd ever seen and the tears increased.

'Darling girl, I'd love nothing better than to stay but we can't afford to. The growing business has been overtaken by the Dutch and we're not earning the money we used to. But we're going to a lovely part of Kent near the south coast and I'm sure there'll be friends and beaches for you to enjoy.'

'Mummy, are you alright? You look so sad.' Emilia's voice broke into her reverie and she turned and smiled at her.

'I'm fine, sweetheart, just thinking about the time when I was a little girl. Shall we go for a walk and I'll tell you more about it.'

Annabel loved the chance to let Emilia know more about her own childhood and for her to see where she had lived. Her daughter asked loads of questions and it seemed to draw them closer together. By the time they returned to the car half an hour had passed and Annabel continued driving around the area, taking in the vast expanse of L'Ancress Bay and its golden beach before heading west to smaller bays she remembered from childhood, Ladies Bay and Le Grand Havre where they stopped for an ice cream and a walk on the beach.

'Don't think there will be beaches and ice creams every day, Emilia, it's a treat to help you settle in. And for me, too, as I've missed Guernsey so much.'

'I understand, Mummy, it'll be an adventure for us both but I have to go to school and you have to work like everyone else. I do think it'll be more fun here than in Manchester.' She laughed and Annabel joined in until they laughed so much they cried.

Ice creams finished Annabel drove back a different, shorter way to end up at the new Vale school. The granite and white building blended in with the nearby cottages and houses and Emilia loved the bright-coloured activity centre in the playground. From there it proved to be only a short drive to their home in Bordeaux, a pleasant surprise for them both.

Later that evening, after Emilia was safely in bed, Annabel went up to the lookout to start unpacking her art materials. The sun had set and she closed the curtains on the night sky before unwrapping the protective plastic around her easel. As she set it up her thoughts strayed to a certain navy captain with the brightest blue eyes. Was he there watching her, ready to announce his presence when it suited him? Oh, this is stupid! 'Daniel, are you here? If so I'd rather see you than have you creep up on me.' She looked round the room and, after the familiar whooshing sound, she saw him, by the window, arms akimbo and smiling at her.

Chapter 5

'Good evening, Mrs Easton. I wasn't sneaking around but I'm never far away, my connection to the cottage being so strong.' He inclined his head toward her.

'Good evening, Daniel. I hope you don't mind me calling you Daniel? We're not as formal these days as in your time.' She couldn't help smiling at him, as if he were really there.

'No, I don't mind. May I call you Annabel? Or though I'm not sure the name does you justice. It should be something more... more European, Italian – I know, Annabella. It has a ring to it, more feminine, don't you agree? I shall call you Annabella,' he said, with an exaggerated Italian accent.

'If you insist,' she said, liking the idea despite the absurdity of it. 'Did you travel to Europe much as a sailor?'

'I wasn't just a sailor, Annabella, I was a captain of my ship from a relatively young age and made a number of voyages to France, then on to Italy and further into the Mediterranean. On my many voyages afar I've seen many sights, some perhaps not fit for a lady's eyes.' He stroked his beard, adding, 'I had meant to write my memoir, describing all my adventures, and see it published but fate had other ideas, as you can see.' For a moment his bravado disappeared and she saw the sadness in his eyes.

'May I ask how you... died? You were so young.'

'I was, perhaps not much older than yourself, if you forgive the impertinence,' he smiled. 'I was injured during the war, commanding a Royal Naval ship caught up in a battle against the Germans. We managed to sink the blighters, but

I was hit by shrapnel and left with a weak right leg.' He paused, his eyes gazing into the distant past. 'I was invalided out shortly before the end and returned here once we'd kicked the Boche out of the island. Made a mess of the old place, they did, having taken it over while I was away and I had to do some repairs. Took me months. Anyway, one day I had been up here, keeping an eye on the ships coming and going,' he patted the telescope, 'and was on my way downstairs when the old leg gave way and I fell right down to the bottom. Broke me neck, apparently.'

'Oh, I'm so sorry, how sad after all you'd gone through.' She wanted to hug him but realised it would be foolish in spite of his seeming solidness.

'That's not the worst of it, stupid doctor thought I'd done it on purpose. Killed myself because I couldn't cope with my disability. Supposed to use a stick, you see, but never did. Too proud and look where it got me. Dead.'

'Oh, is that why you haven't, um, moved on to wherever.' She was beginning to feel out of her depth and not sure what she thought about the "afterlife".

He stroked his beard and frowned.

'It might sound odd, but I didn't think of myself as really dead. It didn't seem possible and I wasn't ready, had lots of plans; wanted to find a wife, have a family, write a book. I did find myself being drawn away, like being pulled with a giant magnet, towards some bright light. Reminded me of a lighthouse. But I had learnt to move away from lighthouses as they indicated danger to us seamen, warning us of unseen rocks or other ships.' He coughed. 'Mostly, though, I was angry. Angry with the blasted Germans who busted my leg but even more angry with m'self for being so pig-headed.' He stomped around the room and Annabel moved away in case the anger became aimed at her. She was the interloper who dared to move into his space.

Daniel came to a stop in front of her and must have seen her nervousness.

'Oh, for God's sake, woman, you don't have to be afraid

of me. I may huff and puff a bit but I'd not hurt you, in fact I'm beginning to enjoy your company. Reminds me of the old days when—'

'You had a girl in every port? Or maybe two or three?' She grinned, relieved at the release of tension.

He let out a roar of laughter and seemed to punch her arm, but all she felt was a light touch. Just as well as a proper punch would have knocked her off her feet.

'You have a good sense of humour, Annabella, and I like your spirit. Perhaps we can be good for each other. We're both sad and somewhat angry about our situations – no, let me finish,' he said as she tried to interject, 'and we need to move on. I need to accept my death and move to wherever comes after and you need to accept life without your husband, who did give you some security but not much happiness, and thrive on your own. You're strong, stronger than he was and you and your little'un will do well here. It's where you belong.'

Annabel's initial thought was, 'How arrogant! Making assumptions about me and my marriage.' And then another thought popped up.

'What makes you think you know about my husband?'

'Ah, in my position I can find out things others can't. It wasn't difficult to learn your husband had been an alcoholic and died from liver failure.' His expression softened as he added, 'I saw the sadness in your eyes and I could imagine how hard it must have been for you. I was surrounded by heavy drinkers in my days at sea and saw first-hand how marriages were destroyed. I learnt to control my drinking as I was responsible for my ship and my crew, who were like a family to me.'

'It's a bit scary that you've learned so much about me. And what made you say this is where I belong?'

Daniel chuckled.

'That's easy. You have to be a local to live in this cottage so I knew you had probably been born here. And,' he coughed, 'I heard two of the agents talking together and they confirmed it.'

She had to laugh.

'So sometimes it's down to being an eavesdropper. Yes, I was born here and my family owned the De La Mare Nurseries at La Moye. You may have come across them when…'

'I was alive? Indeed, yes. Best tomatoes on the island, for sure. A shame your parents had to sell up, but they weren't the only ones. Still,' he beamed, 'you're back now and a proper Guern.'

'Look, Daniel, it's lovely to chat, but I do need to unpack my art materials and get this room straight in case any commissions arrive. I'm happy for you to stay while I carry on.'

He looked nonplussed for a moment.

'You're a professional artist! I hadn't realised, in my day there were not too many female artists around and certainly not on Guernsey. Thought you were only a dabbler.' He waved an arm dismissively.

She took a deep breath. He couldn't help being patronising as he was simply a man of his time. Women had come on a long way since then and she would need to make allowances. Mind you, Clive had been a bit snippy about her art and whether or not she could make it pay.

Forcing a smile, she said, 'I took a degree in Fine Art in London and have been selling my work for some years. I've even had an exhibition in a small Manchester art gallery which attracted good reviews.' As she spoke she started unpacking her paints and the stacking shelves to hold the different paint media. Daniel watched in silence as the display stands filled with bright coloured tubes and pots of paint, boxes of art markers, watercolour pens and an array of brushes.

'Well, I see I owe you an apology, Annabella. My lookout is fast turning into a well-equipped art studio. Do you have any canvases packed away in those boxes?'

'A few.' She grinned, at the last count there were at least thirty paintings, a mix of acrylic, watercolour and alcohol ink.

'I plan to approach the local art galleries as well as continuing to sell from my website online.' There, put that in you pipe and smoke it, dinosaur.

'What on earth is a website? And online?'

Oh, dear, now she had to try and explain.

'It's complicated and I don't have time to tell you now but I will another day, I promise. I really want to get these boxes unpacked and to check my artwork has survived the journey.'

Daniel harrumphed and moved towards the window.

'I can see I'm in the way. I'll leave you in peace. Goodnight, Annabella.' In an instant he was gone.

Chapter 6

The next morning Annabel woke feeling as if she had hardly slept all night. Her dreams, if this was what they were, had been filled with images of Daniel popping up wherever she was. She felt his eyes following her and at one time she ran screaming from the house before waking up to find it had been a dream.

What on earth had got into her? He wasn't even real! At least not a flesh and blood man who might stir her senses as men had done in the past. As Clive had done when they first met. There had been an attraction between them which had led to love. Though it had been doomed thanks to his drinking, it had been real at the time. Sitting up in bed and hugging her knees – no sign of Emilia – she came to the unwanted conclusion that she was attracted to Daniel. It was bizarre, she knew, but there was definitely a spark and he seemed to find her attractive. How was she going to deal with it? It was early days and it was likely Daniel would keep away once the novelty of someone new had worn off.

A knock on the door cut short her ruminations and Emilia peered round the door, saw she was awake and came running in.

After a quick cuddle Annabel sent her off to get dressed while she headed to the bathroom hoping a hot shower would clear her head.

The day followed the pattern of the previous one – unpacking, beach, lunch and then a drive. This time they drove right round the island on the coast road and Emilia couldn't believe how many golden beaches the island possessed. Occasionally they stopped for her to run on one while Annabel sat nearby and enjoyed being still for once, absorbing both the sights and smells of the seaside. Seagulls dipped down looking for food and then rose high in the sky as they moved on, cawing to each other as they regrouped. Annabel wished she had brought her sketch pad and pencils as she built up images in her mind for future paintings. Guernsey offered unlimited scope for seascapes although she also loved painting flora in semi-abstract form and had built up a decent following for her abstract watercolours. For the moment painting would need to come second to her daughter who had been badly affected by her father's drinking and subsequent death.

'Why is Daddy so grumpy, Mummy? He never wants to play with me or read to me like he used to. Have I done something wrong?'

She had sought to reassure Emilia, saying, 'No, sweetheart, Daddy is under a lot of pressure at work to make lots of sales and if he doesn't then his boss is very cross with him.'

'Is that why he drinks that stuff which smells yucky when he comes home? To make it better?'

'In a way, but unfortunately it doesn't work. Don't worry, I'm sure he'll start to feel better soon and then he'll be your old daddy again.' She didn't believe it but what could she say? It had taken her a while to see how much Clive was drinking as most of it happened outside the home. Initially it hadn't seemed to affect him but then his mood changed as the physical effects became more obvious. It was amazing he kept his job as long as he did, until one day two years ago he came home early and told her he'd been sacked.

She had been preparing their supper after putting Emilia to bed. He rarely made it home in time to help these days, explaining he'd had to work late.

'What? But why? You told me you'd gained some new accounts which was why you were hardly home lately.' Thoughts of their mortgage and the other bills filled her mind as she fought to stay calm.

Clive slumped down at the kitchen table, his head in his hands.

'I… I've not been truthful with you. It's been difficult to get new business for months now as there's a new competitor started up and I've been getting more depressed and going to the pub for a drink. Then one drink leads to another and… I can't seem to stop myself. The boss found me asleep in my car at lunchtime cos I was drunk. Fired on the spot and took the car keys and mobile. Told me I needed help and should see my doctor.'

Annabel was numb. She knew she should comfort Clive, tell him they would sort it out, he'd get another job blah, blah, but somehow the words wouldn't come. They had been drifting apart for a few years and it was possible she hadn't allowed herself to see what was happening with him. There was no falling over drunk, simply a lack of interaction, of enjoying time together. She couldn't remember when they had last had sex and neither of them seemed to bother. She had poured herself into looking after Emilia and her art, cocooning herself from reality.

'I'm so sorry, Clive. I should have seen what was happening, been there for you—'

He looked up, his eyes red-rimmed and his face grey.

'No, it's all down to me, love. You didn't drive me to drink, I did. I couldn't cope with the job and being a husband and father. I wanted everything to be as easy as it was initially. But nothing's handed to us on a plate; jobs and marriages have to be worked at, I see that now.' He paused, twisting his wedding ring. 'I had already seen my doctor a few days ago and he's done some blood tests and wants me to have a scan. He suggested Alcoholics Anonymous and I went yesterday. Didn't stop me drinking yet but I think it might help in the long run.'

She had hugged him then and he cried on her shoulder. Once they had eaten they discussed how they would manage their finances until he could get another job. Her art was beginning to sell but not enough to cover his salary. They had some savings which would help for a few months but after that…

Then the blow fell. Clive was diagnosed with cirrhosis of the liver and it was too far advanced to be treated. He went downhill very quickly and Annabel suspected he simply gave up. She did what she could to help him but towards the end he insisted on going into a hospice as he didn't want Emilia to see him looking so ill. He died one night before Annabel could say goodbye.

Sitting there on the beach, with the sounds of the gulls and children's laughter as a backdrop, it all seemed so long ago. Another life. Emilia rarely mentioned her father but Annabel hoped in time they could talk about him. He had not been a bad father or husband, he had been ill and had not sought help until it was too late. Emilia's voice floated across to her wanting her to see the tiny creatures she had found. Shrugging off the sad memories, she called, 'Coming!'

They continued the drive down the coast and Annabel found her mood lifting again at the continued vista of sandy beaches, blue sea and her daughter's exclamations of delight. Eventually, drawing inland from what was the furthest south-western point, they headed along the south where glimpses of the sea were sporadic and cottages and houses more spread out until they reached the road leading to the airport and then through St Martins towards St Peter Port. The view going down Le Val de Terres into Town had to be one of the best on the island and Annabel pointed out Castle Cornet isolated on its emplacement as it guarded the entrance to the harbour and the many boats, local and visitor, moored in the marinas. They had arrived at White Rock Pier via the Condor ferry only days earlier but it already seemed a lifetime.

Emilia's eyes were round with excitement as Annabel parked the car on the Crown Pier and said they could have a browse around the shops and offered to take her to the local library, the Guille-Alles, and register for membership. The library had changed a bit since she went as a child but the staff were as friendly and helpful and the children's section had been extended. They both left with a selection of books and celebrated with a milkshake in a nearby café. Emilia was intrigued to see British shops like Marks & Spencer, Boots and Accessorize among local independents, particularly when her mother explained that Guernsey and its islands were once French and that the local language had been a form of French for centuries.

'Does this mean I have a bit of French in me, Mummy?' They were walking back towards the car and admiring the visitors' yachts bobbing up on the pontoons, several displaying French flags.

'Yes, according to my father, my family arrived here about three hundred years ago from Normandy and may have been fishermen or sailors as our name De La Mare means "of the sea".'

'Ooh, how exciting! Then I won't be as different to the other children here after all.'

She shook her head, smiling.

'No, you may not be a real Guern or local as you weren't born here, but you have a proud Guernsey heritage. It's possible a lot of the children at your school are only here as a parent has come over here to work and has no prior Guernsey connection. I'll try and show you as much of the island as I can before you start school, then you won't feel too much of a newcomer, okay?'

Emilia was happy with that and they were soon on their way back to Bordeaux, staying on the coast road from St Peter Port. Once home Annabel transferred the remains of Colette's casserole into one of her own, washed it and then she and Emilia walked the few yards to her house. It was a similar style but bigger than Seagull Cottage with a separate garage and a large front garden. She rang the bell.

Colette, holding on to a little girl, opened the door with a welcoming smile.

'Hi, lovely to see you, do come in and say hello to Rosie. She's been dying to meet Emilia since I told her about you.' She opened the door wide and they followed inside, and

didn't have one?'

He shook his head.

'Right, I'll try to explain. For about thirty years we've had machines called personal computers, which using something called software, can make vast calculations, create images and even allow us to send letters across the world to other machines while connected to something called the internet. During the war computers were developed as code breakers at Bletchley Park in England and helped us defeat the Germans.'

'Blimey, I don't know what you're talking about, it all sounds like hocus pocus to me. Can you show me?'

Annabel suggested he stand by her while she showed him her website, with images of her paintings, the emails she received and how to write and receive an email. Daniel was clearly a bright man, or rather, he had been, but it took a while for him to accept what, to her, had been a part of her life since forever.

He scratched his head, then his beard and then crossed his arms.

'I'll be blowed, it's beyond me. Makes the stuff we had onboard ship seem pretty basic. Thank goodness I don't need to use such a thing.' He paused to scratch his head again. 'Is it related to the screen showing moving pictures which old Doris had? You've got an even bigger one in the sitting room.'

'Not really, but there are similarities. They're called televisions and have been around for longer, in fact less than twenty years after you died. Did your niece not have one?'

He appeared to be thinking.

'Some years after I died she did have some sort of box which she spent time looking at. Black and white pictures mainly and you could hear people talking and music playing. The boxes got bigger over the years and the pictures became colour. It was a little like going to the pictures in your own home.'

'Exactly. I don't understand the science behind either

computers or televisions, but I can say how much they've transformed our lives and I wouldn't want to be without mine.'

He moved away to stand in front of her and as she studied him it suddenly struck her how enigmatic he was and she would love to paint him. If it were possible to catch the essence of someone who was a ghost.

'Daniel, changing the subject for a moment. Would you consider sitting for me? You know I'm not keen on your oil portrait and I'd like to paint you myself. What do you think?'

Chapter 7

Annabel's question hung in the air for what seemed forever. Daniel did his usual scratching of his head and looked down at his feet as if he would find the answer there. Eventually he looked up at her and smiled.

'Well, I'll be damned. Never thought to be asked such a question when I was alive, let alone now I'm dead. My sister, Peggy, had my portrait painted after I died, from a photograph taken while I was in the Merchant Navy in the late thirties. She and I had similar colouring of eyes and hair and must have told the artist. He was a local chap, an amateur.' He laughed. 'You said it wasn't very good, didn't you? Suppose it won't do any harm to let you have a go. It's not as if anyone else will see it.'

Annabel didn't like to say she might have prints made if it turned out as well as she hoped. A ghost wouldn't be able to make a fuss would he?

'Great. It's a pity I can't work from photos, which is the norm these days so I'll need to start with some drawings. Would it work for you to pop in here in the evenings after my daughter's in bed? We're not likely to be disturbed then.'

'I think I could fit it in within my busy schedule, as long as we don't stay longer than midnight. I can't be held responsible for what happens after that,' Daniel said, straight-faced.

'Oh, do you turn into a pumpkin or something?' She was equally straight-faced but was smiling inwardly at the notion of his "busy schedule".

'Not as far as I know but making myself visible does take a heck of a lot of energy so I might start fading away if we take too long.' His eyes twinkled and she burst out laughing.

'You've not lost your sense of humour, have you? Which is good as I'd like to capture it in the portrait. Could we start tomorrow evening? Unless you have something scheduled?'

It was his turn to laugh, a deep belly laugh which set her off again. It was a few moments before they regained a feeling of calm and Annabel was shocked to see it was after eleven. They said their goodnights, there was a whoosh of air and she was alone. A bubble of excitement floated around her stomach as she thought of the challenge ahead. Daniel seemed so real, all flesh and blood when he was standing near her, but could she translate that into a portrait showing the real man, his soul? Show him as he was over seventy years ago when he was in his prime? She sensed how he made her feel; alive, fizzing with excitement when they met. Her initial wariness had gone and she realised if he'd been alive she would be falling for him. How scary was that? Falling for a ghost? She shook her head. They sparked off each other and maybe it would be good for both of them. As she walked downstairs to her bedroom Annabel hoped she wasn't going mad and heading for the local mental hospital.

The next day, a brisk easterly and a gathering of clouds restricted the time Annabel and Emilia spent on the beach. It was enough to produce pink cheeks and a sense of well-being which had Emilia giggling as they watched two sparring gulls trying to devour the same piece of bread. When one of the gulls eventually managed to claim possession and flew off to nearby Vale Castle, Annabel decided it was time to return home.

'How about if we take a trip to Candie Museum in St Peter Port? If it rains we'll be in the dry and if it stays fine the gardens are lovely with quite a view over the harbour and the islands. And there's a café where we can have lunch. Is it a deal?'

'Yes, please,' Emilia shouted, running towards her as she headed back. With only a week left of the school holiday, Annabel decided a few treats wouldn't go amiss and planned to check what was on at the cinema later.

The museum had changed since Annabel had left the island and she was as excited as Emilia to see it was holding a temporary exhibition titled "Celts and Romans" with lots of artefacts newly brought over to Guernsey. She had loved history as a child and her daughter was showing signs of following her interest and a pleasant hour was passed before they walked through to the café for lunch. Although the rain held off it was too windy to sit outside but they had a great view down over to the islands and Emilia was full of questions about them.

'We'll go over to Herm one day next week and spend the whole day there. It was always my favourite place ever and where we spent summer holidays camping when my parents could spare the time. Sark is beautiful too, but further away and bigger. We might be able to spend a night or two there sometime if I sell some paintings. There's no rush to see everything at once as we're living here, not just tourists, like those people over there,' she lowered her voice, nodding to a French family exclaiming loudly at the statue of the Frenchman, Victor Hugo, a few yards away.

Emilia beamed. 'I'm so glad you were born here, Mummy, and now we're living here. I feel very lucky and if my friends back in Manchester could see me now, I'm sure they'd be jealous.'

'Perhaps, sweetheart, but if someone loved the fast pace of city living then they wouldn't want to live here. Fast, it isn't,' she laughed. 'But I'm glad you're loving it so far. Shall we have a walk round the gardens and I'll tell you why we have a statue of Victor Hugo here. Do you remember we watched *Les Misérables* on television a few months ago?' Emilia nodded and they carried on walking towards the granite statue as Annabel explained Hugo had written the last part of the original book while living in exile in Guernsey and 'he had the most fabulous house in St Peter Port which we can visit...' She continued telling her more of his story as they walked before turning her attention to the various shrubs and flowers vying for attention with their unique scents and colours. Coming from a family of growers, Annabel was keen for her daughter to learn the importance of flora generally and the particular value of growing food. Luckily, Emilia seemed to possess an enquiring mind and loved listening to what she had to say. Except when it was time for bed, of course.

They managed to walk around the whole of the gardens before the first drops of rain fell and they ran for the car, parked nearby. By the time they arrived home the rain was heavy and they were forced to make an umbrella-covered dash for the front door. Once inside it wasn't long before the kettle was on and Emilia was ensconced in front of the television. While she was occupied, Annabel went up to fetch her laptop and check on the cinema, booking two tickets for a live action version of *Cinderella,* for Saturday afternoon. Emilia was suitably excited and plonked a large kiss on her cheek.

'Thank you, Mummy, you're the best ever,' she said, before turning her attention back to the television programme. By the time they had had supper and her daughter was safely in bed, Annabel was excited by the thought of painting Daniel. It had been some time since she had done any portraiture and saw it as a challenge. Her usual subjects, abstract plants, trees and general nature had no means of expressing dissent or dissatisfaction, which Daniel undoubtedly did. She would simply have to do her very best to make him happy with the result.

Once in her studio, she set out her pencils for sketching and selected a large watercolour canvas to fix on the easel. All she needed was the subject.

'Daniel? Are you here yet?' There was no immediate response so she experimented with the position of the easel, wanting to include the telescope in the portrait. Finally she was happy with it when with the usual whoosh, Daniel appeared by the window.

'Sorry, I was busy practising how to stand in front of your bedroom mirror and lost all sense of time.' He flashed her a smile.

'You've been in my bedroom? Honestly! Have you no manners at all? I asked you not to go there right at the beginning and you agreed.' She had to stop herself stamping her foot.

'Ah, but that was if you were also present. And as you were not I thought it could do no harm. I assure you I didn't touch anything.' He splayed his hands palm upwards as if in proof.

'From my viewpoint, my bedroom is off-limits to you whether or not I'm in it. How would you have felt if a female had gone into your bedroom uninvited?' Seeing his eyes dance, she added, 'Don't bother answering that. Please accept we see things differently and I'd appreciate you respecting my privacy.'

He bowed his head.

'Of course. I'm sorry I've upset you and I'm really looking forward to you painting my portrait. Can we begin now? Where do you want me to po… stand?'

Taking a deep breath Annabel managed a smile and asked him to stand by the telescope, with one hand resting on it and the other pointing as if to something he'd seen, his head facing her, the artist/audience. It took a few minutes to get it right before she could start sketching, working quickly to get the main features recorded. Her strength as an artist was her ability to produce lifelike sketches of her subjects in a short time, forming the basis of the more detailed final portrait in which she aimed to reveal the subject's inner self. Definitely tricky with regard to a ghost, she thought as she worked, trying not to catch Daniel's eye and so lose her concentration.

'Right, I think that'll do for today, thanks, Daniel. You've been quite patient and hardly moved at all.'

He grinned, moving his arms to his usual position across his chest.

'I'm the ideal sitter as, having no real body, I have no muscles to ache and, of course, don't get hungry or thirsty. May I take a look?'

'I can hardly stop you, can I? By all means.'

She moved away as he came to stand in front of the easel. She held her breath as he stared at the outline of himself, clothed as he was now, but with a captain's hat perched at a jaunty angle on his head.

'My dear Annabella, I don't believe I looked as handsome in life, let alone in death. You have captured something which is most certainly missing from my other portrait. I applaud you, m'dear.' He clapped his hands, though no sound could be heard.

'Glad you like it. Obviously there's a lot more to be done even before I start painting, but I'm happy so far. As I'm out tomorrow night we can't continue until Saturday evening, if that suits you?'

For a moment his face looked like that of child who has had his new toy taken away, then the cloud lifted and he nodded.

'I shall look forward to it. Of course you're going to the nice neighbours for supper, are you not? She's a good cook so you'll enjoy yourselves.'

'Nothing gets past you, does it, Daniel? And yes, Colette is a good chef. Did you enjoy your food when you were alive?'

'Only when others cooked. Can't abide having to cook for myself. We always had cooks in the navy, o'course. Had to put up with a few stinkers in my time, particularly during the war when food was scarce. Never knew when you were eating boiled rat or chicken.' He grinned. 'It was usually better not to ask. I wish you a pleasant evening for tomorrow and will be back on Saturday.' A quick bow of his head and he was gone.

Chapter 8

After another day of exploration, Annabel and Emilia were looking forward to supper at Colette's, with Emilia more excited about spending time with Rosie rather than sitting at a table eating food with adults. Which was boring. While out driving Annabel had bought some local flowers from one of the hedge stalls scattered around the island, explaining to her daughter this was how her parents had sold surplus tomatoes. It was a custom of long-standing in the island and relied on buyers being honest, which, on the whole, they were. Armed with the flowers and a bottle of wine, they walked the short distance to Colette's at six o'clock.

'For me? Thanks, come on in,' said Colette as she opened the door, kissing them both on the cheek as they passed inside. The door was barely closed when the pounding of small feet on the tiled floor announced the arrival of Rosie, who promptly flung her arms around Emilia, crying, "Melia, 'Melia come and see what I done today.' The two women watched, smiling indulgently, as the girls headed to the play area.

'Rosie was painting at nursery today and has been dying to show Emilia her efforts, her opinion mattering more than ours, it seems. Of course, she doesn't realise we have a professional artist in our midst,' Colette grinned. 'Glass of prosecco to start the evening?' She had a bottle and glasses ready and Annabel quickly agreed.

'Jonathan's running late, as usual, but shouldn't be long. Here's to your new future in Guernsey!' They touched glasses and took a sip of the ice cold wine.

'Lovely.' Annabel sniffed the air. 'Umm, something

smells delicious, let me guess. Red wine, herbs and… chicken?'

Colette laughed.

'Spot on. Chicken Chasseur, but only for the adults. I thought Emilia wouldn't mind eating the same as Rosie which is cottage pie and they can sit together at their end of the table. Rosie won't be too long going to bed, I'm afraid, but I wanted them to have as much time together as possible.' A noise at the front door announced Jonathan's return and he was soon being urged to lift up and hug his daughter before turning to kiss his wife and then, more demurely, Annabel. A glass of prosecco was then pushed into his hand to a cry of 'cheers!'

'That's quite a welcome,' he said, laughing after he took a long sip. 'And it's good to see you again, Annabel. And you, too, Emilia,' he added as a shy Emilia was hanging back behind Rosie.

Colette announced supper was about to be served and ushered the children, after they had washed their hands, to their places at the table. Within minutes everyone was in their place and while Jonathan served the children, Colette asked Annabel to help herself to the main dish and accompanying vegetables. When asked what they had been up to, Annabel described their trips around the island and her plans for the following week in an effort to help Emilia feel more of a local before starting school. The conversation turned to the Vale school, which they had all attended at different times, and how much they had enjoyed it as well as growing up in that area of Guernsey.

Rosie was beginning to flag and Colette excused herself to take her up to bed and suggested Emilia might like to play with Rosie's doll's house while the adults finished their meal. Emilia was only too keen to be spared grown-up talk and went off to the playroom.

For a few moments it was only Annabel and Jonathan at the table and he broke the silence by saying, 'Has Colette mentioned you'll need to register at the surgery before Emilia starts school? They need to know in case there's an emergency at school.'

'No, she hadn't, so thanks for telling me, I'll do it next week. There's so much to think about with such a big move, it's as bad as moving to another country.'

Jonathan nodded.

'Strictly speaking, it is another country with the endless bureaucracy and paperwork that involves. Everything should go smoothly and you can enjoy moving back. Colette will, no doubt, be keen to introduce you to her friends to help you settle in. As she seems to know everyone you could be quite busy,' he said, grinning.

'Fine by me, I've been a recluse for far too long and have missed having girl friends around me. I—' She was interrupted by Colette's return, balancing a bowl of profiteroles smothered with chocolate sauce.

'Couldn't bring these out while Rosie was up as far too rich for her. Please take some to Emilia, though, as there's plenty to go round.'

Annabel returned to find a bowl ready for her.

'Scrummy! I love profiteroles but think of them as a decadent treat. Hello, decadence,' she said, dipping her spoon in the thick chocolate.

Silence reigned as they munched their way through the cream-filled pastries, licking the chocolate sauce off their lips.

'As delicious, as ever, darling,' Jonathan patted his flat stomach. 'Anyone for coffee?'

The women nodded their agreement and he went off to the kitchen with the empty bowls.

'Poor Jonathan has to catch up with some report he's writing so he'll be off to his study in a moment, but it does mean we can have a girly chat,' Colette said, sipping her wine.

'I've been meaning to ask, does he know about, you know, Daniel?'

'Well, let's just say the old lady, Doris, did tell him she saw and spoke to Daniel sometimes but he doesn't really believe in ghosts and thought she was losing the plot. So, I haven't said anything about your experience to be on the safe side. In time, with enough evidence, he might accept it. After all, we do have friends who've had some ghostly experiences,' she shrugged. 'He's too much of a scientist to take it on board yet.'

'In that case I won't be saying anything either. Although there are times I doubt my own sanity.' Daniel's face floated into her mind and for a horrible moment she thought he might have decided to pop round to see what they were up to and her heart raced. Surely he wouldn't? And couldn't? Not knowing how far he could appear from his own home was frustrating. She would have to find out.

'Here we are, ladies, coffee. Sorry for the delay, got a call from the practice manager which I had to take. Now, I'll leave you in peace, but look forward to seeing you again soon, Annabel.'

They exchanged pecks on the cheek and, after kissing Colette, he left.

'Right, now the unbeliever is out of earshot, tell me what's been happening.' Colette leaned forward expectantly.

'I asked if I could paint his portrait and he agreed. Still at the drawing stage but it's going well.' She sipped her coffee as Colette's mouth opened in a large 'Oh!'

'Tell me more!'

Colette hung on her every word, laughing when she told her about Daniel's quip about his body disappearing through lack of energy.

'I like the sound of this guy, he's sure got a sense of humour for someone long dead. Is he sexy?' Colette raised her eyebrows.

'I, er, suppose you could say he is, when he's sitting there, chatting and smiling like a real person he's got quite a glint in his blue eyes.' She felt herself flushing at the thought and hid behind her cup.

'I'd love to meet Daniel sometime. Do you think he might agree to that?'

She shook her head. 'I've no idea, but he has mentioned

you in relation to being the neighbour who looked out for Doris and is also a good cook. I could ask him but would you mind if we wait until I've finished the portrait? I don't want him going off in a huff partway through. He can be a bit prickly.'

'Sure. I can't wait to see the portrait as well... that reminds me, I knew there was something I wanted to suggest. Your paintings. In my restaurant I've old views of the island on the walls and have been thinking of a revamp. Something more colourful and modern. If I like what you've got, I could hang them with price tags so customers could buy them. Kill two birds with one stone – I get free decoration and you get sales!'

'What a lovely idea, thanks. If you come round at the weekend and take a look I'm sure we could find a few for you. I've got prints and originals offering different price points to suit most pockets.' Annabel reached out to squeeze Colette's hand in gratitude. Her new life in Guernsey was definitely coming together. She could only hope nothing would happen to ruin it.

Saturday was full on. In the morning Colette popped round with Rosie in tow to look at the artwork. Emilia took Rosie into the back garden to play while the adults went up to the studio.

'What a wonderful view you have and what a fab telescope. You must love coming up here to paint.' Colette spun round and noticed the easel.

'Is that who I think it is?' Before coming upstairs Annabel had said they mustn't mention Daniel in case he was hovering nearby, as he had tended to do.

'Yes, early draft as yet.'

'I can tell it's going to be good. Now, let's look at your paintings. Ooh, I like that one,' she pointed to a bright abstract of a large array of poppies in a meadow, 'it reminds me of carefree summer days and would look brill on the main restaurant wall.' Annabel pulled out various other originals and prints and Colette ended up choosing four large and five small paintings and prints.

'We've masses of white wall space and these will look gorgeous. I do have some regulars who have an eye for art and are pretty well off, so hope they might be interested in your originals. Your work is so fresh and different I'm sure it will sell and in the galleries if you approach them. And if you have birthday and occasion cards printed, we might be able to sell a few of them, too.'

'Thanks, Colette, I appreciate your faith in me. Now, let's get these paintings downstairs – oh, and would you mind helping me take down a painting in my bedroom which is destined for the garden shed?'

It took a few trips up and down stairs as the large paintings were glazed and heavy. Before going to collect her car for her chosen paintings, Colette helped with the oil painting of Daniel. Warned not to make any comment until they were outside, she simply pulled a face and grinned. As they were putting it in the shed she agreed with Annabel about how awful it was as a painting, but she was intrigued by the subject.

'There's something a bit rakish about him, isn't there? I bet he had no trouble attracting the ladies.'

'From what he's told me, you're right. A bit of a Jack the Lad. Happy to remain single as long as there was a woman waiting for him somewhere.'

Colette took Rosie home and came back with her car to load up the paintings which she planned to take to the restaurant when it was closed briefly before the evening trade. Annabel now had time to prepare lunch before taking an increasingly excited Emilia to see *Cinderella*.

They arrived home by late afternoon and Annabel had to admit she had enjoyed the film nearly as much as her daughter. It had done them both good to be transported into a fairy tale for a while, helping to heal the pain of the past two years. Although Annabel neither wanted nor expected her own fairy tale, she was encouraged by her new friendship with Colette to be more positive about the future. And to have her paintings on display in a popular restaurant was such a boost. She found herself humming a song from the film, "A Dream is a Wish Your Heart Makes", sung by Cinderella, thinking how appropriate it was. She was well past the age when she looked for a handsome prince to sweep her off her feet, but neither did she want to face the rest of her life alone. She didn't *need* a man, she could cope well enough on her own, but seeing Colette and Jonathan together reminded her of what was missing in her life. Easy companionship based on mutual love. Sighing, she started cooking the supper, trying to bat away the image of Daniel which inextricably popped into her head. She wanted a real, live man in her life, not a ghost. However, the thought of seeing him later did make her smile.

It took a while to settle Emilia who was still reliving the film and wanted to tell Annabel of her favourite bits. The pleasure of seeing her eyes shine with delight when she recalled the arrival of the fairy godmother and the coach helped her cope with the impatience to go up to the studio and her allotted time with Daniel.

'You're late,' a voice came out of the shadows as she opened the door and switched on the light. Slowly, a figure appeared by the telescope and he was scowling.

'My daughter—'

'Yes, yes I know. This film, *Cinderella*, is a fairy tale I heard as a boy and thought pretty silly then. I think it even more so now they've made a moving picture with real people in it. Still, I suppose if it amuses the *children*, there's no harm done.'

Annabel took a deep breath. What arrogance. How dare he! Tempted to leave, she reminded herself she was the one who wanted to paint his portrait and hoped to make money from it. Money she very much needed.

'Serves you right for listening in to a private

conversation. I'm not ashamed to say I enjoyed the film, as did the hundreds of parents and children present. Now, if we're to make any progress tonight, would you mind taking up the position and we'll carry on.'

Daniel seemed about to say something but changed his mind and took up the pose of the previous session without needing any adjustment.

Annabel focused on the drawing and the detail she was adding, slipping into her own world as artist at work. She had already decided to add a different background, with the telescope pointing to an early twentieth century merchant ship in the bay, adding much more substance to the portrait. For the moment she rough sketched a steam liner until she found an appropriate image.

'Right, I think that's enough for tonight. I was wondering if there's a photo of any of your ships in the cottage?'

He came over and stood by her side, stroking his beard.

'It's coming on and I like the idea of a ship in the background. My sister inherited my photo albums but I don't know what happened to them. Thrown out, I suppose. Could be in the shed or may have been donated to the Priaulx library. They like to collect anything with a local connection.'

'I'll search the shed first.' She started tidying up, not keen to chat but needing more information from him. 'Did you sail trading or passenger ships?'

'Both. Some ships carried both freight and a limited number of passengers and I learned my craft on them, sailing the Mediterranean mostly. Over the years, as I gained experience, I moved to the bigger shipping companies, like White Star Line and not long before war broke out I was captaining ships on the transatlantic route. That was the crowning glory of my career for a few months.'

In spite of herself, she was impressed. She'd imagined Daniel sailing around on dirty, rust-bucket freighters not posh ocean liners.

'I didn't realise, in the portrait you're not wearing the

smart uniform of ocean liner captains.'

He shrugged.

'The photo it was based on was taken when I was lower down the ranks on an old freighter, but don't worry, I'd rather you painted me in the same way. I never felt as comfortable in the smart uniform of liners and having to spend a fair amount of my time being nice to passengers, who thought me inferior to them as they were so wealthy.' He threw up his hands and muttered what sounded like an expletive.

'It's a pity you never got the chance to write your story, it could have been a bestseller and made you rich,' she said, with a laugh.

He looked pensive and started pacing up and down while he seemed to be chewing something over.

'Perhaps it's not too late, Annabella. I could dictate the story to you and you type it up on your fancy… computer thingy. Then you can send it to a publisher and make loads of money, enough perhaps to buy this cottage.' His eyes were sparkling. 'What do you say?'

She stood there open-mouthed, trying to take in his idea.

'You're suggesting I write the memoir of a ghost who was once a seafarer, eventually becoming a captain of an ocean liner? How could it work? Not only am I a woman but I wasn't alive at the time you were. It would seem pretty fishy.'

'I'm sure there's a way round it. You could say you found my diaries in my cottage and thought what a good story they made. Or write it as fiction, like *Moby Dick*. I loved that book as a boy.'

'Well, I'll think about it. I'm grateful for you thinking of me as a way to earn money, though.' She had a thought. 'Did you write any diaries?'

'Ah, alas, no. Too busy enjoying myself when I was younger and too busy running a ship when older. Never fear, my memory is fully intact, better than when I was alive. And there are some particularly racy memories of—'

She raised her hand.

'Stop, I can imagine. Or rather I can't, not being a sailor nearly a hundred years ago. If, and it's a big if, I do decide to type up your memoir, it may need some judicious editing.'

Daniel raised his eyebrows.

'I don't see why, as no-one from that time will be alive to sue and I thought people were more broad-minded these days. No more simpering misses blushing at the slightest hint of a male torso and the women these days wear skirts short enough to leave nothing to the imagination.'

Glad she was wearing jeans, Annabel couldn't argue his logic.

'It's getting late and I'm tired. Next time I'll be starting the colour washes if you want to come along, but I could manage without you if you're busy.' She had already worked out the colours needed so she could carry on without him now, but, infuriating as Daniel could be, she enjoyed their time together.

He pretended to check an invisible diary, turning over the pages with furrowed brow, until she burst out laughing and he joined in.

Calming down, he said, 'No, I'm free and I look forward to meeting you here tomorrow evening. Sleep well, Annabella.' He blew a kiss and disappeared.

Chapter 9

Sunday dawned bright and warm and even Annabel experienced the urge to get up and spend time on the beach, much to Emilia's delight. They made a picnic of their breakfast; cereals, toast and juice packed into a basket and grabbing a big rug walked the few yards to the beach and, wearing big smiles, settled down to eat. The toast was cold and it was messy but fun and Annabel found herself giggling with Emilia at the slightest thing. The meal was rounded off with a coffee for mother and an ice cream for daughter. After a very quick paddle, the water still freezing, they returned home to shower and change.

For Annabel the spontaneity of the breakfast on the beach made her realise she was letting go of her usual cautious self, someone who had to think everything through before making a decision. It felt good, like shedding an old skin which was too tight and restricting. Sitting in the kitchen munching fresh, hot toast she recognised the change had been creeping up on her since the decision to move back to Guernsey. She loved her new life and the cottage, complete with resident ghost, was encouraging her to try new things, like possibly writing the memoir of said ghost. The thought made her smile and reminded her to check out the shed for any family memorabilia, including old photos. It was utterly bonkers but... what had she got to lose?

After making sure Emilia was settled with a library book, Annabel walked to the bottom of the garden where the shed was half hidden by overgrown shrubs and the ubiquitous ivy which attached itself limpet-like to any non-moving surface. The shed was in reasonable condition and housed the lawn mower and various tools she was meant to use to keep the garden tidy. She hadn't taken much notice when she and Colette had left the portrait there and now took a good look around. There were old tins of paint and a toolbox holding a hammer, screwdrivers and odds and ends. All very boring and the usual suspects for the contents of a shed. She sighed, trying to peer through the gloom, the one window was badly in need of a clean and the lightbulb appeared to be dead. Switching on her phone's torch illuminated an old dresser against the far wall, with cupboards and drawers. Encouraged, she cleared a path through and opened one of the drawers. The usual mess of old tools and string. The next drawer proved harder to open as something was sticking and she ended up with bruised fingers in the attempt to free it. Eventually the drawer opened, revealing an old-fashioned photo album. Pulling it out she saw sepia photos showing what looked like Victorian or Edwardian people. Putting it to one side, Annabel searched the other drawers and cupboards, being rewarded with another two albums plus some loose snaps. Finding an empty box, she put everything in and locked the shed, a buzz of excitement propelling her back to the cottage. Emilia was still engrossed in her book so she took her finds upstairs to the studio for a proper look.

The sepia photos were likely of Daniel's parents or close relatives, according to their dress. Later on in the album black and white photos replaced them and the change in fashion indicated the 1920s. Although it was fascinating to see them, Annabel was disappointed not to recognise anyone resembling Daniel. A number of photos were labelled and the name 'Gallienne' appeared frequently. Another album took over from when the first ended and then she saw it. The photo of Daniel in his seaman's outfit used for the oil painting. The photo was damaged and slightly blurred, but recognisable. It was taken outside and there was a shape in the background which could have been a ship. Removing it carefully from its corner tabs, she put it to one side and carried on turning the pages. Whoever had taken the photos was an amateur who hadn't mastered the art of focusing properly, and other photos, which could have been of Daniel, were unclear. Then over the page there was a larger photo of a ship, a steamer moored in port and identified as 'SS *Felixstowe* 1926'. Other photos of smarter, bigger ships followed together with groups of sailors posing in front on the dockside. She couldn't tell if any were Daniel.

There was a gap of years before more photos followed and Annabel assumed it was thanks to the German Occupation and the war. The next photos were of a family, mother, father and baby sitting in what looked like the garden of Seagull Cottage, in the late 50s, she guessed from the clothes. Likely to be Daniel's sister, husband and daughter, Doris. Looking at her watch she was surprised to see it was nearing lunchtime so she put the albums in a cupboard and went down to see if Emilia was hungry.

'What are we doing this afternoon, Mummy?' her daughter asked as she finished the last mouthful of soup.

Her head so full of old photographs, Annabel hadn't given it much thought. Her mind whizzed through the options for a new arrival to the island.

'How about Castle Cornet? You know, it's on that long sticking out bit at the other end of the harbour. Really old with dungeons and other creepy things you find in castles.'

Emilia's eyes lit up.

'Does it have any ghosts? All decent castles have ghosts, don't they?'

Wondering how she would react if she said they had their own in-house ghost, Annabel shrugged. 'To be honest I don't know but we can find out when we go round. Anyway, I don't think ghosts appear during the day so we wouldn't see them.'

Emilia was not put off and rushed off to get ready. Annabel had only been to the castle a couple of times as a child and her memories of the visits were vague but she did remember being fascinated by the tales told by the lady who took them round. For some reason children were especially enthralled by gory and ghostly stories, the more gory the better.

As they approached the breakwater connecting the castle to the town, it appeared so much bigger as the dark granite stonework loomed above them. Emilia hopped around as they parked the car and approached the entrance. The slimy, twisting walls set the scene as they led the way through a portcullis and onto an outside area housing the shop and ticket office as well as providing great views towards St Peter Port. Wherever they walked there was the pervading smell of the sea.

'Wow, Mummy, this looks brilliant. And it's so big!' Emilia gazed up at the castle's many levels spread before them.

'Yes, there are loads to see. Come on, let's get our tickets and I want to book a tour if we can.'

They were lucky, the next tour began in fifteen minutes, giving them time to mooch around the shop and buy a guide book before joining the tour group. It was interesting for Annabel to see the castle through her daughter's eyes as her own memories began to return. The eight-hundred-year-old castle was inherently the same, but she noted how much more technology was used in presentations for the tech-savvy children of the day. Nothing could improve on the dark tunnels and twisting staircases which thrilled the children but caused the parents to stop and catch their breath when they had a chance. The guide knew her stuff and facts and figures flowed effortlessly from her lips as she led the way, answering questions with patience and a smile.

'Thanks, Mummy, this place is so cool. It's a shame there isn't a ghost, but the lady said she'd not heard of one. But perhaps there is and no-one has seen it. That could be true, couldn't it?' Emilia looked crestfallen and Annabel was torn.

'I suppose it could, sweetheart, though even without a ghost I think it's pretty cool, too. Now, shall we go and see what the café has to offer us starving tourists?' Emilia's face lit up and no more was said about ghosts as they looked at the range of cakes on display. Tea, juice and cake rounded off the afternoon nicely and Emilia was still full of the castle's charms as they headed back to the car. Another successful trip, Annabel thought, with a smile.

After she had kissed a very tired daughter goodnight, Annabel made her way to the studio, a flutter of anticipation dancing in her stomach. The same feeling she used to get in the early days of her romance with Clive. She knew it was daft and silly and a bit spooky, but she couldn't help herself. And if it helped her recover her sense of self, of worth, then what harm could it do?

The room was empty and she wondered if Daniel was making a point about lateness. She hoped he wouldn't be long as she was dying to share with him about the photo albums which she now retrieved from the cupboard.

There was a whoosh and the familiar deep voice from behind her.

'You found them! Good girl. Were they in the shed?'

As she turned round he materialised, beaming.

'And a good evening to you, Daniel. Don't you have any manners?'

'Sorry, yes. I tend to forget the social niceties these days. Good evening, Annabella,' he said, with a slight bow of the head. 'I trust you are well?' His eyes were twinkling.

She laughed.

'Okay, you've made your point. I'm well, thank you and yes, I found the albums in the shed and there are photos of you and what I think may be your ship.' She laid out the relevant photos for him and moved aside. His forehead was creased in concentration as he examined them.

'Yes, obviously this one,' pointing to the one in uniform with the ship in the background, 'is the one my sister used for the painting. Not sure about the ship, it's too blurred. And these others could be of me but again, they're not clear. I remember asking a young sailor to take the photos with my camera, a Box Brownie, which I thought was the bees' knees until the film was developed and saw how poor the photos were. Ended up buying another camera later and the photos improved.' He continued looking and then pointed to the one of the steamer, SS *Felixstowe*.

'Wonderful, she's the tramp steamer I spent years on from a young lad, going wherever the charters took us, round the Mediterranean mainly and then to the Far East when trade improved. Could tell a few tales, she could.' He looked up. 'Reminds me, have you thought anymore about typing up my memoir? We've got a few photos which could be used to back it up as genuine.' Before she could answer he went on, 'Oh, there's my last ship!' He pointed to a more modern liner in one of the later photos. 'The SS *Baltic*, of the White Star Line, which I captained for a number of cross-Atlantic cruises and had to wear a fancy gold-trimmed uniform to impress the passengers.'

'Brilliant, I hoped it was your ship, though there's no photo of you in uniform. Pity.'

Daniel shook his head.

'No, I'm glad. I looked like a ponced up actor in a bad film.' His eye caught the last photo of the family group. 'My sister, Peggy and her husband Albert and their little'un, Doris. We have a few photos here we can use, so what about it? My best-selling memoir?' He cocked his head, waiting.

'I suppose so. With the proviso if I'm not happy with any of it, then I can change it. For example, I'm not writing anything pornographic even if it does sell well these days.'

'Great to have you on-board! Pity about the porn, though.' As Annabel opened her mouth to say something, he laughed. 'Didn't mean it, honestly. But it might be a little risqué in parts or it wouldn't truthfully reflect a sailor's life of that time. Or before or since, I'd guess.' He winked and she found herself flushing and turned away to collect up the photos. Dear God, what had she let herself in for?

'I can't wait to get going. When can we start?' Daniel did

his usual pacing up and down.

'I'd like to finish your portrait first as it might be suitable for the cover.'

He clapped his hands.

'Brilliant! Oh, you're a clever girl, you are. Brighter than a lot of my officers and if you were a man, though I'm glad you're not, you'd go far.'

Gritting her teeth, she said, 'Believe it or not, but being a woman wouldn't hold me back these days. In fact women even captain ships in the Royal Navy as well as in the Merchant Navy.'

'Well, I'll be damned! A woman in charge of a ship?' He shook his head in disbelief. 'Things have moved on a bit too far from my day. Certainly can't see myself being told what to do by a woman.'

'No, I can't see that, either. Now, how about we get back to the painting and I'll use the photo of the SS *Felixstowe* for the ship in the background.'

Daniel perked up and was soon in his usual position by the telescope. Annabel had to force down her instinctive reaction to his misogyny and bigheadedness in order to focus on the painting. What worried her more than finishing the portrait without losing her cool, was how she was going to cope with typing his memoir, likely to be full of self-praise and hardly complimentary about women generally. And not wanting to kill him. Again.

Chapter 10

It was Monday and the beginning of the last week of the Easter break. The first thing Annabel did after breakfast was book a day trip to Herm for Tuesday; the forecast promised a warm, sunny day. Today was cloudier and she decided it was the ideal time to pop into St Peter Port to buy Emilia's school uniform. She had been putting it off as it signalled not just the end of the holiday but the start of a new life for her daughter, who she knew was nervous about it. It was understandable and she had felt the same when her parents had moved to England. They were due to meet the head teacher on Wednesday for a look around before term started the following Monday. His letter confirming the appointment had also explained the school had, like many schools, a House system, and Emilia had been placed in Balmoral. Annabel had smiled at the use of the names of the Royal palaces as, although Guernsey was a Crown protectorate, it had its own government. She vaguely remembered a Royal visit when she was at Vale school, but couldn't recall who it was or the reason. It had, however, given them a half-day's holiday so had been welcomed by the children at least.

Annabel left the kitchen to tell Emilia about the plans for the next few days and, as expected, was met with delight at the trip to Herm but with decided coolness with regard to uniform shopping.

'It won't take too long and we can have lunch in Town afterwards. And we might even have a look at the new summer clothes in the shops as last year's will be too small…'

Emilia gave her a hug, saying, 'Oh, thank you, Mummy, I'd love that. You're the best mummy ever!'

Annabel knew it was bribery but thought it was justified after all the upset of the past couple of years and the changes yet to come. But as soon as Emilia was in school she would have to focus on earning some money. She would need a lot more visibility for her paintings than in a local restaurant.

After parking on the Crown Pier they walked the short distance to the Commercial Arcade and the sports shop selling the uniforms. The summer uniform was a checked dress in red for Balmoral students and the main school colour was red too, making it easy to match with a red cardigan. Then there was the PE kit and a logoed school bag. At least there was no need to buy the winter uniform yet and a couple of dresses would see Emilia through to the autumn. It wasn't too painful, Annabel thought, as they left with fewer bags than she had expected.

A short walk to the High Street led them to an assortment of clothes shops displaying their summer ranges in all their bright colours. Emilia virtually skipped into the first and most expensive one, and Annabel sent up a silent prayer for a bargain. Her prayer was answered as there was a mini sale on for girls' dresses and they found a couple for Emilia to try, together with a skirt and top. Mother and daughter both approved the clothes which looked very pretty on a smiling Emilia and Annabel considered the cost reasonable. It was such a pity her daughter's clothes were outgrown before they were outworn. Annabel remembered her own mother lamenting the same thing when she was a girl. She studiously avoided checking the women's section, knowing it was better to avoid temptation. If and when she sold some paintings she would come back.

St Peter Port offered numerous eateries and Annabel had liked the look of Dix Neuf in the Arcade and minutes later they had retraced their steps and were waiting for a table. They were shown to one in the open window and had only been seated a few minutes when Annabel spotted Colette hurrying past.

'Colette! Hi!'

Colette looked round and smiled.

'Hi, Annabel. Can't stop as I have a meeting but I was going to phone you later. Might have a buyer for one of your paintings. Catch up when I'm free.' A quick wave and she was soon out of sight.

'Wow, Mummy, that's so cool. Wouldn't it be wonderful if you're going to be a famous artist?'

Annabel had a lump in her throat as she gazed at Emilia.

'It would, sweetheart, but it's early days and I'd be happy to be able to pay the bills and have us a bit of fun. On that note, have you chosen something for lunch?'

A leisurely drive round the island finished off the afternoon and Annabel found herself remembering the almost forgotten places from her childhood and pointed them out to Emilia who continued to lap up all the memories she shared.

After supper she unearthed their rucksacks, ready for the trip to Herm and advised Emilia what to pack in hers. Her daughter could hardly contain her excitement as she rushed around grabbing clothes and a swimsuit. Another island – and so small! No cars or bicycles and they could walk the whole way round in a couple of hours! After being bombarded with questions for what seemed hours, Annabel persuaded Emilia to read one of her library books before bedtime. Escaping downstairs, she had just poured a glass of wine when her phone rang.

Her stomach fluttered when she saw it was Colette.

'Hi, Annabel, sorry I couldn't stop to chat earlier, but I was already late for an appointment with my accountant. The good news is one of my regulars who's a big fan of art and has her own gallery, has fallen for your paintings. How about that?' Colette sounded as excited as if she herself were the artist.

'Why, that's wonderful, thanks, Colette. Is there one in particular she wants to buy?'

'She absolutely loves the big poppy painting and wants to buy it, but not only that she would like to talk to you about a possible exhibition in her gallery! Result or what?'

'Wow, I don't know what to say. It sounds too good to be true. I've only had one gallery exhibition before and although I had good reviews, I didn't sell many paintings.' Thinking about it, she hadn't had many paintings for sale at that time, anyway.

'It's definitely genuine. She's not only a lovely person but has pots of money and has supported a number of local artists over the years. To be honest I was hoping she'd like your work.'

'Well, if this comes off, I'll certainly owe you big time.'

'I'm sure it'll be fine and I'm only too happy to help a friend. Got a pen and paper? Right, her name's Laura Ogier and her gallery's called The Scully Gallery, and is at L'Islet, on the opposite corner to the supermarket. Here's her mobile number…'

Annabel made a note of the details and promised to phone her the next day.

'Laura insisted on paying a deposit and I've marked the painting as sold. Although you and I didn't discuss any financial arrangement I'm not looking for commission on paintings sold, I'll leave that to Laura.'

'It's very kind of you, Colette, but I would have been happy to pay commission.'

'Your paintings have given the restaurant a real lift and saved me decorating, so I'm happy with the current arrangement. Might have to rethink if you sell too many paintings!' she giggled.

Annabel joined in with the laughter. 'Don't worry, I've loads more and I can always provide more prints to keep you decorated.' She agreed to let Colette know what happened with Laura and they said goodnight on a high. As she reached for her wine she realised how time had marched on past Emilia's bedtime and the usual rendezvous with Daniel. Grabbing her glass she sped upstairs and was relieved to find her daughter fast asleep, her book open and the light on. Closing the book with a bookmark, she switched off the light and made her way upstairs to the studio, wondering if she would find an angry Daniel pacing up and down.

'Ah! There you are. At last. My word, you women can talk, can't you? Pity I can only hear half the conversation but I gather you've sold a painting and have a gallery interested in you. Well done.' Daniel was leaning against his telescope and gave her a broad smile.

Taken aback by his good mood, it was a few moments before she registered the meaning of his words.

'Daniel, how dare you listen in to my private conversations! Am I not allowed any privacy in my own home?' she said, flushed with annoyance.

'It's my home too, you know, and I only wondered what was keeping you as it was past our usual time and slipped downstairs to check. I couldn't help but hear what you were saying into that funny little gadget you call a mobile. Clever, aren't they? I don't think Doris ever had one but her son did, before he left for university. Only came back the once to tell his mother he was off to Australia—'

'All right, Daniel, we don't need to waste any more time. But please do respect my privacy. What if I'd been talking to a... a boyfriend?' It suddenly occurred to her it would be an even bigger problem if she ever did have a boyfriend and wanted him to stay the night. Her flush grew deeper as she fiddled with her brushes and pencils.

'Understood. If and when the situation arises, I promise to remain out of earshot.' He raised his eyebrows. 'You are thinking of remarrying then? You should, as you're far too young and damned attractive to remain a widow. Why, if I wasn't dead, I'd be first in the queue,' he said, with a wink.

'Ah, but you told me you weren't the marrying kind so I find that hard to believe. You didn't want commitment.'

'It might have been true once, but as I grew older I began to like the idea of family life, although it may have been difficult to make it work with me away at sea so much.' He sighed. 'Then war broke out and I hardly saw a woman for five years. If I'd only known how short my life was going to be, I would have tried harder to find a woman prepared to take me on.'

Annabel wanted to give him a hug, he looked so sad. And in spite of his old fashioned approach to women, he was still sexy. If he wasn't a ghost... Pulling herself together, she said, 'We're supposed to be getting on with this painting. No more talk of whether or not you'd have married and please take up your usual pose. I'll be able to carry on without you after this evening if we just crack on.'

He looked taken aback but did as he was told and stood by the telescope in silence. She went to work, filling in the details of his features, clothes and the telescope ready for the next stage of painting. The room was silent except for the scratching of her pencils on the paper. An hour later she was finished.

Flexing her fingers, she said, 'That's it for tonight, thanks, Daniel. I'll paint during the day once Emilia's at school.'

He came and stood by her to examine the picture, remaining silent.

She couldn't read his face and after a few minutes said, with some impatience, 'Well? What do you think?'

'Um? I think it's very good and I look forward to seeing the finished painting. But I was really thinking that perhaps it would be a chance for us to start working on my memoir. In the evening, that is, when your daughter's in bed. I can dictate while you type on your laptop thingy and you can paint during the day, as you said. What d'yer think?' His eyes bored into hers as she wondered how she had let herself be taken over by this man. No, not a man. A ghost.

Chapter 11

The shrill and unwelcome sound of her phone alarm brought Annabel out of a dream which seemed so real she was left shaken. She had been with a man – she couldn't see his face – and they were enjoying a passionate embrace in what had looked like her bedroom. Awake, her heart was pumping fast and her body was left tingling with anticipation of their lovemaking. What on earth? she asked herself, taking deep breaths as she fought aching disappointment. It had been well over three years since she and Clive had had sex and it had been perfunctory and unsatisfying. Annabel was trying to work out what had triggered such a sexy dream when Emilia rushed in telling her to get up as they didn't want to miss the boat to Herm.

'It's okay, we have plenty of time. Go and get dressed while I jump in the shower.' Emilia gave her a big kiss and ran off while Annabel headed for the shower, thinking she should really make it a cold one but couldn't face that and settled for as hot as she could stand it. By the time she had showered and towelled herself dry, the memory had faded and she was looking forward to the day ahead and the return to paradise.

The forecast had been right, the sky was cloudless and the sea sparkled under the sun's rays as they drove down towards St Peter Port and White Rock for the boat. Once the car was parked they walked the few yards to join the queue at the Trident ticket office. Being the last week of the holidays it was busy with excited children in the charge of their mothers with only the occasional visible father. The scene brought back happy memories for Annabel of when she and her mother went camping on Herm for a week in the summer, to be joined by her father at the weekend. They never went abroad but didn't need to, living on an island with fabulous beaches and with a jewel of a tiny island a boat ride away. Looking now at Emilia's happy face, she was glad once more of the chance to give her daughter a taste of what she had enjoyed, and taken for granted until the time her parents had sold up and left.

Knowing the sea breeze could be cool so early in the year, Annabel opted to sit inside the ferry by a window and Emilia knelt on the seat beside her, her nose pressed against the glass. Minutes later the passengers were all aboard and they cast off, moving towards the entrance of the harbour with Cornet Castle on their right, or starboard for the nautically inclined. Annabel was content to sit and watch her daughter's animated face as they drew further from St Peter Port, enveloped by the conversations of the grown-ups, the laughs of children and occasional cries of babies and toddlers. Overall there was a sense of anticipation, of "going away" even though for the majority it was only for a day. Some had backpacks and sleeping bags and Annabel envied them their forthcoming camping experience. As long as it stayed fine, as not quite as much fun in the rain, she remembered.

The ferry, a catamaran, sliced through the waves as they hit open water and Herm grew large in front of their eyes, lying peaceful under the spring sun. Seagulls ducked and dived alongside the ferry, cawing loudly to each other as they kept a look out on any possible snacks. The tourist season had barely begun and Annabel imagined the island waking up from the winter hibernation like a bear, flexing its muscles and opening its eyes to see what spring was bringing. Emilia's eyes grew wide with excitement as they neared the small harbour sheltering a handful of boats mostly belonging to Guernsey folk who could come and go as they pleased all year long.

The skipper brought the boat close to the harbour steps and once it was tied up the crew helped the passengers disembark. Some were pushing through the crowd, elbowing people aside while the more polite and relaxed waited their turn. There was no rush. Moments later Annabel, holding Emilia's hand, was helped ashore and moved away from those waiting for their luggage to be unloaded.

'Come on, we'll head for The Mermaid Tavern as I need a coffee and I'm sure you'd like an ice cream, yes?' Emilia's wide grin said it all and they followed the path leading to the shops and the pub. It looked as if most of the day trippers had the same idea as there was a crowd mingling around the courtyard benches and tables but the service was quick and they were soon sitting down with their refreshments.

Annabel let out a contented sigh, gazing around and noting what had changed since she was last there.

'They've added a new room at the back and it all looks bigger than I remembered. When we were over here camping Mum would do most of the cooking on a camping stove but occasionally we'd come here for a meal as a treat. It was always busy with a great atmosphere and music in the evenings.'

'I think you were very lucky, Mummy, and I can't wait to explore.' Emilia concentrated on her ice cream but a few minutes later her, looking thoughtful, she said, 'I'm feeling a bit nervous about school as I won't know anyone.'

Annabel pursed her lips.

'I know, sweetheart, but remember you didn't know anyone at your last school either as we'd moved to the area in the middle of the year. And you soon made friends, didn't you?'

'I suppose so, but it took a while and I felt very lonely for a long time.' She frowned as she licked the ice cream.

'Here's an idea. I'll ask Colette if she knows of any children in the area who go to Vale school and if so arrange a meet up. Even one friendly face would help, wouldn't it?' Annabel mentally crossed her fingers.

'Yes, thanks, Mummy. But I'd prefer a girl to a boy as boys are loud and bossy.'

She had to hide a smile at her daughter's view of the male sex and prayed Colette would come up with a girl or she would be in trouble.

A few minutes later they set off onto the path leading westward towards the common and onwards to the paths to the beaches and the north of the island. They had only gone a few yards when a voice called out, 'Excuse me, you left this behind!'

Annabel turned to find a man waving her sunhat in the air and smiled.

'Thanks, I brought it in case the sun gets too strong, but…' she pointed to the sky where the sun was partly hidden by cloud.

As she moved to take the hat from his outstretched hand, Annabel gave the man her full attention. She liked what she saw. He was, she guessed, early forties, tall with a sprinkling of silver in his fair floppy hair, a tanned face and a well-toned body clad in T-shirt and shorts.

'Well, you might need it later as the sun's always stronger in Herm than Guernsey,' he said, giving her a broad smile.

'Yes, I remember from my childhood. I'm showing my daughter around Herm for the first time.' She took her hat and, not sure what to do, shook his hand. It was like an electric shock.

'Ah, are you a local or frequent visitor? Pleased to meet you, I'm originally a local. My name's Richard, Richard Naftel.'

'And I'm Annabel Easton, but I was born a De La Mare, so originally a local too. And this is Emilia.' She took her daughter's hand and gently pushed her forward. Richard smiled and shook Emilia's hand, causing her to blush and look down at her feet.

'Nice to meet you, Emilia. What a pretty name, I don't think I've met anyone with that name before.' Richard looked over her head to Annabel, who mouthed 'she's shy' as she let her daughter draw back to her side. Richard, focusing on

Annabel, went on, 'Are you over for a day trip? Just the two of you?'

'Yes, it's just the two of us and we're here for the day. And you?' Conscious they were blocking the narrow path she moved to the side to allow a family to pass. Normally not one to engage in conversation with a stranger, her body's reaction forced her to stay. She hadn't felt like this with a man for so long, apart from Daniel, and a ghost didn't really count.

'I'm renting a cottage, up in the Manor village. I'm a writer on retreat and only come up for air occasionally.' He pushed his hair back, coughed and went on, 'I know this seems a bit pushy, but would you like to pop in for a drink later? I'll be in for the rest of the day and it would give me an excuse to take a breather.'

'Right, well, yes that would be nice, thank you. If we're in the village, perhaps after lunch? Which cottage is it?' Her stomach did a flip-flop.

'Pennywort, and you can't miss it…' he went on to explain how to find it among the cluster of buildings which formed the Manor village in the middle of the island. After making their farewells he turned back towards the lane leading up the hill to the village and Annabel and Emilia continued on the coast path.

'Are you okay with us popping in to see Richard later? If you'd rather not, I'd understand.' Acutely aware of her daughter's slight wariness of men, she didn't want to push it, although for her own part she welcomed the chance to spend more time with him.

'It's alright, Mummy, he seemed a nice man and he obviously likes you,' Emilia grinned slyly.

'Don't be silly. I think he's a bit lonely staying here on his own and would like a bit of company. Anyway, let's see how the day goes, shall we?' She strode ahead, trying not to think too much about Richard's charming smile and soft brown eyes.

The temperature slowly rose as the sun forced its way through the cloud and everyone they met smiled a greeting, seduced by the charms of the tiny island. Annabel kept a watchful eye on Emilia as she ran ahead over the open common, warning her to be careful of the numerous rabbit holes. She caught up with her at an incongruous little cemetery on the edge of the common and explained it was thought to be where two young men who had drowned 200 years ago were buried. They stood in silence for a moment before the sight of a rabbit jumping out of the long grass nearby made them laugh. Emilia tried to chase it but it was soon away and out of sight down one of the holes.

Laughing, Annabel said, 'Come on, we need to turn right soon and take the path to Shell Beach on the other side of the island. It was my favourite beach as a girl and I'll explain why when we get there. It has a little café so we'll have lunch there before going on to the Manor village.'

Five minutes later they arrived at the dunes edging Shell Beach and Annabel told Emilia to remove her shoes as she took off her own. 'Right, now we can feel how special this beach is,' she said, wriggling her toes and laughing as she ran down the beach. Her daughter ran after her and they both collapsed together onto the sand.

'Have you noticed anything different about this beach?' Annabel said, laying out their towels. Emilia screwed up her face and shook her head.

'Well, the sand isn't sand, it's actually millions and millions of tiny, tiny shells which have been swept here by something called the Gulf Stream. If we had a microscope we'd see all their different shapes.'

Emilia immediately scooped up a handful and peered at it closely.

'It does look a bit like tiny shells, now you've told me. Can I take some home to keep?'

'Only a small amount as we're not supposed to take any away. Just what's in your hand now, I'll give you a bag.' She dug out a small plastic bag from her rucksack and Emilia carefully poured in the sand, looking round to see no-one was watching. Once stored safely in the rucksack she was happy to start digging in the damp sand nearer the water's edge while Annabel settled down with a book, keeping one eye on her daughter. Later, they moved to the café for a light lunch, enjoying the feel of the warming sun on their bodies.

Leaving Shell Beach they took a path on the left, signposted Belvoir Bay which wound uphill along the coast. The bay was rocky with little sand and more secluded than Shell Beach and they only paused for a moment to take a look before continuing on the upwards path. To the right were open fields and they reached a path cutting through towards the Manor Village in the centre of the island. They didn't see a soul and Annabel was struck by the silence, only interrupted by the occasional song of a bird or the squeal of a gull.

'It's such a beautiful place, Mummy, can anyone live here?'

They were standing by a hedge looking across the fields and down towards the harbour. A group of buildings were just visible to their left.

'Only the people who work here can live on the island all the year round. I would imagine it gets a bit too quiet in the winter and bad weather would stop the ferry coming over with supplies which could be a problem. Tourists can stay in the hotel or in the self-catering cottages for weeks at a time if they can afford it. There's even a small primary school here for the children of the inhabitants with older children staying with host families in Guernsey during term time. We'll see the school when we reach the village. Come on, not far to go.'

It had been more than twenty years since she had been to Herm and her memory of the cottages and other buildings was hazy, and she had heard a great deal of renovation work had been carried out over the years. A buzz of excitement grew inside her and Annabel wasn't sure how much was due to seeing the lovely village again and how much was due to seeing Richard again. Tough call.

The little granite cottages were bathed in sunlight and their gardens were bursting with bright spring flowers and

Annabel could see why they were so popular with tourists, offering peace and seclusion hard to find in most places these days. The village was edged by granite walls and the southern entrance led the way to a miniscule chapel on the right, St Tugual's, going back centuries.

'Come on, this is one of my favourite places on the island and I'd love to know what you think.' She led the way through the heavy wooden, but modern, door and suddenly it seemed very dark. Small windows restricted the light coming in, not helped by the mass of granite walls. Above the granite, the arched walls and ceilings were white. At the far end stood a cloth covered altar with a cross and candlesticks. In front were rows of chairs. The chapel was empty and Emilia checked it out, wide-eyed.

'It's so sweet, like something out of a fairy tale.'

'Well, Herm has long been linked with fairies, along with pirates and monks so…' Annabel shrugged, waving her hands.

Emilia's eyes grew even wider and she sucked in a breath. Annabel could almost hear her daughter's brain digesting this information, which when a child herself, she had been sure was true. Yes, monks and pirates had definitely lived on the island, but fairies? However, since she was now apparently living with a ghost, then anything was possible.

Leaving the chapel they only had a short walk past more cottages before reaching Pennywort across the courtyard, adjoining the Manor House.

'Hi, glad you decided to call round. Come in, please.' Richard opened his arms wide to usher them in through the small kitchen and then into the sitting room.

'This is lovely, Richard. It looks so cosy,' she said, taking in the granite fireplace and soft painted walls displaying bright coloured paintings.

'It is, ideal for one or a couple. Please, sit down,' he pointed them to the leather sofa, adding, 'Can I get you a drink? I've tea, coffee, wine or fruit juice.'

'I'll go for juice, thanks, as we've still got some walking

to do,' Annabel said, conscious it might not be wise to drink alcohol while with Richard, a stranger, particularly with Emilia in tow.

'Fair enough,' he said, fetching two glasses of juice for them and a glass of wine for himself and then stretching out in an easy chair.

Annabel had noticed the dining table was covered with pages of typescript next to an open laptop.

'So, what do you write?'

Richard smiled. 'I've come here to try and finish my latest book away from life's distractions.' He turned towards Emilia, 'I write books for children, under the name P E Newton, my most popular series is—'

'"The Marvellous Academy"! Oh, I love those books in fact I've read them all.' Emilia flushed pink and looked down at her feet.

Annabel's mouth dropped open, recognising the name and the books. And here she was, sitting near one of the most popular children's writers of the day!

'How wonderful! Emilia's always telling me about your books and how the children at the academy have special skills or powers and enjoy amazing adventures.'

'Thank you both, I never expected to find a local fan, and I'm flattered.' Richard's eyes sparkled with genuine delight and Annabel felt the tug of attraction grow stronger.

He put down his glass and went over to a briefcase on the table, pulling out a hardback book and a pen and returned to the chair. 'This is my newest published book, only came out last week and I'd guess you haven't read it yet, Emilia?'

She looked up and gasped. 'No, I haven't. I didn't realise it was out already and was going to order it from the library.'

'Then it's my pleasure to give you a signed copy.' Richard opened the book to the title page and wrote, "For Emilia, With Warmest Wishes, P E Newton".

As he handed her the book, she managed to mumble, 'Thank you very much.'

'That's so kind, Richard, thank you and I'm sure the

other children will be jealous when she starts school next week.' Seeing his puzzled look, she went on, 'We only arrived in Guernsey a few weeks ago and Emilia will be starting at the Vale school, which she has been a little nervous about.'

'I see.' He smiled at Emilia and, leaning forward, said, 'Why don't you act as if you're a student of the Marvellous Academy and nothing and no-one can get to you. Pretend you're invincible and that's what you'll become.'

Emilia, clutching her book nodded, her eyes bright.

'I will, thank you.'

Annabel guessed her daughter was dying to start reading the book and suggested she might like to sit outside in the courtyard while she and Richard carried on chatting. With a quick, 'Thanks,' she was off.

'You've absolutely made her day, if not her year, and I can't thank you enough. Since her father died, life hasn't exactly been smooth sailing although moving to Guernsey seems to be helping,' Annabel said, softly.

Richard frowned.

'I'm so sorry, I hadn't realised. Guess I assumed you were divorced. Must have been hard on you both and brave of you to make a fresh start in Guernsey.'

'Well, I loved my childhood here and I wanted Emilia to enjoy the things I did and it's so safe here compared to a city like Manchester.' She paused. 'Do you live in Guernsey?'

He shook his head.

'No, like you I grew up here but left to go to university. I… I live in London but come over here when I need to focus on my writing. There're too many distractions in the big smoke.'

'I suppose.' She was puzzled. Surely he didn't need to come as far as Herm for peace and quiet? Some of her Facebook friends were writers, sharing how they managed to write their books around children, husbands and even day jobs. A week or even a weekend away on a retreat would be considered by them as a great treat. A thought struck her.

'Do you have a family, Richard?' Her stomach clenched.

He sighed, a look of sadness replacing the cheerfulness.

'Yes, I have two children but my... wife and I are divorced. I see the children when I can but because the divorce wasn't exactly amicable, it's not as often as I'd like.'

'I'm sorry to hear that. It must be very difficult. I'd hate to be separated from Emilia. Do you ever bring them here with you?' She couldn't help feeling relief that he was divorced, it meant they were both free for... whatever.

'No, I only ever come here to write. And they'd find it too quiet, being teenagers used to the high octane of London and its unlimited attractions.'

'I'm a country girl at heart and I think my daughter is, too. My aim is to provide her with a safe environment in which to grow up and then she'll be free to make up her own mind.' The thought of Emilia going off to England and not coming back was something she couldn't contemplate. 'Are you staying long in Herm?'

He spread his hands out.

'Depends on a couple of things.'

'And they are?'

'How long it takes me to finish the book and,' he paused, his eyes locking on to hers, 'if I can persuade you to see me again.'

Chapter 12

Annabel was distracted when she and Emilia left the village to walk the last leg of the tour round Herm. As they followed the path leading to the Seagull campsite she was thinking of Richard and the date they had planned for the following week when Emilia would be at school. He was coming over to Guernsey for the day and they would meet for lunch. Was it too soon? She hadn't been on her own for long and would it upset Emilia? The thoughts skittered though her mind as she tried to focus on where they were going and answer the questions her daughter asked about Herm.

'What do the people who live here do in the winter when tourists don't come?'

'As I said earlier some things stay open, like the cottages and The Mermaid. And I understand there are always lots of jobs needing doing, like refurbishments, decorating and repairs. I guess it could get a bit boring after a while, though. What do you think, sweetheart?'

'I'd miss the shops and cinema and being at a school with lots of children. I'd want to go over to Guernsey quite often.'

They spent a few moments discussing the pros and cons of spending the winter there as they entered a tree-lined lane leading to the campsite.

'Ooh look, Mummy! They have lots of tents here and they look so big you can even stand up in them. Please can we stay in one in the summer?' Emilia jumped with excitement as she pulled at her arm.

'Perhaps. If I can afford a holiday this year I'd love to come here. It looks so much bigger and better organised than when I came with my parents.' She noted the rows of large frame tents with their own picnic tables and even spotted a small shop near the shower and toilet block. Very civilised. And what a view over Puffin's Bay!

She had to almost drag Emilia away to continue through to the cliff path and the very last stretch down to Rosaire Steps where they would be catching the ferry home. Up on the cliffs they had a great view over the sea towards Guernsey, looking more golden as the sun's rays warmed the granite buildings.

'Come on, I can see the ferry leaving St Peter Port. We should be back at the cottage in an hour.'

Annabel, too tired to cook, opted for a fish supper from the chippie on the Bridge, and it was delicious, eaten off paper in the garden. Emilia, keen to read her book, was happy to go to bed early, leaving Annabel free to unwind with a glass of wine as she contemplated the evening ahead. As she thought about Daniel and his portrait she suddenly remembered the gallery owner and called the number. It was answered by a woman with a distinctive Irish accent.

'Annabel, good to hear from you. To be sure, Colette will have told you how much I love your work and want to talk with you. It would be grand if we could meet at the gallery, say tomorrow morning?' Laura sounded as bubbly as Colette.

'I'd love to, if you don't mind me bringing my daughter who's ten, well-behaved and happy to read a book while we talked.'

'Sure, that's no problem, I could wish my son was into reading instead of video games which drive me mad!' she laughed. 'Would eleven o'clock work for you?'

Annabel was happy to agree and put the phone down feeling energised and excited. Finishing her wine she went up to the attic to see if Daniel had turned up.

The room was empty.

A bit deflated after the excitement of the day she spent a few moments sorting out the colours she would use for the portrait and checking her brushes were all in good condition.

Tempting though it was to make a start now, she knew it would be better to wait until Emilia was at school and she had clear days.

'Good evening, Annabella.'

Startled, she looked up to see – no-one.

'Come on, Daniel, don't play games, it's been a long day,' Annabel said, torn between being irritated and pleased he was there. Well, sort of.

Gradually his figure materialised in the usual place near the window and he proffered a salute and a smile.

'It's good to see you, *bella mia*, the house has been so quiet without you both today. How was Herm? Overrun by tourists I presume.'

She smiled, warmed by the endearment and the twinkle in his eyes.

'Herm was lovely, even better than I remembered and hardly overrun by tourists.' She had a thought. 'In your day it was a private island wasn't it? Were locals allowed to visit?'

'Indeed it was, leased by Sir Compton Mackenzie, a writer who enjoyed the sea. I met him a couple of times when islanders were allowed to visit though we were restricted on where we could walk.' He rubbed his chin, his eyes looking back to the past. 'It's a beautiful little island and Mackenzie was quite a character, shared a dram or two while we traded tales.'

'To think you met Sir Compton Mackenzie! It must have been about a hundred years ago.' She shook her head.

'Yes, remember I've been dead quite a while,' he said dryly.

She flushed. 'I tend to forget sometimes as you're so… real.'

'Lucky for you I'm not, Annabella, as I would have to kiss you,' he said with a grin.

'Yes it is, isn't it?' Her voice was light but inside her stomach turned over as she wondered what it would be like to be kissed by him. If he was alive. Then Richard's face popped into her head and she smiled. Now he was definitely alive – and available.

She realised Daniel was staring at her, his head on one side and arms crossed.

'Something's different tonight. Did anything happen in Herm?'

Blimey, for a man and a dead one at that, he's very perceptive, she thought.

'We met a man who writes children's books, one of Emilia's favourite authors and he gave her a signed copy of his latest book. Really made her day.' She started rearranging her brushes to avoid looking at him.

He pursed his lips and nodded.

'I'm sure it did. I've noticed how much she likes reading. Is this guy a local then?'

'Sort of, he was born here but lives in England and visits Herm to write.'

'You liked him, didn't you, *bella mia*?'

Still fiddling with the brushes, she nodded.

'But that's wonderful news! And do you think he likes you? Are you seeing him again?' Daniel leaned forward, his face close to hers and she whispered, 'Yes.' Somewhat taken aback he was pleased she had met someone, she asked herself why. After all he wasn't available even though he made it clear he found her attractive.

He clapped his hands, saying, 'I hope it works out for you as you deserve happiness with someone even if it means you leaving my house. I shall miss you, Annabella.'

'Hey, not so fast! I've only just met this guy so it's too soon to see me walking down the aisle or whatever. And I do love living in your house and would miss you too so let's slow things down, right?' She smiled and reached out to touch his hand, only to touch air. They both laughed.

'Sorry, you're right. It's early days, but I do want you to be happy and not leave it too late like I did. In the meantime, how about my idea of you typing my memoir? They'd include the times spent with Compton Mackenzie and perhaps more well-known names will come to mind once we start.'

'Okay, you've twisted my arm. I must admit I'm curious to learn more about your adventures, at least those which are publishable.'

'Let's start tomorrow evening; you must be tired after your day in Herm. Ciao.' He winked and moving towards the window, disappeared.

The following morning, promptly at eleven, Annabel and Emilia arrived at The Scully Gallery, only a short drive away. Sleek and tastefully decorated, for a moment Annabel felt out of place in what was obviously quite a classy establishment. Before she could turn and run a woman about her own age, immaculately turned out in a designer skirt suit and with a chic haircut, came forward and reached for her hand.

'You must be Annabel! I'm Laura, so good to meet you and your lovely daughter.' She smiled at Emilia who, hugging her book, smiled in return. 'I understand you love reading, which I think is grand. I devoured books when I was younger but, unfortunately, have little time to read these days. You'll be quite happy sitting with your book while your mammy and I have a chat about her marvellous paintings?'

Emilia nodded, looking overwhelmed.

Laura led the way to a desk in the corner and after offering Annabel a coffee, disappeared to an adjoining kitchen and returned with two cups.

'Right, tell me about yourself, Annabel, and how long you've been painting.'

She gave a brief overview of her background, including her art training in London and how she had developed her own style over the years since.

'I particularly love watercolour as a medium but also like experimenting with mixed media to create more depth. I've been focusing on natural subjects lately, such as the giant poppy painting you like and think I'll be spoilt for inspiration here in Guernsey. And I also paint the occasional portrait if I like the subject.'

Laura listened intently, making notes as she sipped her coffee.

'It's refreshing to find an artist who likes to create art they love as opposed to churning out what art critics view as fashionable. Although Guernsey's small, you'd be surprised how many islanders appreciate modern art and build their own collections.' She waved her arms to embrace the paintings on display and Annabel noted what an eclectic mix they were. Some were stunningly beautiful with probably stunning prices to match. 'My clients love to discover artists unknown to them and I'm sure they'll love your work. Have you a portfolio to show me?'

'Yes, it's here on a memory stick. I also offer Giclée prints of my most popular originals and could work to commission.'

'That's grand, let me take a look.' Laura inserted the stick into her laptop and browsed the display. Looking up, she smiled. 'These are beautiful and are enough to form your own exhibition, if you're interested.'

Annabel's heart raced. Her own exhibition! In such a smart gallery! It would be every artist's dream.

Breathing deeply, she replied, 'I certainly am interested, Laura, if you could give me more details.'

'For sure. This is good timing as I've had an artist who's had to cancel an exhibition through illness and I can slot you in sooner than normal. I usually highlight an individual artist for two weeks in the upstairs gallery and we work out prices for each painting between us. At the moment your prices are too low.' Annabel's jaw dropped. Too low? She had been worried they were too high!

Laura grinned and continued, 'Which is understandable when you haven't had professional representation. Sold paintings will remain on show until the exhibition ends as they might initiate a commission. If all goes well, there should be only a few paintings left and I'd be happy to continue showing them with the other artwork downstairs.' She paused, making a note on her pad. 'Any questions?'

Annabel grinned. 'Yes, when can you arrange an exhibition, and how much commission do you charge?'

Chapter 13

Annabel floated on air as she left the gallery, explaining to Emilia about the contract for an exhibition.

'I told you, Mummy, you'd be famous after Colette displayed your paintings. The lady and her gallery are very posh, aren't they?'

'Posh in a nice way, sweetheart. How about we go to Colette's restaurant to tell her the good news and celebrate with some cake?' Emilia squeezed her hand in response and they were soon in the car on the way to the Bridge. Her mind racing, Annabel found it hard to focus on the road. Things were happening so fast: Daniel and his portrait and memoir, meeting Richard, and now her first proper art exhibition. It seems Guernsey was her good luck charm. As long as it lasted…

The restaurant was enjoying the calmer time between morning coffee and lunches and they soon found an empty table. Annabel asked the young waitress if Colette was available and, after taking her name, the girl went to find her. As she waited she looked at her paintings on the walls, which did indeed complement the restaurant, and wondered what to do about them. She was still thinking when Colette came out of the kitchen and rushed over, exclaiming, 'Well, how did it go?'

'Brilliant, thanks. Laura's going to host an exhibition in late June to include every painting I have and wants me to charge about three times what I do now. But how did you know I was meeting her?'

'She phoned me last night. Oh, I'm so pleased for you, Laura's exhibitions are renowned for launching previously unknown artists, with buyers even coming over from Jersey.' Clapping her hands, she said, 'We must celebrate. Champagne and cake and what would Emilia like? We have some scrummy ice cream milkshakes and I can recommend the strawberry in particular.'

'Yes, please, Colette, can I have the milkshake and cake?'

'Of course, I'll go and see to it and will be back in a jiffy.'

Five minutes later and Colette came back with a bottle of champagne in an ice bucket, while the waitress bore a tray with two glasses, a milkshake and three slices of cake and three plates.

'This looks amazing, thank you. Is this one of your lady's special cakes?'

'It is, our bestselling coffee and walnut cake, which is to die for. We're not counting calories today,' Colette said, pouring the champagne into two flutes.

'Salut! And now tell me all the details.'

Between sips of champagne and bites of cake, Annabel told her friend what had been agreed with Laura.

'As it's all down to you displaying my pictures, how would you feel if we only displayed my prints here and then I can exhibit the originals? They're much cheaper but you'd still have the same decorative effect and I'd happily pay a commission on any sales. I owe you that much,' Annabel said, savouring the bubbles in her mouth.

'That's a great idea, a win-win for us both. You need to be seen primarily as an up-market artist but isn't above selling limited edition prints for the less well-off. Like me!' Colette chuckled, waving her glass around. 'I'd be happy with a print in my home, although perhaps I should buy an original as an investment as when you become famous the prices will rocket.'

It was Annabel's time to laugh. 'I don't see any chance of that happening, but I appreciate the thought. By the way, I was expecting Laura to be local, not an Irish colleen. Though she is lovely.'

Colette nodded.

'I forgot to mention it. She came over some years ago to work at the Candie Museum, setting up some exhibitions, and met and fell in love with a local chap, Gerry Ogier. He's a very successful businessman who helped her set up the gallery. Lovely guy, too, they come to the restaurant quite regularly.'

The celebration continued for a joyful fifteen minutes before Colette was needed in the kitchen, insisting Annabel take the remaining champagne home with her to finish later, they had only had a small glass each. She and Emilia arrived home still feeling on a high and after lunch spent the rest of the day on the beach at L'Ancresse. A little paddling and sandcastle making together followed by reading (Emilia) and dozing (Annabel) made for a delightful afternoon.

Colette popped round after work and they finished the champagne accompanied by some nibbles she brought with her.

'I'm having some friends round on Sunday and would love you and Emilia to join us. Weather permitting, it'll be a barbecue and very relaxed as there will be other children, including a couple near Emilia's age. I've already told them about you and they can't wait to meet you and I know you'll get on brilliantly. Do say yes.' Colette squeezed her arm in encouragement.

'Thanks, we'd love to come and I can't wait to meet them either. My life is opening up so much I'm almost dizzy!' She laughed. 'Although perhaps it's the champagne!' She lowered her voice so Emilia, in the next room, couldn't hear. 'I met someone in Herm and we're meeting for lunch next week in Guernsey and he's quite nice…' She went on to tell her more and Colette listened wide-eyed.

'You're right, your life is taking off and I couldn't be more pleased. This guy Richard sounds ideal and I hope to meet him if it works out between you. I'd been wracking my brains to think of any eligible men and couldn't think of any. All the best ones are taken.' She topped up the champagne.

'Here's to love and friendship!'

They raised their glasses for the toast.

'How many are coming on Sunday?'

Colette counted on her fingers; 'My brother Nick and Jeanne with their two kids Harry and Freya; Charlotte and Andy with their son James; and Tess and Jack with baby Mia. Gosh, that's ten without us. Will be a bit lively, I'm afraid.' Colette grinned.

'The livelier the better, I've led too quiet a life for too long. Is there anything I can do to help?'

Colette shook her head.

'Nope. But thanks for asking. The boys will take care of the barbecue, naturally,' she rolled her eyes, 'and I will prepare salads, jacket potatoes and the usual accompaniments while Jeanne and Charlotte are providing desserts. Mind you, any bottles of wine are welcome,' she said, grinning.

'No probs, happy to contribute.'

'Forgot to ask, how are things with, you know, the ghost?' Colette looked around nervously, as if he might appear at any time.

'Going well, actually. His portrait is coming on and it's been interesting listening to his stories. I've agreed to write his memoir and find a publisher if I can. Daniel's agreed for me to keep any royalties as I think he wants me to buy this cottage one day.' She paused, seeing a mix of emotions cross her friend's face. 'Is there a problem?'

'I don't know. It all seems so unreal, you painting a portrait of a ghostly sea captain who's pretty delish and then also writing up said ghost's memoir of his, probably nefarious, exploits while he sailed around the Med. Hard to get my head around.' She gulped some champagne and choked and Annabel had to thump her back for a few minutes. After a deal of coughing and wheezing she calmed down.

'Thanks. Do you not see how it looks a bit weird to me?'

'Yes for sure. I guess I'm so used to Daniel being around it's like he's part of the furniture.' A whooshing sound near her head made her gulp.

'What was that?' Colette looked around, wide-eyed.

'That was Daniel showing he's listening in which he has agreed not to do, haven't you?' She raised her voice as much as she dare not wanting to alert Emilia next door. A whispered, 'Sorry, I'll go' and a soft touch on her arm and she knew he'd gone.

'He's gone. I'm sorry, Colette, but he's quite harmless, just finds it hard to believe this is no longer his house.'

Colette took a deep breath.

'Well, rather you than me. I'm not sure I'd cope, no matter how good looking he is or was. Could make it difficult if you ever brought a boyfriend home, though,' she said, winking.

Annabel grimaced

'Yes, I know, but it's something to face if and when it happens. Daniel knows I've met someone and seemed pleased for me. A prospective boyfriend may see it differently.'

'I should say so! My, your life is hardly boring, girl.' Colette stood up, saying, 'On that note I'd better trot back home before Jonathan sends out a search party.'

After a sisterly hug, she went and Annabel was left realising she had to make supper and soon.

Later in the evening Annabel went up to her studio practising in her head what she wanted to say to Daniel. Honestly, he really had no manners or sense of propriety! She couldn't risk him turning up, or listening in, when she had friends round as she hoped to if and when she had some. Colette would understand but Jonathan? By the time she reached the top floor she was raring to let rip.

'Daniel, are you there? It's no good hiding because you know I'm annoyed with you. We have to sort this out if you want me to write up your precious memoir.'

She stood, hands on hips, and waited.

Slowly, he began to appear, taking his place between the

window and the telescope, as if needing protection. Even if she did want to throw something at him, and she did, it would be pointless.

'Hello, Bella, I know, I know you're mad with me and I'm sorry. I couldn't help myself, I wanted to know what you told your friend about me. A lovely lass, by the way—'

'I know, you told me, remember? It's hard for you, I realise that, but you absolutely must stick to our agreement and stay away from downstairs or anywhere other than in here. Colette knows about you but as you heard, she does find it hard to understand. And most people would simply flip and make a scene and I might lose friends or have to move.' She took a deep breath. 'Do you understand, Daniel? This is very important. It's my life which could get messed up. Mine and my daughter's. Not yours. Yours is... over. Caput. I'm sorry, but that's how it is.' She found herself trembling and crossed her arms to steady herself.

He looked so sad and his shoulders slumped and she wondered if she'd gone too far. After all, the poor man had died in his prime, before he could enjoy a family life...

'You're right, as usual, and I can only say how sorry I am. Being a ghost can be hard, a curse. I can see the life carrying on around me but I am no longer a part of it, can't join in, hold a conversation. You are the only one I can talk to, who can be my friend, but I have to keep my distance, play by the rules. And as you've probably gathered, I've never been one for rules,' he said, managing a grin. 'You mean a great deal to me and I wouldn't knowingly do anything to cause you harm or distress. You make my non-life bearable. It's why I want to help you, help you and your daughter have security and your own roof over your head.' He spread his palms upwards. 'If I promise to keep utterly and completely to our agreement, will you forgive me and type up my story? When I was alive I had talked briefly to a publisher who'd expressed an interest in it, saying it had the makings of a bestseller.' Shrugging, he went on, 'Of course times have changed and my story might not be of interest to readers today, but we won't know unless we try. It's up to you.' He stood still, his hand seeming to stroke his precious telescope as he waited for her response.

Annabel slumped into her chair. It had been quite a speech and it would take a very hard heart to dismiss it. And her heart was far from hard. In fact it was beating fast with the emotion stirred within her. Once more, she felt the desire to throw her arms around him, comfort him, as one would a small, lost boy. Finally, looking up, she smiled.

'We'd better get started then. No time like the present, is there?'

His eyes lit up.

'You mean it? You'll type my story on that computer and then find a publisher?'

'I'll do the typing but I can't guarantee we'll find a publisher.' She opened her laptop and powered it up. 'What are we calling it?'

He stroked his beard.

'How about, "Adventures of a Swashbuckler"?'

'Swashbuckler? Doesn't that mean a pirate?'

'Not necessarily. It can mean an adventurer who sails the seas to seek his fortune. Or it did in my day.'

'Right, it'll do for now but a publisher might wish to change it.' She typed in the title and asked, 'Author name?'

'Oh, I can't use my own name. I was in the Royal Navy, remember. Can we make one up?'

'I suppose so, though pen names are usually used by fiction writers.' She thought for a moment. 'How about Captain Daniel Gregg? It keeps your initials which might be useful.'

'Yes, it'll do. What next?'

'Now you start telling me your story, and don't go too fast.'

Daniel took up the stance of an actor about to deliver a speech and Annabel started giggling.

'What's so funny?' he said, frowning.

'Sorry, but you look a bit theatrical and it's putting me

91

off. Pretend you're reading from a book. Keep it natural.'

Taking her literally, he opened his hands as if holding a book and began his story.

'I had dreamt of going to sea since I was a small boy. Couldn't wait to join the ships I saw coming in and out of St Peter Port in Guernsey. What adventures were to be had in foreign lands...' He continued dictating and as she typed his deep voice thrilled her like a lover's caress. This isn't going to be easy, she thought, trying to concentrate.

It was the last weekend of the Easter holidays and Annabel noticed Emilia swinging between excitement at making new friends and periods of withdrawal, keeping in her room and not wanting to talk. Unfortunately, Colette hadn't been able to come up with anyone Emilia's age at the school and so she would be going into the unknown alone. She cheered up on Sunday when they were due to go to Colette's for the barbecue. Apparently Freya and Harry, Colette's niece and nephew, were seven and nine so they could play together.

'Why don't you take your new book as Harry might also be a fan of those stories. It will give you something to talk about.' Annabel was plaiting Emilia's hair after she had changed into her new summer dress. Although not yet summer, the past few days had been heating up and it was forecast to stay fine for the day.

'Okay, I will. It'll be nice to have someone to share with, even if he is a boy. Thank you, Mummy,' she said as Annabel finished the plaits.

Sighing, Annabel couldn't help worrying how her daughter would cope at the new school. At least moving to Guernsey had proved to be a positive experience for Emilia so far and as long as she made friends soon, school should not be an issue.

'Right, time to go, sweetheart. You fetch your book and I'll get the wine.' Annabel wasn't feeling as upbeat as she appeared. It had been a long time since she had socialised with a group, not since Clive had become withdrawn and stopped inviting people around or going out. She had used to love meeting other couples but now – well, she had to admit she was scared. A close group of friends like Colette's might not want to welcome a stranger into their lives, in spite of what her friend said. Just because Colette liked and welcomed her didn't mean her friends would. And if they didn't like her, how would it affect her friendship with Colette? There was more riding on this barbecue than she had originally imagined. Her hands were sticky with sweat and she had to grip the wine tightly. She was also worried they would be heavy drinkers, not wanting to be with drunks after Clive. Normal social drinking she could cope with, not averse to a glass of wine herself.

As they approached Colette's house they could see several cars parked in the drive and Annabel whispered to Emilia, 'Time to go and make some friends, yes?'

Emilia, grinning, nodded. 'Sure thing.' Annabel kept her fingers crossed for them both.

The front door was ajar and they walked into the hall, following the sound of voices into the conservatory and the garden. Annabel spotted her hostess in a group near the barbecue and headed towards her.

'Hi, Colette, I come bearing wine to go with this wonderful food you've prepared,' she said nodding towards a large table groaning under the weight of colourful salads and finger foods.

'Thanks, we have a large ice bucket here for wine and beer,' Colette pointed to a builders' bucket of ice, depositing the bottle of white wine and then giving her a hug. 'What would you like to drink?' She chose a glass of chilled white. 'Good, everyone's here now so I'll make the introductions then you can all get to know each other while I keep an eye on the boys and the food,' she winked at the menfolk huddled around the barbecue.

The three women were grouped with the children around a sandpit set far from the barbecue and they looked up and smiled as they approached.

'This is my lovely new neighbour, Annabel, who I've told you all so much about.' Seeing the look on her face she added, 'Only kidding. Just the good bits. And her daughter, Emilia. So, this is my sister-in-law Jeanne who has to put up with my brother Nick, bless her,' pointing to a dark-haired woman with a warm smile, 'then Charlotte, who's from England but we don't hold that against her,' pointing to a woman with beautiful chestnut hair and a creamy complexion, 'and finally Tess, who's a doctor working with my husband. She was born here but moved to the mainland and came back a few years ago.' Tess, a brunette with short hair was sitting with a baby girl in the sandpit. 'Right, girls, I'll leave you to it,' Colette gave them a big smile and turned to go back inside.

Jeanne was the first to speak.

'We're all so pleased to meet you at last as Colette has assured us we'll all get on like the proverbial house on fire. The trouble with living on an island is we keep meeting the same people and it's great to expand the pack.' She turned to the two older children who were helping a little boy with a sandcastle. 'These are Freya and Harry and they'd love to say hi to Emilia, wouldn't you?' The girl looked up and grinned at Emilia who smiled back. Harry said a quick 'hi', and carried on with the sandcastle. 'Harry, Emilia's brought an exciting looking book with her, why don't you come and see what it's about while Freya helps James?' Turning to Emilia, she said, 'Harry loves reading, he inherited it from me as I'm a writer and adore books.'

Harry, looking intrigued, came and joined Emilia and they went to find a space further away on the lawn.

Charlotte chipped in.

'Colette tells us you're an artist who's just landed an exhibition with Laura Ogier, which is brilliant news. I shall pop down there to take a gander as soon as it's open as I love adding to my collection.' She gave a throaty laugh. 'I was brought up in a house with loads of old oil paintings, putting me off art for years. Now I admire anyone who can create something beautiful. Talking of which,' she said, turning towards the little boy, 'this is my son James, who started school last year and loves it, don't you, darling?'

James looked up and smiled at Annabel.

'Hello, are you the new lady? Mummy's right, I do like school and can't wait to go back tomorrow. I've missed my friends.' He went back to the sandcastle.

Annabel turned to Tess, who was filling up small shapes with sand making her baby giggle.

'Hello, Tess, lovely to meet you, and what a gorgeous baby. What's her name?'

'Hi, great to meet you, too. This is Mia and she's nearly a year old. Bless her, it's been teething time lately so there's not been much sleep for any of us has there, eh, poppet?'

The women soon slipped into an easy conversation and Annabel began to relax. They all had so much in common being young mums with interesting backgrounds. Charlotte was a writer who happened to own a publishing company which, she thought, might come in useful when Daniel's memoir was finished. Jeanne had written several books, fiction and non-fiction, set on Guernsey making them quite a creative group all round.

'Time for food, everyone – come and get it!' called Colette, waving from the table. The women joined the men who were then introduced to Annabel as the cooked meat was handed out.

'Annabel, please meet Nick, my brother who builds boats and is quite handy with a barbecue.' Colette pointed to a tall man with curly, dark but greying hair and deep blue eyes set in a tanned face. They exchanged a quick 'hi' and cheek kiss before Colette went on to introduce Andy, a slim man who was an architect and married to Charlotte. Another cheek kiss and then finally, Jack, tall and muscular and a property developer married to Tess.

'Good, now everyone please help yourselves,' Colette waved her arm over the food, 'and there's plenty of wine and beer on ice.'

Annabel had to chivvy on Emilia who was deep in conversation with Harry, her precious book open between them.

'Come on, eat now and chat later, sweetheart, as I'm not cooking tonight.' Emilia reluctantly closed her book and went with Harry to queue for food, continuing to chat.

Jeanne and Annabel exchanged a glance and burst out laughing.

'I think we can say they've hit it off! Emilia's been so anxious about making friends over here and I had the same problem when we moved to the mainland. It would be lovely if they could have playdates as I assume Harry goes to a different school?'

'Yes of course. We're in Perelle and I'm sure we can arrange something. You could come to me and we can chat while the kids play.' Jeanne smiled.

'Love to, thanks. Colette says you have an amazing garden and I've never been great with plants. Much better at painting them than growing them.'

Jeanne nodded. 'I can garden but can't paint and, to be honest my beautiful garden is mainly thanks to my late grandmother who had a flair for gardening. We each have our own skills, Annabel, we can't be good at everything.' Annabel laughed.

'You're so right! But looking around everyone here, I'm impressed by the various talents and skills possessed by you all. Quite a mix.'

'We may be a small island and not as high-flying as Jersey, but we have a lot going for us, isn't that right, Tess?' She turned to the other woman who had been listening while filling her plate.

'Absolutely. Like you and Jeanne, I left the island young and never expected to return, but life throws us curve balls sometimes and now I'm back I wouldn't want to be anywhere else. Are you settling in okay? It's hard at first, but making friends will help,' Tess smiled at Annabel, as they finished loading their plates.

'And as an expat who will never count as a local,' Charlotte butted in, laughing, 'I endorse what the others have said about Guernsey and was welcomed into this fab group of people with warmth and acceptance. I'm looking forward to getting to know you better as you learn more about us.'

Annabel looked at the smiling faces around her and her earlier fears melted away. She was home and nothing could spoil he new-found happiness.

Chapter 14

The alarm emitted its shrill buzz, tugging Annabel from a dream involving an ocean liner of years gone by where the passengers were dressed to the nines for dinner. She appeared to be a favoured passenger, invited to the Captain's table and as she took her seat recognised the Captain as none other than Daniel. Just as he turned towards her with a broad smile the alarm went off. It took her a moment or two to orientate herself in the present and remember this was Emilia's first day at Vale school.

Annabel shot across the landing and knocked on Emilia's door before opening it and to find her daughter already wearing her red checked dress and the new school sandals.

'I woke early and thought I might as well get ready. I don't want to be late on my first day, do I?' She was smiling but Annabel noticed it didn't quite reach her eyes.

'No, sweetheart, you don't and you look lovely in that dress. I'm very proud of you and I'm sure you'll love your new school.' She squeezed her in a hug, tears pricking at her eyes for some reason. 'Right, I'll be downstairs as soon as I've showered and dressed. How about if I make pancakes for breakfast to celebrate your first day?' The huge grin on Emilia's face said it all.

There was a real buzz outside the school gates as the children greeted each other after their three-week holiday. Annabel took it as a good sign the children enjoyed school and she couldn't see even one glum face. And the parents, virtually all mums with the occasional visible father, looked even happier – no surprise there! The gates were opened and after quick goodbyes the children went through, chattering loudly. Annabel waited to escort Emilia in and find her teacher, as the head had suggested. Once that was accomplished and Emilia gave her a quick last hug, she left.

Driving back, she thought about how her daughter would cope. She could only hope the lack of a friend would soon be remedied. Annabel knew she had been lucky to meet the great group at the barbecue, promising new friends ahead. She wanted the same for Emilia.

It was strange to be on her own back in the cottage until Annabel reminded herself she wasn't technically alone. Deciding to check she went up to her studio keen to start the painting. A few minutes later, after she had painted a light wash over the drawing, a cough alerted her to his presence.

'Oh, so you are here during the day. I wasn't sure as I'd always assumed ghosts only appeared at night, unless they were trying to frighten potential tenants.' She looked up to see Daniel perched by the telescope, smiling broadly.

'You should know by now, Bella, I am not your usual ghost and can come and go as I please. However, as a gentleman I do respect your privacy and stay out of the way most of the time.' She shook her head, tutting. He moved silently to her side. 'I understand little Emilia is at school now and cannot be scared by my presence and I wanted to see the painting.'

'There's not much to see yet and, to be honest, no artist likes anyone breathing down their neck when they're painting, particularly if it's a portrait.' She wagged her finger at him, 'and before you say you're not able to breathe, you know what I mean.'

He grinned and moved away.

'You're right and I'll leave you in peace. But are we still meeting this evening to continue with my memoir?'

'You don't give up, do you? Yes, okay, but I do need some time to myself so let's only meet for an hour in the evenings, agreed? And there may be times when I'm out.'

Daniel tapped his nose.

'Aha! Are you seeing the mysterious gentleman from Herm again?'

'Not that it's any of your business, but I expect to. Anyway I can't go out at night because of Emilia, unless she's also invited.' She had hoped Richard would have rung by now to confirm meeting on Wednesday and told herself he was probably deep in his writing but Daniel's comment touched a nerve. 'Now please go away and let me work undisturbed,' she snapped.

Flinging up his hands, he nodded and disappeared.

Cross she had let herself lose her cool, Annabel went back downstairs and made herself a cup of coffee before returning to the studio and focusing on the portrait. Once she was immersed in her work, calm descended.

About an hour later her phone rang.

'Hi, Annabel, it's me, Richard. Is this a good time to talk?'

Her stomach tied itself in knots but she managed to sound calm.

'Yes, this is great,' she said, quickly putting the brush to one side. 'How are you?'

'Fine, thanks, been beavering away at the latest masterpiece the past few days and pleased with the progress. What have you been up to?'

She told him about the gallery offer and the barbecue at her neighbours and he offered congratulations on the former and asked if she had enjoyed the latter.

'Yes, it was fun and I've made some new friends my own age which is lovely.'

'I'm pleased for you but I do hope you can still spare the time to meet up this week. I'm still planning on coming over on Wednesday if you're free?'

She chuckled.

'My social life hasn't taken off quite just yet. Wednesday would be perfect, thanks. What are your plans?'

'To be honest it rather depends on you. Do you have a car?'

'Yes.'

'Good, then I thought we could perhaps have a coffee in Town when the boat gets in mid-morning and then tootle off for a drive before having lunch somewhere. As you probably know, there are quite a few decent eateries to choose from.' There was a pause. 'What do you think?'

'I think it sounds lovely, as long as I'm able to pick up Emilia at three. I'll need to drop you off in St Peter Port first.'

'Of course, duly noted. Shall we say meet at ten thirty at Dix Neuf? Do you know it?'

'Yes, I do. See you then. Bye.'

Left smiling after the call part of Annabel wished Daniel had been around to witness it. Silly, she knew, but she would quite like Daniel to be jealous and not as keen on her forming a real relationship. There was obviously no future for them, but she did have feelings for him and wanted them reciprocated. Stupid bitch, she told herself, shaking her head and picking up her brush to continue painting her ghost.

Emilia came out of school smiling and holding hands with another girl about her own age.

'Hello, Mummy, this is Jennie and she was chosen to be my friend and show me around today. And she only lives down the road from us, isn't that great?'

'Hello, Jennie, nice to meet you and thanks for taking care of Emilia. Have you had a good day today?' She looked from one to another.

'Brill, my teacher, Mrs Marchant, is very nice and the school itself is great. And guess what? Jennie loves the "Marvellous Academy" books too.' Emilia beamed at her new friend.

'Wonderful, you'll have lots to talk about. Is your mum here, Jennie?'

She pointed to a young fair-haired woman who was waving from the gate. Annabel approached her and explained she believed they lived nearby and would be happy to have Jennie round on a playdate sometime. The woman, Wendy, confirmed they lived around the next corner, a few minutes from Seagull Cottage and thought it would be great for the girls to play together. After an exchange of phone numbers they went off in their respective cars.

Once they were in the car, Emilia began to describe her day in more detail and Annabel was only too glad it had gone so well. Long may it last, she thought, thinking back to her own schooldays at Vale. Although it had been a happy time for her and the teachers were great, there had been a couple of boys who enjoyed teasing the girls. Not enough to report, but enough to make her dread going to school some days. Glancing across at her animated daughter in the passenger seat, her heart clenched at the idea anyone would hurt her. She had gone through enough.

To celebrate the successful start to her new school, they spent time on the beach before Annabel ordered in a pizza, much to Emilia's delight, and they sat in the garden to eat it. It was warm for April but the evenings drew in early and Annabel found herself remembering the long, hot sunny days of her childhood summers. Long hours on the beach, exploring rock pools for sand crabs, swimming in the sea which felt warm even when it wasn't, sandy sandwiches and delicious ice creams. Hopefully she would be able to offer similar experiences to Emilia. As the air cooled, it was time to decamp into the house and for her daughter to get ready for bed. There was little objection as Emilia was keen to read her book before lights out.

Later, after checking she was asleep, Annabel went up to the studio for the session with Daniel. She found him examining his portrait.

'It's coming on, isn't it? When do you think it'll be finished?' He was perched on her desk with his arms crossed.

'And good evening to you, Daniel.' She sat down and opened her laptop and clicked on the file. She scanned what she had typed. It was about his early childhood when his father, a sailor, would be away for months at a time and return with tales of strange places which fired Daniel's imagination.

Sadly, when Daniel was eight his father never returned, drowned at sea. His poor mother struggled to cope and died a year later, leaving him and his baby sister orphans. An elderly aunt who lived at Rue Robin, not far from Seagull Cottage, took them in. Daniel admitted he was 'a bad 'un' and would run wild, climbing trees and anything tall and dangerous. Annabel thought his aunt must have gone through hell, although when she died she did leave him some money, enough for him to buy a plot of land and build his cottage when he was still in his twenties. He was sixteen when she died and this prompted him to take an apprenticeship as a boy seaman on an old tramp steamer and so began his adventures.

'Annabella? Did you not hear me?'

She looked up, her mind still imagining him as a small, lost boy and then an equally lost youth going out into the big wide world.

'Sorry, I was just reading through the last session. The portrait? Should be finished in a day or two, perhaps longer as I'm out on Wednesday.'

'Aha! Has the man from Herm phoned?' He crouched down level with her eyes and stared at her.

'Yes, if you must know we're meeting up on Wednesday and I don't intend to discuss Richard now as we're supposed to be writing your book.' She glared at him.

He stood up.

'Fine, fine. I was only trying to show I cared about you. Right, where had we got to?'

'You had joined your ship, the SS *Felixstowe*, and about to start your first voyage.'

'Ah, yes. Now what an adventure that was! We were headed for the Mediterranean and when we hit the Bay of Biscay and the turbulent waters around there, I was sick as a dog for days. Thought I was dying, I did. The First Mate took pity on me and forced some concoction down my throat which tasted foul but did the trick and once I found me sea legs I never lost 'em again. First stop was Bilbao, a port in

Spain, and I got ready to follow the others off for a bit of shore leave but the Captain called me back, said as how I wasn't to go ashore yet, muttering something about being green behind me ears as yet. Told me he'd decide when I was ready. Bitterly disappointed I had no choice but to stay behind and do the Captain's bidding…'

As Daniel continued dictating, her mind was filled with images of rough sailors, hardened by a tough life at sea, and the naïve youth who was about to follow in their path. The other thing which amazed her was Daniel's impressive memory; she had difficulty remembering what she had done even a few years before. Did dying somehow improve one's memory?

'Bella, are you listening to me? You've stopped typing on what did you call it? A keyboard?' Daniel stood, arms crossed, in front of her his face red with suppressed anger.

'Sorry, my mind keeps trying to picture what you describe and I stop hearing you. What did you just say?'

He repeated it and she shook her head.

'No, you can't use that word, it couldn't be published. Your language needs to be less salty, Daniel, if you're to see the book in print.'

He threw up his hands.

'Ridiculous! Words like that were common among sailors back then and probably even today.'

'Maybe, but we don't want to put off potential publishers, do we? I'll change that and you carry on. We only have another half an hour.'

Still grumbling Daniel picked up the thread and she had to make a fierce effort not to visualise the scenes he described. This was going to be a lot tougher than painting his portrait, she thought, gritting her teeth.

Chapter 15

Wednesday morning was warm and sunny and Richard sent Annabel a text to confirm he was on the morning ferry. She had dithered over what to wear – what does a nearly forty-year-old wear on a first date? – in the end she settled for jeans and a silky blouse topped with a light jacket. Emilia had trotted into school with a perfunctory wave, keen to catch up with her new friend, leaving Annabel glad she had her own new "friend" to meet and spend a few hours with. As she finished applying her lipstick she felt heat rise in her face at the thought of a possible intimate relationship with Richard. After being unwillingly celibate for more than two years it hit her that might be about to change and unbidden erotic images flashed into her mind. Her hand trembled and the lipstick swerved. Tutting, she grabbed a tissue to repair the damage. Reminding herself she was approaching middle-age, Annabel gathered what she needed into her bag and ran downstairs. About to lock up, a voice called out, 'Have fun!' accompanied by the familiar rushing sound and a deep laugh.

Muttering, 'Honestly, Daniel,' she hopped in the car and set off for Town as images of Richard and Daniel insisted on floating into her mind. At least Richard was a living, breathing man who was available for a full relationship. Apparently. Sighing, she drove almost on auto-pilot to find a parking space on the Crown Pier. Five minutes later she was in Dix Neuf and her stomach began flipping at the thought of seeing him again. Pretending to read the proffered menu, she remained alert to any newcomers and when he duly appeared, their eyes locked onto each other's and he strode towards her wearing a broad smile and kissed her on both cheeks, French fashion.

'It's so good to see you again, Annabel. This past week has dragged even though I've been writing furiously. How are you? And your lovely daughter?' His hair flopped forward and he pushed it back, grinning.

'We're both fine and Emilia's settled into school well, thanks to your book, which has made her very popular,' she said, tucking her own hair behind her ears.

'Pleased to hear it and I'm glad I was able to help. Now, what would you like to drink?'

After placing their orders they chatted about their respective activities since they had first met.

'I've spent most of the time chained to my laptop while I wrestled with a tricky plot issue. Won't bore you with the details, but my editor picked up a particularly gaping plot hole which meant I had to rewrite thousands of words.' Richard paused to sip his coffee, frowning at the memory. 'It was my own fault, of course, took my eye off the ball so to speak and it's reminded me to stay more focussed when I'm writing.' He reached out to touch her hand, saying, 'However, I'm a great believer in the old saying, all work and no play…'

Annabel felt something like an electric charge flow through her hand and arm and for a moment could not speak.

'Couldn't agree more, but I do hope you spending time with me didn't cause your plot a problem.'

He shook his head. 'No, when I met you in Herm I was already struggling with it. In fact it's the main reason I came over here, to help me focus. And it's working so well I can afford to give myself some time off for R&R.' He grinned, still holding her hand.

The surge of electricity eased but Annabel continued to feel flustered. Annoyed with herself for behaving like a teenager on a first date, she could only nod.

Richard didn't appear to notice anything and went on to describe how he had managed to avoid bumping into his neighbours in the cottages by taking his daily walks before six in the morning, when it was still dark and with the aid of a torch. His account of near misses were so amusing she started giggling and the pair were soon laughing together, helping her feel more at ease with him.

'I thought we could drive out to the west coast and find somewhere to have lunch, if that's okay with you?' he asked, finishing his coffee.

'Fine, but remember I have to be at Vale school by three.' Annabel hesitated. 'After I've dropped you back in town.'

For a moment his face clouded and then he smiled, saying she was right, he didn't want to risk being bombarded by a horde of children. She had been more concerned about Emilia seeing her with him again, but he had a point, as her daughter would find it hard not to tell everyone who he was.

They headed out to the west coast via Route de Saumarez, leading to King's Mills and onwards to Vazon Bay. The sun continued to shine through a thin veil of cloud and Annabel could hardly believe she was shortly to have lunch with such an attractive and successful man. Heady stuff after the past couple of years. Richard kept her entertained by stories of his writing career, never touching on anything too personal. Before they reached the main road at Vazon she asked if he had somewhere in mind for lunch.

'Yes, I thought we'd go to La Grande Mare and hopefully eat outside by the pool. Okay?'

'Fine, I've never been there but driven past, it looks nice.' She knew it was an upmarket hotel with its own golf course and not normally one she would choose, but happy to go along with it. As a successful writer living in London, Richard was bound to have more sophisticated tastes than her.

The hotel was only a few yards on the left from the junction and they were soon parked and walking inside. Richard had obviously been there before as he led the way past the bar to the restaurant and asked for a table outside. Fortunately, being early in the season, there were several tables available and Richard chose one in splendid isolation.

'What a lovely view,' she said, taking in the sparkling pool and the distant green of the golf course hedged with shrubs and trees as far as the eye could see.

'It is indeed and one of the reasons I enjoy coming here when I'm on the island. Now, what would you like to drink? I thought a bottle of Pinot Grigio?'

'Only a small glass for me, thanks.' Not only was she concerned about the drink driving limit, but Emilia had once been mortified when her father had picked her up from school stinking of alcohol although not obviously drunk. She couldn't do that to her daughter again.

The conversation palled while they perused the menus but as soon as they had given their orders and the wine arrived it picked up. Richard asked her more about her childhood and the move to England and she was quite happy to tell him. He steered clear of the years of her marriage and as she picked up on his reticence regarding his own, she avoided asking about what was probably a sore subject. She hadn't got any sensitive secrets herself, except the fact she was living with a ghost and writing his memoir, and, oh, was painting his portrait. Nothing out of the ordinary. That thought and the effect of the wine brought on a choking fit. When Richard asked if she was okay, she had to pass it off as the wine going down the wrong way. He raised his eyebrows but made no further comment.

The food arrived and took all their attention. Annabel had chosen sea bass while Richard had chosen duck.

'Mm, delicious,' Richard said after taking a bite. He then took a sip of wine before going on to describe a terrible meal he had at a top London restaurant once and after making a huge fuss, they agreed to waive the full cost of the meal, including the wine. 'Actually, the food hadn't been that bad, just a bit overcooked, so I was quite happy to accept it for free. And the wine was a superb Burgundy,' he said, grinning.

Annabel smiled but inwardly squirmed at the idea of making a fuss without real reason. She hoped he wouldn't repeat it here as she wouldn't be able to face coming back. Although it was unlikely she would be able to afford to. Then she remembered the gallery offer and thought anything was possible.

Richard chatted throughout the meal, mainly about his

success as an author and the perils of being well known, particularly in London. Thinking of her Facebook writer friends she thought they would be only too delighted to be fêted and to have fans asking for autographs or selfies. It was becoming obvious to her that Richard liked the sound of his own voice and was secretly pleased to be so successful. Still, it saved her from sharing more than she wanted about her own life and its complete lack of success. So far. Her only real accomplishment to date was her daughter and it would be nice, she thought, if she were to achieve a modicum of fame and fortune as an artist. Enough to buy her own home and not worry constantly about money. Sighing inwardly, she picked up her glass and sipped the excellent wine.

When they had finished their main courses, Richard insisted she tried one of the fabulous desserts on offer. 'I have a terrible sweet tooth and always eat desserts so please join me.'

She was only too happy to oblige and was soon tucking into a plate of mixed desserts sure to satisfy anyone's sweet tooth.

It was only when he asked if she wanted coffee that Annabel checked her watch. Two thirty. She panicked.

'I'm sorry, Richard, but we have to go. I'm only just going to have time to drop you off in Town before collecting Emilia.' She picked up her bag ready to dash while he asked for the bill, not looking at all pleased. 'Why don't you stay longer and enjoy a coffee? You could get a taxi to St Peter Port.'

He shook his head.

'No, I'll go with you, at least we'll have a few more minutes together. I hadn't realised how time had flown and it's been such fun.' He pushed his hair back and smiled.

She let out a sigh, feeling guilty for ending the lunch abruptly but knowing it wasn't her fault. The drive back to Town was subdued, both aware they were soon to say goodbye, but for how long? She pulled up outside Marks & Spencer on the front and he reached across to kiss her. Properly, on the mouth. It had been a long while…

'Thank you for joining me today, Annabel. I'd love to see you again and will ring you later, if it's okay with you?' He stroked her face and her insides melted.

'Yes, that's very okay. And thank you for the wonderful lunch.' She gave a quick wave as he left the car and drove off with damp eyes. It was the wine. It always made her emotional.

Annabel kept quiet about Richard, not wanting Emilia to know anything in case it fizzled out. And it did seem too soon to bring another man into her life. Fortunately Emilia was more interested in her own day at school, chatting about the new friends she was making and how soon could Jennie come round for a playdate. After she and Wendy, Jennie's mum, agreed on Friday, Emilia was happy to watch some television while Annabel cooked supper. She was full from lunch and only ate a small portion of the pasta bake. Once her daughter was in bed she made her way to the studio, planning to continue her portrait if Daniel failed to appear. But he was waiting, arms folded and a big grin on his face.

'Did you enjoy yourself today, Annabella? I understand the food's good at La Grande Mare.'

'What! Did you follow us there? But... how?' She sank into her chair, her face reddening at the thought of how much he had seen.

'It's a common misconception that ghosts are restricted to the place where they died, but I have found over these many years that I can go anywhere on the island if I'm,' he made a coughing sound, 'near someone connected to me. For example, I used to keep an eye on my great-nephew when he went out on his motorbike, making sure he stayed safe.'

Taking deep breaths to calm herself, she replied, 'But we're not connected, we're not family so you shouldn't be able to follow me.'

Daniel shuffled his feet, and avoided meeting her eyes.

'We may not be connected in the familial way, but I... I do care about you... and Emilia and would want to make sure you didn't come to harm.'

'I see.' A thought struck her. 'Does this mean you followed us over to Herm?'

'No, I discovered I'm not allowed to cross over water. Ironic, don't you think, considering I was a sea captain and spent most of my life at sea.' He looked downcast and for a moment she felt sorry for him.

'That's a shame, I admit, but it doesn't give you the right to follow me around like some kind of stalker!'

'Stalker? What's a stalker?'

'Oh, someone who is obsessed with a person and follows them wherever they go and sends messages on social media.'

'Social media?'

Waving her hands, she said crossly, 'Never mind, it's too complicated to explain. The point is, you've invaded my privacy by following me and it's upsetting. You might have been looking out for me, but I was in no danger, unlike your nephew, and now I don't know if I can trust you.'

Daniel stroked his beard.

'I think I understand what you're saying and I'm sorry if I've caused you offence.' He moved closer to the desk to stand in front of her. 'You can trust me, Bella, I only wish to protect you. Would be happy to lay down my life—'

They stared at each other as his words sank in. And then, as one, they burst out laughing until tears ran down Annabel's face. Daniel, of course, couldn't shed tears.

'Oh, Daniel, you idiot.' She wiped away the tears and blew her nose. 'Even if you had a life I wouldn't want you laying it down for me. But I do appreciate the thought and only ask you to stop following me around. And if ever I do bring Richard home, you must swear to keep away. Can you do that?'

'Yes, I swear I'll keep away if you bring Richard here.'

Chapter 16

The next couple of days passed peacefully as Emilia continued to enjoy school and Annabel had uninterrupted time in the studio working on Daniel's portrait. Life was settling into a new, more relaxed pattern after the trauma of Clive's illness and death. Annabel hardly thought about those days now, it was as if they had been lived by someone else. The island was working its magic, accepting her as one of its own. She hummed as she worked, delighted as ever when the painting continued to gain depth and realism under her brush. She chuckled at the memory of the 'magic painting books' she had been given as a child, using only water to bring to life wild animals or sea creatures. The little books had planted the germ within her of becoming an artist when she grew up, and it survived in spite of the negativity of teachers who said it wasn't a viable career choice and she would need a day job to survive. In a way they were right. Even though her parents had been more supportive, Annabel knew after gaining her degree she would need more skills and completed a secretarial and business course. This led to an office job giving her financial independence until she met and married Clive. Then it helped pay the mortgage until Emilia arrived.

Standing back to take in her progress, Annabel couldn't help smiling. The twinkle was visible in Daniel's eyes and his lips were split in a broad grin. Quite seductive, she realised, but why not? For a ghost he was incredibly sexy when he wasn't in a mood. And the effect was much more in keeping with the 'real' Daniel than the awful oil painting it was supplanting. If they were to find a publisher for the book, it would make a brilliant cover. She had just begun to fill in more of the background detail when her phone rang. Looking at the caller ID she was tempted to ignore it then realising it was putting off the inevitable, she took a deep breath and answered, saying, 'Hello, Deirdre, nice to hear from you. How's your mother?'

She visualised her sister-in-law, her face set in a permanent frown, gripping the phone as she forced herself to speak to the person she disliked with a passion. The feeling was mutual.

'Mother is quite well, thank you, considering. It's been a very difficult time for her since... since we lost poor Clive.' There was an audible sniff over the phone. 'And it's not been made any better since you upped and left with dear Emilia, her only grandchild.' Another sniff. 'Anyway, she wanted me to find out how you both are and if you now realise you may have made a mistake in leaving Manchester.'

Annabel rolled her eyes and counted to ten.

'We're both very well, thank you. Emilia absolutely adores it here and loves her new school and is making lots of friends. And I'm falling in love... with the island again, making friends and have an exhibition at a local art gallery soon. So, all in all we have absolutely no regrets about leaving Manchester.'

There was a long pause.

'I see. But surely you must be finding it difficult... financially speaking. I've been reading how Guernsey is as expensive as London where property's concerned.' Annabel heard the note of desperation in Deirdre's voice. Her mother-in-law, Cynthia, had no doubt told her to convince them to return to Manchester where a better, less expensive life awaited them. Also a life where Annabel was expected to worship Clive's memory to the point of sainthood, while helping Deirdre care for the aged widow who had lost her only son. No way, José.

'No, actually I've been lucky enough to find a reasonably priced cottage to rent and am continuing to sell my paintings locally and online and managing quite well, thanks.' She crossed her fingers. It was almost true...

Another long pause. Annabel could hear a voice in the background and guessed it to be Cynthia giving further instructions.

'Mother says she wants to come and see for herself where you're living and to see dear Emilia, who we both miss so much.'

Annabel put her hand over the phone in order to release some choice swear words.

'Won't the journey be a strain for Cynthia? I thought she was having problems with her legs. And I'm sorry but I can't put you up, we only have two small bedrooms.' And a ghost turns up in one when he feels like it, she thought, smiling to herself.

'Mother's legs are improving now the weather's better and naturally we wouldn't dream of imposing on you and will book a hotel for a few days.'

'Oh, right. Let me know when you've booked your trip. Emilia will be happy to see you.' It was only a little lie...

They said their goodbyes and Annabel was left staring at the portrait wondering what she'd done to deserve a visit from Cynthia and Deirdre. They had never got on and after Clive's death they had tried to take over her life, offering them a home in the large detached house where Cynthia was looked after by Drippy Deirdre, as Annabel called her. It was bad enough having to sell her home as she couldn't pay the mortgage and Clive hadn't kept up the insurance payments which would have covered it. There was no way she could have lived under the same roof as her in-laws and this prompted her to think of Guernsey, and the modest amount she had cleared after the sale. A pity it was as expensive as London, Deirdre was right there. But, if her paintings did begin to fetch higher prices, then they might survive. Oh, and there was always the forthcoming bestseller. She could see Daniel's memoir were shaping up well; he was a natural story-teller with a good sense of humour although a touch risqué at times, she thought. It was opening her eyes to the ways of sailors in the 1920s and 1930 and what they endured for the sake of the end consumer.

Daniel had been narrating the ship's arrival in Marseilles and said something which made her stop typing.

'You can't say that! And certainly can't go into detail, I don't think a publisher would publish it.'

'Why not? It's what happened, after all, and was common among all sailors at the time. I'm not going to whitewash anything to please people's sensibilities. If they don't like it, then blast their eyes, they don't have to read m'book.'

Annabel took a deep breath. It wasn't easy arguing with a long-dead ghost who had a different perspective on the world.

'Okay, I'll type what you want, but don't blame me if the book is rejected because of foul language and… and unsavoury descriptions. I'm aware almost anything goes these days but it might make it harder to find a publisher. I thought you wanted it to be a bestseller so I can buy this cottage, that was our deal, yes?' Her voice trembled. She so wanted to stay here.

Daniel flung himself around the room, muttering something foreign she fortunately could not understand and then came to an abrupt halt in front of her, red in the face.

'I will endeavour to modify my language, Annabella, as I do not wish to upset you. I will also try to, er, be less fulsome in my descriptions of what happened in various ports. As long as I can still give an indication of what went on. Agreed?'

She smiled. 'Thank you, I agree. Shall we continue?'

A slight bow of his head in response and they picked up where they had left, in Marseilles.

Back in the present Annabel continued with her painting while ruminating over the phone call which had dredged up memories she had tried hard to bury. Her earlier sunny mood had evaporated and she began to question whether or not everything was as rosy as she had said. It was true about the low rent, for sure, but her tenure wasn't secure and dependent on the whim of a faraway landlord. Chewing her lip she pushed down the frisson of fear creeping through her veins. The agent had confirmed the lease was for a year, with the possibility of renewal, but with the owner receiving such a low rent, surely he would want the market rent of nearly double at that point? Did he know about the ghost? She decided to ask Daniel when they next met. And then she had been a tad over-optimistic about her sales. Admittedly, she was still selling some online and now a couple through the restaurant, but hardly a full-time income. Even with the promise of the gallery exhibition, there was no guarantee of sales. The lovely Laura might have misjudged the market. Art was so subjective, as she knew herself. There were several well-known successful artists whose work she thought was rubbish.

Throwing her brush down in despair, she went downstairs to make a coffee, trying to recover her earlier positive mood. Bloody Deirdre! She had a knack of spoiling anything good. She had attended her and Clive's wedding dressed entirely in black as if for a funeral. Annabel only later realised how much Deirdre adored her brother and hated to see him happy with another woman. To give Clive his due, he was aware of how unhealthy this was and had moved south. However, over the years and after his father's death he had been pressurised to move back north to provide support for his mother.

Taking her coffee back upstairs Annabel decided it was no good worrying about the future and she must enjoy the present moment and what she had to be thankful for. Including a rather dishy man presently staying in Herm. With a smile on her face she continued to paint until it was time to fetch Emilia.

A few days later Annabel received another call from Deirdre, announcing their arrival a week later on the Friday and they would be staying for four nights at The Peninsula Hotel.

'How nice. You must come round for lunch on the Saturday when Emilia's home. We could even go to the beach after, weather permitting, as it's only across the road.' Her heart plummeted into her stomach at the thought of entertaining them in her home, but knew she had no choice. They were, after all, Emilia's grandmother and aunt. If only it was my parents coming to visit, she thought, it would be so different. But there wasn't much chance of that for a long time as they were on a three-month cruise after her uncle had died and left them some money.

'Thank you, we'd like that. I'm not sure Mother will be keen on the beach, it depends how tired she is from the travelling. We're renting a car, if you could give me directions?'

She duly gave Deirdre the directions before they ended the call.

Annabel had been about to go up to the studio after putting Emilia to bed and now went back to the kitchen to pour herself a glass of wine to take with her. When she entered the room Daniel was already waiting and he raised his eyebrows at the sight of her glass.

'Good evening, Annabella. Has something upset you? You appear a little flustered.'

'Hello, Daniel. Yes, my awful sister-in-law phoned.' She told him about the imminent arrival, taking sips of wine to calm herself. He listened attentively.

'Oh dear. I have no experience of in-laws, of course, and indeed little of family relations at all. There were some advantages of being away at sea for months at a time,' he said, grinning. 'My sister and I were fond of each other but barely saw one another during my lifetime. And after my demise, we rubbed along quite contentedly whenever I dropped in.'

'Ah, I've been meaning to ask you about your family. So your sister saw you as a ghost, then? What about her family, did they see you?'

He stroked his beard, his eyes taking on a faraway look. 'Well, I was careful about showing myself to anyone other than my sister, who, although shocked at first, came to accept me. Her husband wasn't able to see me, and nor were visitors to the cottage.' He shrugged. 'I don't know why some could and others couldn't and you're one of the few non-family people who can see me. As you know, Doris saw me but not her husband. And then they had a boy, Matthew Daniel,' he smiled, 'named after me, he was, and he seemed to sense my presence when he was a young'un but didn't seem to actually see me. His mum told him about me and how I built the cottage, my sister having told her, but I'm not sure how much he took on board. Serious lad he was, good at school, not like me,' he said, laughing, 'and went off to university and never came back, except to say goodbye to Doris when he emigrated.' He paused, and for a moment the sparkle left his eyes. 'Doris was beside herself, for sure. Her husband, a good for nothing sort of bloke, had cleared off with another woman while Matthew was quite young. To be honest, I thought she'd marry again but she never looked at another man. I kept her company a bit when no-one else was around but,' he said, shrugging, 'she withdrew into herself and saw few people except when she was still working.'

'Oh, that's so sad about Doris. My friend Colette's told me how she kept an eye on her over the past few years. She said she had a lot of tales to tell, including about you.' She looked him in the eye, saying, 'Because the cottage was rumoured to be haunted people kept away and Doris was left alone.'

His jaw dropped.

'You mean because of me Doris was alone? How awful! I had no idea and Doris never said a word. If I'd known I'd have stayed away, for sure.' He pushed his hand through his hair, shaking his head.

'Hey, Daniel, don't blame yourself, you were around for her and she obviously liked you being there otherwise she'd have said something to you. The problem lies with those folk who couldn't cope with the idea of a ghost, even though they probably wouldn't have seen you anyway.'

'Harumph. Maybe, we'll never know. But it's a shame her boy Matthew now owns me cottage as he skedaddled off to the other side of the world without a backward glance. No true Guernsey-man would do that.' He paced up and down, an angry frown on his face.

Annabel gave him a few moments to calm down before replying.

'I think we'd better get on with your memoir as time's getting on. Are you ready?'

He stopped pacing and drew himself up straight before offering a salute.

'Aye, aye, Cap'n, I'm ready.'

Chapter 17

The playdate with Jennie was a success and the mums agreed Emilia could go round Jennie's house the following Wednesday after school. Annabel chose that day as Richard had phoned to say he hoped to be over then and wanted to have lunch with her. It meant they could have more time together and perhaps even come back to the cottage, which opened up all kinds of possibilities...

On Saturday Jeanne phoned to invite them round on Sunday afternoon for tea and a chance for the children to play together. Apparently Nick was away on business and the women would be able to 'have a good goss', as Jeanne put it. Annabel was left smiling broadly as she caught up with the household chores. Life was good and even the thought of her in-laws arriving the following weekend didn't dampen her mood.

The drive down the west coast was becoming more familiar by now and Annabel had no problems finding Jeanne's house in Perelle. Perched near the top of a lane it was a traditional Guernsey cottage similar to Seagull, but bigger and looked to have a good-sized orchard to the side. They had no sooner parked in the drive when Harry and Freya ran out of the front door to greet them. Their mother stood smiling in the porch.

As the children rushed through to the garden, Jeanne gave Annabel a quick tour of the cottage.

'I inherited it from my grandmother and it was in a bit of a state, but I had such fond memories of it from my childhood I decided to do it up and live in it. Nick helped a lot when it came to fitting cupboards and decorating and we've loved living here.' She finished up in a large sunroom at the back, saying, 'We added this on last year so we can feel as if we're in the garden when it's too cold or wet to be outside.'

Annabel admired the view of a large cottage garden, complete with vegetables, herbs and bright splashes of flowers among bushes and shrubs. To one side she spotted a pergola covered in vines and flowers.

'It's absolutely gorgeous, Jeanne, and I can see why you love it. It makes my cottage look tiny but as I only rent it I can't make changes.' And with a resident ghost to boot, she thought.

'Let's go outside and we can chat while the children run around in the orchard. Can you help me carry out the drinks?'

They settled into comfortable chairs next to a table holding a jug of fresh lemonade, glasses and bowls of nibbles. They were able to see nearly all the garden including part of the orchard, from where could be heard the excited shouts of the children.

Annabel heaved a sigh of contentment.

'This is blissful, Jeanne, and I'm so glad you invited us round. I probably spend too much time on my own,' she said, sipping the chilled lemonade.

'You're welcome. I'm a bit like you, as a writer I usually spend hours in my study on the computer and hardly talk to anyone when the children are at school. Nick's at the boatyard all day and when he's extra busy he might not be home until late at night.' Jeanne gave her a sympathetic look. 'It must be worse for you, on your own.'

If you only knew, she thought!

'Yes, I guess it is. Which is why I'm determined to build friendships and get out of the house more. Now, tell me more about your writing?'

Jeanne talked about the books she had written, both non-fiction and fiction, all with a Guernsey connection. Annabel listened, wide-eyed.

'Wow, I'm impressed. Good for you, particularly as

121

you're raising a couple of children as well. I need to up my game!' she said, laughing.

'Hey, you're doing fine. I saw your paintings in the restaurant and thought they were lovely. So good, in fact I wondered if you'd consider painting either our house or the garden or both? In watercolours. It would be so special to me.' Jeanne touched her arm.

'Oh, of course, I'd love to. They're both beautiful and would make a great painting.' She looked around, eyeing the potential. 'I think the garden with the back of the cottage would be best. Do you agree?' Her heart thumped. A commission! How great was that?

Jeanne clapped her hands.

'Perfect. I'd already asked Nick and he was totally up for it and said we'd better get our request in before your prices went sky high!'

'Smart move, as after the exhibition who knows what'll happen,' she said, with a laugh. Calming down, she added, 'I do have a painting to finish before I can start, but that should only take a week or so. It would be lovely to show the spring flowers at their best, so would you mind if I took some photos now with my phone?'

Jeanne agreed and Annabel took out her phone and walked around snapping away trying to capture the essence of the old cottage and garden. She could hardly wait to start.

That evening Richard phoned and they arranged to meet for coffee at The Boathouse on the Crown Pier on Wednesday. As they chatted, Annabel began to fantasise about bringing him back to the cottage after lunch, her body experiencing buried feelings of sexual desire. She grew hot and clammy simply talking to him. God, this is crazy! Am I really ready to sleep with someone again? And if we did end up in bed together, what happens next? He'll go back to London and carry on with his successful life and probably forget me. I'll be simply a holiday fling. After ending the call she went into the garden for a few minutes to cool down. It was dark and as she leaned on the gate gazing over the bay the full moon cast its light on the sea and the bobbing boats, creating a magical scene which made her gasp. She breathed in the salty, seaweedy air as she stood, beguiled and calmed by the moon, part of her thinking what a brilliant painting it would make. It wouldn't be easy, but if she were to—

'Good evening, Bella. And what an evening it is.'

She spun round to find – nothing.

'Daniel? Where are you? Stop playing games.'

'I'm not but would you really like me to materialise, wearing my old-fashioned uniform. It would be just my luck if a neighbour or passing motorist were able to see me.' A laugh erupted somewhere near her left ear.

'Okay, you win. Were you looking for me?' It was unnerving talking to thin air. In the dark.

'Yes, were we not due to meet this evening? To continue my memoir?'

She struck her forehead.

'Sorry, I was… distracted and forgot. Shall we go in now or leave it until tomorrow?' Part of her was still thinking of Richard and their next date and her professional side was trying to work out how to capture the beauty of the moonlight on the bay. Neither conducive to typing a ghost's memoir.

'I'm happy to continue tonight, *bella mia*, there's still time.' The voice was now near her right ear.

She sighed. Well at least it will take my mind of Richard.

'Okay, let's go.' The familiar whoosh announced his departure and Annabel walked slowly back inside and up the stairs.

On Wednesday morning Annabel shot out of bed before her alarm went off, keen to start what promised to be a special day. She had pushed down the niggling doubts and worries about starting a relationship with Richard, deciding to go with the flow, as people were always saying. Perhaps a fling would suit her better, acting as a warm-up for a more serious relationship. At least her self-confidence was being given a big boost, she consoled herself as she chose her outfit. Something sexy but not overtly "come and get me I'm yours". Mm, tricky, she thought, checking her wardrobe. With May fast approaching, the temperature was rising and she settled on a summery knee-length dress which emphasised her slim figure topped with the jacket she had worn last time.

'You look nice, Mummy, are you going somewhere special today?' Emilia came into her room still in her pjs.

'Thank you, sweetheart, just meeting a friend for lunch. Are you looking forward to going round to Jennie's after school?'

'You bet, it's so nice to have someone my age to play with. Jennie's got a much older brother who goes to the grammar school so she's almost an only child like me. I think it's why we get on so well.' She turned and went back to her room leaving Annabel facing the guilt as the mother of an only child. She bit her lip, remembering her devastation when she miscarried three years after Emilia's birth. Clive was also upset, but assumed she would get pregnant again quite quickly. Sadly, it wasn't to be. Seeing Tess's baby had triggered latent broody feelings, unhelpful for a single woman approaching forty. Telling herself she had to get over it, she went downstairs to make breakfast.

The Boathouse proved to be a perfect choice as Annabel was able to park virtually outside. As she walked towards the café, Richard arrived, giving her a kiss before escorting her to a table.

'You're looking lovely today, the dress suits you. Brings out the blue of your eyes,' he said, as they sat down. He was wearing chinos, a cream open-neck shirt and a linen jacket.

'You look good, yourself,' she said, smiling, 'and more relaxed than when we last met.'

A hovering waiter asked if they were ready to order and went off inside.

'Ah, and the reason for that is I've finally cracked the plot problem and am racing towards the finish line. Only about five thousand words to write and it can go off to my editor.' He leant back in his chair and sighed.

Her stomach clenched as she asked, 'Does this mean you'll be leaving soon?'

Richard smiled, saying, 'Would you miss me if I did?'

She flushed, wondering how to answer such a loaded question. If she said yes, would it make her sound needy? If she said no, would he simply walk away?

He must have seen the confusion on her face as he leant forward and said, 'A bit of an unfair question, I'm sorry. Shouldn't put you on the spot like that. After all, we hardly know each other, yet.' He gripped her hand, adding, 'Something I'd like to remedy. If you want to, that is?'

'Yes, I… would like to. But… when are you leaving?'

'Now, that depends on how well we get to know each other. There's no rush for me to leave yet.' His eyes focussed on hers and her breathing quickened. *God, I'm no better than a silly teenager! Was I like this with Clive?* She couldn't remember, it was too long ago.

She was saved from replying as their coffees arrived and she took a sip to distract herself from her heightened emotions.

Richard took a sip of his coffee before saying, 'I feel like I'm pushing you into a corner, Annabel, which wasn't my intention. But I do find you very attractive and genuinely wish to spend more time with you. Don't let's worry about my leaving yet, agreed?'

'Agreed.'

'Good. Now, about lunch, I realised The Marina Restaurant at Beaucette is not too far from your home and thought we could go there. Then you might have time to show me your cottage before collecting Emilia.'

'Oh, I forgot to tell you, my daughter's on a playdate after school so I don't need to collect her. The other mum will bring her back after tea as they only live around the corner from us.'

His eyes lit up.

'But that's wonderful. We can spend the afternoon together, what fun!'

Yes, she thought, it could certainly be fun. If I don't chicken out.

After coffee they took a stroll around the harbour, admiring the many boats moored in the visitors' marina before returning to the car. Time for an early lunch. Annabel drove along the coast road through the Bridge, round to Vale Castle and round the bend, pointing out Seagull Cottage as they passed.

'It looks lovely and must have a great view from the top window. Can't wait to see it properly later,' Richard said, squeezing her arm. She smiled, trying to focus on the road and not what might happen later.

Beaucette Marina was part of her childhood, having run free around the area near her parents' property. It had always held a bit of magic for her compared to the bigger marinas of St Peter Port. Formed out of an old quarry, it was small and unique in offering live-aboard moorings on the island and held some impressive yachts and a collection of quirky boats. As Annabel parked by the restaurant they had a clear view of the moorings in their sheltered granite embrace.

'Wonderful view, isn't it?' she said, getting out of the car.

'Indeed, but we may have to sit inside as there's a strong breeze today. I'll ask for a table by the window.'

They were in luck and were soon settled at a table set by a window overlooking the marina. The menu had an Italian flavour and Richard ordered two glasses of Prosecco while they made their choices. With the meal he ordered a bottle of white wine and Annabel only allowed herself a small glass, leaving him to drink the majority. It made her uneasy as it brought back memories of Clive's drinking, but it didn't seem to have any adverse effect on Richard. On the contrary, he became more tactile as the meal progressed. Although aroused by his attentions, Annabel couldn't quite let go of her nervousness.

They took their time over lunch, managing three courses and coffee before Richard called for the bill.

'Thank you so much, Richard, that was wonderful. I've not been used to dining out at smart restaurants except to celebrate a birthday or anniversary.' Even the celebration meals had been dwindling in recent years as not only was money becoming tighter but they were drifting apart.

'It's been a pleasure and we're very lucky Guernsey has such a great choice of quality restaurants.' He stood up, reaching his hand to her. 'Ready? I'm dying to see your lovely cottage.' His eyes conveyed his true desire and she felt the heat rise in her throat. She smiled, allowing him to lead her by the arm out of the restaurant and towards the car. Minutes late they arrived at Seagull Cottage and she led the way inside, praying Daniel would stay true to his promise. They began with the ground floor and Richard liked what he saw.

'It's strange, this is almost like being back in my childhood home in St Martins. We lived in a traditional cottage which my parents gradually extended over the years and the layout is so similar. Obviously the kitchen looks brand new, but it probably had one similar to ours originally.' He gazed around, an almost rapt expression on his face and Annabel, who had been worried he'd think it shabby, was relieved. Although technically not her house, she was possessive of it and hoped to own it one day.

After they had explored the ground floor he asked to see the garden and they went out to the back garden and walked around while she pointed out the shed and he admired the flower beds and shrubs.

'I do like gardens though I'm not a great gardener. When I'm in Herm it's like being in the middle of a huge garden which makes it so relaxing. Do you agree?'

'Yes, totally. Shall we walk round to the front and you can begin to appreciate the view over the bay to Herm.'

They headed towards the garden gate and stood for

a few moments looking out to sea.

'Wonderful. I do envy you this view. Shall we go inside and see what it's like from upstairs?' Richard reached for her arm and they were about to turn back when Annabel heard a shout.

'Mummy! You're home and oh, Richard's with you. I'll come over.'

She saw Emilia waving from across the road, with Jennie and Wendy in the distance behind her. Before she could say anything, her daughter darted into the road and hadn't gone far when a speeding car came round the bend and Emilia was lost from sight.

Chapter 18

Annabel was frantic, trying to push through the gate but by the time she was through the car was speeding away and Emilia seemed to float through the air and land on the path by the cottage.

She rushed to her daughter, only vaguely aware of Richard standing frozen in the garden while Wendy and Jennie were running across to join her.

'Oh, my God, sweetheart, are you alright?'

Emilia was white with shock but seemed unhurt, though her legs were wobbly.

'I'm… okay, Mummy, but I thought the… car was going to hit me and closed my eyes. Then it was as if a wind… lifted me up and blew me across the road and… then I landed on the path. It was like being carried by someone. I was so scared! And I'm sorry… I know I shouldn't have… run across like that. Won't do it again… promise.' Then the tears fell and Annabel hugged her tight, soothing her with gentle words as Wendy and Jennie arrived, pale with shock and disbelief. Annabel knew instantly what had happened and silently thanked Daniel as a small whoosh of air by her ear marked his departure.

'Oh, Annabel, I'm so sorry. I'd taken the girls to the beach to play before going back home for tea, I—'

'Please, Wendy, it's not your fault. And by some… miracle, Emilia's come to no harm. I need to get her inside and look after her so I'm afraid the playdate will have to finish now.'

'Of course. Here's her bag and I'll take Jennie home, too. I think we've had enough excitement for one day. It was a miracle that car didn't hit her. I turned round as it was speeding away and Emilia was on the path.' She shook her head, looking dazed. 'We'll arrange another time later.' Handing her Emilia's school bag, she led Jennie away to their house around the corner.

Annabel remembered Richard, and turned to see he had disappeared inside. Hmm. Not being very supportive, is he. She could only hope he would accept, like Wendy did, that the car had only missed Emilia by a miracle. She looked up to the attic and caught a glimpse of a bearded, smiling face and smiled back. Then it was gone. With her arms around her daughter, she went inside, keeping up a flow of soothing words hoping to stem the tears.

Richard was in the kitchen just coming off his mobile. All the earlier signs of desire had vanished and he was pale and looked decidedly uncomfortable, she thought.

'Is Emilia okay? For a while there…' he whispered, spreading his hands.

'I know. She's fine, just shocked. I'll just take her up to bed and tuck her in and be back soon.'

She went to leave and he stopped her saying, 'Look, I've phoned for a taxi, as it looks like you'll be busy now. I'll ring you later when I'm back in Herm.' Before she could reply he gave her a quick kiss on the cheek and left. Shaking her head in disbelief, she supported Emilia upstairs to bed, not bothering to undress her. Within moments she was asleep. Letting out a long sigh of relief, she went down to the kitchen and poured a small tot of brandy, always a good standby in cases of shock, she had found. She did not like the taste but it worked. Calmer, she went upstairs to the studio.

He was waiting for her.

'Oh, Daniel! How can I ever thank you. You… you saved her life.' Then she burst into tears, and slumped into the chair.

'My dear Annabella, I am only too glad I was able to help. I was hovering around the garden when you returned with the… gentleman and had seen Emilia and the others go to the beach. Something, some sort of sixth sense, if ghosts can have such a thing, made me stay when I had promised to leave if that man was with you.' Daniel moved close to her, as if to take her in a hug. She experienced a warmth flow through her, even though there was no physical contact. Her tears began to slow as she let herself be "held".

'Then that car came round so fast and I saw Emilia begin to run across the road and I used all my strength to lift her and over to the other side. It was over in seconds.' He "hugged" her tighter.

'It was awful,' she whispered. 'I've never been so frightened in my life. And nor has Emilia. I can only hope she'll be more careful now and it's going to be hard to let her out of my sight.'

'I understand. But as long as I'm here I will watch over her. Both of you. As I said before, I'm fond of you both and will make sure no harm comes to either of you. If you will permit me, of course.' He stood back and smiled.

She looked into his deep blue eyes, so full of what looked akin to love. If a ghost can love.

'Of course, Daniel. I'll feel safer with you around.'

Later that evening Annabel was in the sitting room after making a scratch supper for herself. Emilia had slept on, not even waking when she changed her into her pjs. As there had been zero impact with either the car or the road, Annabel had decided against calling a doctor, even Jonathan, as it would have meant too many questions she couldn't easily answer. The less fuss the better, she thought. Her phone rang. Richard.

'Hi.'

'Annabel, how are you? And Emilia?' His voice sounded distant, as if from across an ocean rather than over the bay in Herm.

'We're both okay, thanks. Emilia's been sleeping, which is always the best remedy for shock. Physically, not a scratch.' She was cool, not sure how she felt about his lack of help and abrupt departure.

'What a relief, I've been worried about you both.' He coughed. 'I'm so sorry for rushing off like that, but to be honest I've never been any good in a crisis or sickness. Not an attractive trait, I admit, but it's the way I am. Please don't think I don't care, I do. When I saw the car racing round the corner as Emilia was coming across the road I froze, dreading the worst and closing my eyes to avoid seeing what... happened. When I opened them I saw her lying dazed but safe on the path. He must have missed her by inches. A miracle.' She heard him take a breath. 'I've been a coward and I'm sorry. I shouldn't have left you on your own.'

No you shouldn't, she thought, trying to decipher her feelings towards him. It was too soon and she was still in shock, replaying the scene over and over in her head. Suddenly she was consumed with an utter weariness and wanted her bed.

'Well, thank you for phoning and explaining, Richard, but I'm exhausted and going to bed. We'll talk another time, okay?'

'Yes, of course. Goodnight, Annabel.' The phone went dead and she hauled herself up and headed for the stairs as tears pricked her eyes. Whether for herself, Emilia or Richard she didn't know.

The following morning Emilia seemed restored by her lengthy sleep, if a tad subdued. Annabel thought it best not to mention the near accident, knowing her daughter would talk about it if needed. Dropping her off at school she saw Wendy wave off Jennie and approached her.

'How's Emilia this morning? Still shocked I expect,' Wendy said, quietly.

'She's okay, thanks. Hopefully she'll be more careful crossing a road now. How's Jennie? She was obviously upset at the time.'

'We had a chat last night and I drummed it in about road safety and hoping, like you, they'll learn lessons from what happened. And I've told her not to talk about it with anyone else in case it upsets Emilia. Least said, soonest mended, as my mother used to say.' She smiled.

'Thank you for that, Wendy, I was worried about her becoming the centre of gossip. We have family coming over from England tomorrow for a few days, and it would be lovely if the girls could have a playdate later next week, if you're happy for another try.'

'Of course. How about next Wednesday? And we won't venture to the beach this time,' she said, with a laugh.

'Good idea!' Annabel said, relieved. She had been worried Wendy would query what had happened yesterday, and was reassured. Richard hadn't seen it all either so it was going to go down as a lucky (or miraculous) near miss. She was saved from having to explain an invisible rescuer.

It was a much happier girl who came out of school later and Emilia was full of the day's events and how she was really enjoying history in particular.

'I loved it too when I was at school. All those kings and queens and their castles,' she said, as they walked to the car. 'Oh, and I had a chat with Wendy this morning and she's happy for you to go round for a playdate next Wednesday which I said would be fine. Okay with you?'

Emilia nodded enthusiastically and Annabel said no more.

Later that evening Annabel went up to the studio for the usual memoir dictation looking forward to seeing Daniel.

'Good evening, *bella mia*, I can see you are more cheerful today. And how is the lovely Emilia? Fully recovered, I hope?' He was propped by the telescope, his arms folded in his preferred position and wearing a broad smile.

She returned his smile and sat down.

'My daughter's fine, thanks to you, and seems to be back to her normal self. I'm getting there, although I am disappointed in Richard and how he behaved yesterday.' It had nagged at her all day and she was no nearer what to do about it.

Daniel nodded, his face solemn.

'He didn't appear to be what you might call of a heroic disposition, did he? I saw him close his eyes as Emilia ran across the road. Not the act of a gentleman, in my book.'

She sighed.

'I know, he did at least confess to me about it. But it has affected how I think about him. It had been going so well…'

'Dearest Bella, don't give up. If he isn't the right man for you, then I'm certain another will present himself soon. I'm amazed you haven't been inundated with suitors as yet.' He came and stood by her, resting a hand on her shoulder. Again, she felt a surge of warmth flow from him and relaxed.

'Oh, Daniel, what a pity you're a ghost! If you were alive I'd quite fancy you.' She smiled at him and he waved a hand.

'There are times I wish I was alive, Bella, but then I remind myself I would be one hundred and thirteen years old and look like an Egyptian mummy.' He shook his head. 'You wouldn't fancy me at all then.'

She smiled. 'I guess not! We'll simply have to go on as we are and your book will make me rich and famous and you'll have to scare off the fortune-hunters.'

This set them both into fits of laughter and it was a while before they calmed down enough to talk.

'And before we start the dictation, Daniel, my beloved in-laws are arriving in Guernsey tomorrow, although I'm not expecting them here until Saturday lunchtime. Could you lay low please when they're here even though I'd love to see you appear and scare them off, it wouldn't be fair on Emilia. And might cause me a problem or two.' Her stomach dropped at the thought of them in the cottage – it was her space and they were invading it.

'Of course I'll lay low as you put it, but if they start giving you any trouble I might be tempted to encourage them to leave, remaining invisible, naturally.' He grinned and she noticed a glint in his eyes.

'I think I can look after myself, thank you. Now, shall

we do some work?'

On Friday afternoon Deirdre rang to say they had arrived safely and had checked into their rooms at The Peninsula.

'Good, how was the flight?'

'It was quite pleasant, thank you, though Mother is a little tired now and resting in her room. I'm about to take a little walk to get some fresh air after the enclosed area of the airport and the plane.' She sniffed. 'How is darling Emilia? We can't wait to see her tomorrow and you of course, Annabel. What time would you like us to come round?'

Never was the thought which popped into her mind, fortunately not into her mouth.

'How about twelve o'clock? And we're both looking forward to seeing you.'

'Perfect. Goodbye until then.'

Annabel had just arrived home after collecting Emilia from school and now found her in the sitting room watching television. She simply nodded when told they were coming for lunch the next day. Annabel could not resist smiling at the underwhelming welcome the in-laws were likely to receive tomorrow lunchtime.

Annabel made an effort with the lunch, not wanting to be accused of meanness. A selection of salads and cold meats followed by a homemade chocolate mousse and served with white wine and juice. She knew the women were partial to wine and anything chocolate and both suited her own tastes. She covered the old dining table with a bright cloth and set out four places with her best china and glasses. After blitzing the downstairs rooms she decided they could not complain Emilia was living in unsuitable accommodation. Something they seemed to be most concerned about. Although her in-laws had no legal rights where Emilia was concerned Annabel wanted to ensure they could not cause her problems if they considered her an unfit mother. She had told Emilia not to mention her running across the road and the near miss.

Dead on twelve the visitors arrived in their hire car.

'Go and greet them, sweetheart, with your biggest smile while I finish off in the kitchen.'

As she carried the last plates to the dining room she could hear Cynthia and Deirdre exclaiming over Emilia and how much she had grown. Going back into the hall she fixed on a bright smile to welcome her guests.

'Cynthia, good to see you and so brave of you make the journey over. How are your legs these days?'

Cynthia, in her mid-seventies, was stout and walked with a stick, though otherwise in reasonable health she professed struggling to cope domestically, hence the need to have Deirdre move in.

'Not too bad, thank you, Annabel. The journey did take it out of me but I'm better today and seeing dear Emilia's made it all worthwhile,' she said as they met in an awkward embrace. Her face bore a permanent frown even at supposed moments of pleasure. Deirdre, coming up behind, had a similar facial expression. In her mid-forties, she looked older, with lank greying hair touching her shoulders.

'Hello, Annabel, thanks for inviting us round.' After a brief hug Deirdre turned to look around the kitchen, saying, 'I hadn't expected you to be living in such a pleasant cottage, and with such a view, too. You were lucky.'

'Yes, I was very lucky. Would you like to look around before we have lunch? There's also a good sized garden at the back, ideal for Emilia to play. Sweetheart, would you like to lead the way?'

Emilia, who had been hanging back, came forward and led the guests around the ground floor while they offered muted words of appreciation. Annabel then took them into the garden, pointing out its generous size, larger than the one they'd owned in Manchester, and the added benefit of a shed.

'Well, my dear, I have to admit, it looks quite snug. And Deirdre tells me you're settling in well, is that right?' Cynthia stood, resting both hands on her stick, near the garden wall and surveyed the cottage.

'Yes, we love it here, don't we, sweetheart?'

Emilia responded with a resounding 'Yes!'

Annabel noticed a faint whoosh near her right ear and waved her hand, hoping Daniel would take the hint and leave.

Deirdre, pursing her lips, suggested they went back inside and they trooped into the dining room and Annabel served up lunch. The conversation during the meal was stilted, focusing on the weather and what Cynthia and Deirdre thought of Guernsey so far. They did admit to thinking it was 'quite pretty, with some nice beaches' they had seen on a drive that morning. When lunch was finished, Emilia asked to be excused to watch a particular film on the television and Annabel agreed, glad of the chance to talk openly to the women.

She topped up Cynthia's glass of wine and her own. Deirdre declined as she was driving.

'Well, I do hope you're both satisfied we're not living in a slum and Emilia's happy and enjoying this new phase in her life. And, of course, I'm delighted to be back home.'

Deirdre and Cynthia exchanged glances.

'Yes, I'm reluctant to admit it, as I had hoped you'd be keen to return to Manchester, but you appear to have settled in here and Emilia's obviously happy.' Cynthia sighed and Annabel couldn't help feeling sorry for the woman who had doted on her only grandchild. Cynthia was an unhappy woman who had been dealt hard blows, losing her husband at a relatively young age followed by the totally unexpected death of her son and now separated from her granddaughter. Annabel couldn't warm to Cynthia, but she did sympathise with her.

Deirdre cleared her throat.

'I have to agree with Mother, and… I'm glad for you but I'll miss seeing Emilia.'

'Perhaps you two could come over a couple of times a year for a long weekend, staying in a nice comfortable hotel, and spending some time with us.' Now I've done it, she thought, I won't be able to go back and un-suggest it. What was I thinking? I must be mad! Cynthia's eyes lit up.

'What a marvellous idea! We haven't had holidays for years and it would do us good to get away a bit more. What do you think, Deidre?'

Deirdre cracked a smile.

'I agree, Mother. We could check availability with the hotel while we're here and be back before you know it.'

Chapter 19

Before they left Cynthia invited Annabel and Emilia to join them for lunch at the hotel on Sunday and Annabel was happy to accept. The added bonus was the chance to use the hotel's outdoor pool and Emilia admitted to her mother that 'Grandma Cynthia was actually quite nice.' Annabel nodded, without comment. She realised she had been demonising the pair of them since Clive's death and having moved to Guernsey their apparent power over her had diminished.

Sunday dawned in hazy sunshine and as the morning evolved the haze disappeared and the sun grew stronger. Annabel sent up a silent prayer of thanks for the good weather, allowing her in-laws to experience Guernsey at its best and boosting her argument for returning here. After filling a beach bag with their bathers and towels, she and Emilia set off in the car to the Peninsula Hotel. Emilia was particularly excited to swim in a heated pool after only managing to paddle in the still decidedly cold sea. When they arrived Cynthia and Deirdre were relaxing by the pool with what appeared to be glasses of sherry, fully dressed.

Cynthia smiled as they approached their table, set with four chairs. Annabel couldn't remember the last time she had seen her mother-in-law smile and wondered if sherry was the key to her softening. Or perhaps it was being waited on in a comfortable hotel. Either way, it was a relief to see and there was even a smile hovering around Deirdre's thin lips.

'This looks lovely, Cynthia. Do you plan on having a swim? We've brought our bathers.'

Shaking her head, Cynthia said, 'No, my swimming days are over and Deirdre was never keen, were you, dear?' Her daughter nodded. 'We're happy to watch you two enjoy yourselves building up your appetites before lunch.'

'Okay, we'll go and change. Back in a minute.'

Wearing their bathers they returned to leave their towels and clothes with the others before entering the pool. Emilia was a good swimmer but initially was happy to splash about with Annabel before swimming a few lengths under her mother's watchful eye. There was only one other woman in the pool and she was enjoying a stately progress from one end to the other. About twenty minutes later, Annabel and Emilia emerged, laughing and pink-faced after their exertions.

'What good swimmers you are! It's been such a pleasure to watch you having fun,' Cynthia said, passing them the towels. 'We'll go in for lunch as soon as you're dressed.' She smiled at them and Annabel found it hard to believe this was the sour-faced woman who had made life so difficult for her after Clive's death. Even Deirdre looked to be enjoying herself, drying Emilia with the towel. They went off to change and on their return went through to the restaurant which overlooked the pool area. After they had made their choices from the set menu Deirdre ordered juice for Emilia and a bottle of wine for the adults with Annabel only accepting a small glass.

The meal passed pleasantly with the focus on Emilia and school and what she enjoyed the most. Annabel was happy to let the conversation flow around her as she enjoyed the food. When coffees were ordered they took them outside to sit by the pool again and Emilia asked if she could go swimming.

'It's too soon after lunch, sweetheart, but you can go in the shallow pool for a paddle.'

She nodded and went off to change.

Cynthia leaned over to Annabel.

'I wanted to have a word with you about Emilia. I've been giving some thought to the future.' Annabel's heart raced. Please don't let her suggest Emilia spend time with them in Manchester. She couldn't bear it and nor would her daughter. 'She's my only grandchild and Deirdre won't be providing any more, sadly, so I propose to set up a trust fund for her, to mature when she's eighteen. It could help her through university or provide a deposit on her first home. It will be up to her, no strings.'

Annabel opened her mouth but nothing came out. It was hard to take in, but as she looked from Cynthia to Deirdre, both smiling, she realised it was for real.

'It's... very generous of you, Cynthia, and I hardly know how to thank you. Are you going to tell her?'

Cynthia shook her head. 'No, I think it's better to wait until she's eighteen. If I'm no longer around to tell her, then she will receive a notification from my solicitor—'

Deirdre interjected, 'Of course you'll still be around, Mother, you'll only be in your eighties.'

Cynthia shrugged. 'Perhaps. I'd love to see her grow up, but nothing is guaranteed in life, is it?' Annabel felt compelled to squeeze her arm in support.

'I'll be instructing my solicitor as soon as I return home and he will then send you a copy of the legal documents.'

'Thank you,' she said, still wondering what had brought on this act of generosity. More than a glass of sherry, for sure.

Perhaps Cynthia read her mind as she went on, 'I've had time to think since we lost dear Clive. He admitted to me not long before he... died,' she sniffed, 'how much he had let you both down by not seeking help for his... problem and asked me to help you. At the time I thought encouraging you to stay nearby was the answer, but now seeing how you're both so happy here I understand I was wrong and if I can offer some future security to Emilia, I will be helping you both, as Clive asked.'

'I see.' Before anyone could say anymore, Emilia arrived fully clothed but with dripping hair. Annabel spent a few moments drying her hair while Cynthia and Deirdre discussed how they would spend the afternoon.

'We thought we'd take a drive and stop somewhere later

for afternoon tea and would love Emilia to join us. It will give you some time to yourself, Annabel, so you can catch up on your painting or simply relax,' Cynthia said, with a smirk.

'Of course, what a good idea. You have a lovely time, sweetheart, and I'll see you later at home.' Emilia simply nodded and after an exchange of goodbyes, Annabel left. She knew exactly what Cynthia was up to, giving her no chance to refuse and hoped her daughter wouldn't be too bored. However, it was a small price to pay for the promised trust fund offered to ease her mother-in-law's conscience although not in any way actually easing her own current financial situation. She didn't mind, she was an independent woman and could, with a bit of luck, and the backing of the lovely Laura and the handsome ghost, Daniel, make enough to provide for them both in the coming years.

Emilia was dropped back late that afternoon and admitted she had enjoyed spending time with her grandmother and aunt. Cynthia confirmed they would be back in late September and planned to stay at the Peninsula again.

Annabel said she would look forward to seeing them and they said their goodbyes. As she waved them off she heard a whooshing sound come from the cottage and seemed to head towards Cynthia and Deirdre as they were getting into their car. She whispered, 'No, Daniel, don't,' and the whoosh came back and tickled her ear before fading away. Letting out a deep breath she turned and went back to the front door where Emilia had been waving.

'What was that noise, Mummy? Like someone had released the air from a balloon.'

'Not sure, sweetheart, probably a bird flying low and too fast for us to see. Now, come and tell me all about your afternoon.' Inwardly she was fuming. How could Daniel be so foolhardy as to risk arising suspicion with his whooshing around!

Once Emilia was in bed Annabel took the stairs to the studio rehearsing what she would say to him. The room was empty.

'Okay, Daniel, we both know I'm cross with you. Don't play silly buggers and show yourself.'

Slowly a figure materialised near the window.

'Well? What were you thinking?'

Daniel stood with his arms crossed, a sheepish expression on his face.

'You told me your in-laws were part of the reason for you leaving Manchester and you dreaded their visit. I thought I'd encourage them not to return, not to bother you again.'

Annabel threw her hands up, releasing a sigh.

'It's true I didn't want them here, but my mother-in-law's setting up a trust fund for Emilia and is no longer the problem she was. We still don't like each other but she's helping my daughter and that's all that matters. Unfortunately they'll be back later this year and it's likely to become a regular occurrence which I'll cope with. I have to.'

'Sorry, I was trying to help.' He paused. 'Isn't a trust fund something to do with lots of money?'

'Usually. I've no idea how much money is involved but it could offer Emilia some security.' She plumped down at the desk, drained of her anger.

'I see.' He scratched his beard before saying, 'Are we continuing with the book this evening? I'd understand if—'

She lifted up her head and saw the concern in his eyes and taking a deep breath, said, 'Yes, we are.'

Chapter 20

The next few days passed quietly with Emilia continuing to settle in well at school while Annabel finished painting Daniel's portrait. Then she planned to start on her commission of painting Jeanne's house and garden before concentrating on building up her portfolio for the gallery exhibition. To this end she took advantage of fine days to seek inspiration from the natural beauty of the island. She made a number of sketches which would form the basis of her semi-realistic abstract paintings. Planning new work helped take her mind off not hearing from Richard although the sense of hurt surfaced at unguarded moments. She knew he was behaving like a coward but wasn't quite able to let go her feelings for him.

Colette popped round for an occasional chat which boosted Annabel's mood. Later that week Colette asked if she would like to join herself, Charlotte and Jeanne at Charlotte's home on the following Monday morning.

'We try to meet up a couple of times a month when the children are at school or nursery, giving us time to be girls together and we'd all love you to join us. Tess is back at work at the surgery in the mornings so can't join us.'

'Sounds great, thanks for asking me.' Annabel hesitated. 'You know this ghost, the sea captain called Daniel, who sort of lives here, don't you?'

'Sure, he sounds quite something. Why, what's happened?' Colette's eyes grew round in anticipation as they drank wine in the kitchen.

'Well, I've finished his portrait and his memoir's coming along great. I think the portrait would make a wonderful cover picture. Would you like to see it?'

'You bet I would! I'm still finding this a tad mind-blowing, to be honest.'

'Just a sec, will be right back.' She went upstairs to fetch the portrait and her laptop, hoping Daniel would behave and stay away.

'Here we are. I used an old ship of his as background.'

Colette studied the painting, wide-eyed, for a few moments, before turning to Annabel, saying, 'It's brilliant! No-one would guess this guy is a ghost and boy, is he handsome, eh! And your portrait is way better than the oil painting we took to the shed.' She sniggered. 'Just as well he isn't alive, or I'd be tempted to misbehave.'

'I know the feeling. It's been weird, like having a real live man around who then disappears into thin air. We've been careful not to let Emilia see or hear him as I don't want her frightened but he's not always followed the rules I set at the beginning and there's been some tricky moments.' Like when he saved her daughter's life...

'He seems to have become almost part of the family, just as his niece thought of him, which was natural, I guess. How you've coped, I don't know. I'm not sure I would have.' She shook her head. 'So, any particular reason you're bringing it up now?'

'Well, Charlotte has a publishing company and Jeanne's a writer, and I will soon be looking for a publisher for Daniel's book. I'm not going to tell them he's been dictating it to me, in case I'm hauled off to the funny farm, but will say I found his memoir and was so taken with the stories I've been transcribing them to publish as a book using a pseudonym. What do you think?'

'I think it sounds brilliant. I take it there are no diaries or written journal?'

'No, he admitted he hadn't ever written anything, too busy running a ship. But his memory is brilliant, better than a live person's. Look, here's a sample to show you.' Annabel booted her laptop and opened the file for "Adventures of a

145

Swashbuckler" by Captain Daniel Gregg and turned it towards Colette. She read for several minutes, smiling, frowning and at one point laughing. She looked up and grinned.

'He's a good story-teller, isn't he? A bit like the boys own adventure stories my brother used to love as a kid. Though this book has more grown-up stuff.'

'Oh, it does. I've tried to rein in his language and some of the saucier tales but it's aimed at adults and he wants some spicy bits left in. Do you think I could mention it to Charlotte or Jeanne with regard to a potential publisher?'

'Charlotte might be the better bet as her company publishes historical non-fiction. If she isn't interested then talk to Jeanne as she has contacts in the industry. Ooh, exciting stuff, eh?'

Annabel sipped her wine, looking thoughtful.

'Yes, I hope so, but it could all be a waste of time as I've no idea if such a book would appeal to modern readers. Daniel was encouraged by a publisher when he was alive, but seventy years have passed. He's pushing me to publish entirely for my sake, to be able to buy this cottage, which is rather sweet of him. He's not happy his great-nephew lives in Australia and is not interested in his heritage.'

'I'll be keeping my fingers crossed for you, girl. And, by the sound of it, this Daniel has feelings for you, though I didn't think ghosts could have feelings, did you?'

She felt herself flush and turned away to pick up the bottle of wine.

'We do get on well though I'm not sure about him having feelings for me. I think he simply wants to help me, like a friend.' A faint whoosh of air followed by a whispered, 'I do love you, Bella,' caused her to nearly drop the bottle but her friend didn't seem to notice.

Colette pursed her lips as she accepted more wine.

'Thanks. I'm not convinced about no feelings, but then, what do I know about ghosts? They're usually portrayed as quite sinister, scary things in films apart from that wonderful film, *Ghost*, with the gorgeous Patrick Swayze as the ghost. He tried so hard to tell his girlfriend what had happened to him but she didn't seem to notice. Not like your Daniel at all. You've certainly noticed him!' she said, laughing.

'I could hardly avoid it as he turned up while I was viewing the place and is determined to stay, it seems.' She looked around, afraid he'd appear in front of them, but perhaps he sensed Colette couldn't see or hear him and there would be no sport in it for him. She was slightly disappointed her friend couldn't see him as it would have lent credibility to her own experience to have a witness.

She turned the conversation back to the coming get-together at Charlotte's, asking where she lived and would they go there together.

'Charlotte lives at Le Guet, with amazing views over Cobo and I'm happy to take you.' Checking her watch, Colette stood up, saying, 'Hadn't realised the time. I'd better be off and look forward to Monday. Thanks for the wine.' Annabel escorted her to the door where they said goodnight and shared a hug.

Going back to the kitchen Annabel hissed, 'Are you still here?'

For a moment there was silence, then she heard him say, 'Yes, but I'll go if you want me to.' The voice came from near the oven.

'You just can't help yourself, can you? So many promises not to turn up when other people are around and definitely not downstairs.' She moved towards the oven, her hands outstretched in front of her but found nothing. Of course there was nothing, she chided herself, even if he was there he had no substance. Grrr. What she would give to be able to slap his face.

'I've moved,' he said, from behind her, 'and I think it's best if I leave you in peace this evening. You're cross and in no state to work on that computer. In my defence I had already realised your friend wasn't able to see or hear me and couldn't resist telling you I do have feelings for you. I don't know if that's normal for ghosts or not, but it's how it is for me. Goodnight, Bella.'

She felt a soft touch on her cheek and with a whoosh he was gone.

On Sunday morning Annabel's phone rang. Richard. Should she answer it – or not? Hesitating for all of five seconds she answered.

'Hi, Richard.'

'Annabel. Sorry for not ringing sooner but I've been up to the proverbials in edits and hardly had time to come up for air. How are you?'

'Okay, thanks. Had the in-laws over which was – interesting.'

'Oh, yes, I remember you don't get on, do you? Still, you survived?'

'Yes, I did.' She was about to ask why he was ringing when he said, 'Would you be free on Tuesday morning for coffee? Can't do lunch I'm afraid but would love to see you.'

Her stomach flipped in spite of herself.

'Yes, okay.'

'Great. Shall we say ten thirty at The Boathouse?'

She agreed and after mutual goodbyes he rang off. For several minutes she sat still, wondering what to make of the call. It had been so brief, no real chat and no endearments. More like making a doctor's appointment than a date. Not that a cup of coffee was much of a date to be honest. Annoyed with herself for saying yes, she went in search of Emilia and suggested they pop over to the beach before lunch. Her daughter's big smile cheered her up and they collected a rug, a bucket and spade and fishing net and left. It proved a good distraction as they searched for tiny crabs and starfish in the rock pools and then turned their attention to shells. Emilia was building up quite a collection which she was displaying on a shelf in her bedroom, just as Annabel had done as a child. The happy memories flooded in and she managed to forget Richard and the unsatisfactory call. They celebrated having fun by buying ice creams at the kiosk and arrived home flushed by the uptake of ozone.

In the evening Annabel went up to her studio wondering if Daniel would show his face after the upset of the previous day.

'Daniel? Are you here?'

'Yes, but I can go if you're still cross with me.' The disembodied voice came from near the window.

'It's okay, you can show yourself. I suppose if you knew Colette couldn't see or hear you it wasn't as bad as I thought. But please don't do it again.'

She watched as he slowly materialised by the telescope, a half-smile on his lips. He bowed his head.

'Good evening, Bella, I'm pleased to see you again and glad you forgive me. I hate it when we fall out.'

'Humph. And whose fault is that, eh? Shall we crack on with this memoir of yours as I might have someone in mind to publish it.' She wasn't going to admit she had missed him, too. It would have made him insufferable.

Daniel's eyes lit up.

'Brilliant! How on earth—'

'I'm not saying anymore so don't get too excited. But the more I can show them the better. Ready?' She booted up the laptop and opened the file.

'Now, where were we? Ah, yes, I remember. We had taken on fresh cargo at Istanbul…'

The next morning Colette picked her up after the school run and headed off west along the coast road towards Le Guet. They chatted about their weekend and Annabel mentioned Richard had finally called. Colette was all ears and insisted on knowing what was said. Annabel gave her the gist of it, saying she had found it a bit odd. Colette agreed.

'He seems to run hot and cold, doesn't he? Do you think he's going back to the UK?'

'Possibly. Though he could have told me over the phone.' She sighed, beginning to wonder if she should have said no to meeting him.

Colette shot her a glance.

'You really fancied him didn't you?'

'Yes, I guess so. He… he was the first man I've sort of dated since Clive and I'm not sure how to feel with someone else now. It's like being a teenager again. Bloody awful!' She bit her lip.

Colette reached to press her hand.

'It must be difficult for you to cope with so soon after making such a big move, too. Let's hope he'll have a good explanation when you meet up tomorrow,' she said, turning into a long drive leading to a large detached Victorian villa.

'Wow! What a gorgeous house.'

'Isn't it, just? A combination of Charlotte's good taste and Andy's architect skills. Speak of the devil,' she added, as Charlotte appeared at the front door.

'So glad you could come, Annabel, we do love our girly get-togethers, don't we Colette?' Charlotte gave them both a hug before ushering them towards the door.

'I'm honoured to be asked so soon after meeting me.' Annabel smiled at her as they entered the hall. Gazing around at the immaculate period décor, she said, 'And what a beautiful home you have.'

Charlotte smiled, spreading her arms.

'Thank you. I'm very lucky to have a husband who gave me carte blanche to decorate what was a pretty run-down house when we bought it. Now, come on through to the conservatory where Jeanne is waiting, desperate for coffee so she says.' She laughed, a deep throaty laugh which proved infectious. Laughing, they went through a formal sitting room to a Moroccan-style conservatory with brightly coloured divans and chairs set around a low slung wooden table. Jeanne, who had been reclining on a divan, jumped up to greet them.

'Hi, girls. Isn't this lovely, getting together without a child in sight? And I believe the coffee's pretty good here, too,' she said, grinning at Charlotte.

'Okay, I can take a hint. Back in a jiff, ladies.'

Joining her on the divan they were soon in catch-up mode, asking after the various children and partners. Annabel couldn't help feeling the odd one out even though the others seemed happy to moan about their spouse's perceived shortcomings. Charlotte returned with freshly brewed mugs of coffee as Jeanne was saying she hardly seemed to see Nick these days as he had a deadline on a boat delivery and was virtually living at the workshop.

Charlotte nodded in sympathy.

'Andy's up against it, too, he's been spending long hours at the office,' she said, then pausing, added, 'Honestly, we women are never satisfied are we? We moan if they're never around and then complain if they get under our feet!'

Annabel stared down at her mug while the others smiled in agreement. There was a time when she had resented Clive spending long hours away from home but in later years was relieved to be on her own with Emilia. It had been much calmer…

'I'm so sorry, Annabel, that was tactless of me. You must be missing your husband all the time.' Charlotte looked stricken as she reached to squeeze her arm.

She shook her head.

'No, please don't apologise. The last few years of my marriage weren't happy and we'd probably have divorced if Clive hadn't died. I do miss having a man around sometimes, though,' she said, grinning.

'They do have their uses, for sure,' Jeanne chipped in.

The conversation then flowed around a variety of topics, accompanied by much laughing and giggling as they drew Annabel into their group and they opened up about their individual ups and downs of the past weeks.

'Have you been able to do any painting? I'm so looking forward to your exhibition,' Charlotte asked.

'Some but I've been more focussed on a writing project which I wondered might be of interest to you.' She looked to Colette who gave her the thumbs up.

'Sounds intriguing. Tell me more.'

She described finding what appeared to be the memoir of the long-dead original owner of her cottage, detailing in somewhat graphic detail his adventures at sea in the early twentieth century and how she had been transcribing it on her computer with a view to possible publication.

'His story's fascinating, charting the years spent as a teenager on tramp charters, moving upwards to being a captain on merchant cruise ships and his final time in the Royal Navy during the war.' She paused, took a deep breath, and went on, 'I wondered if it was something your publishing company might be interested in.'

Both Charlotte and Jeanne were leaning forward, listening intently to what she said.

Before Charlotte could reply, Colette broke in, saying, 'I've read a small bit myself and he doesn't pull any punches, giving quite graphic descriptions of, the, er, brothels in Marseilles, for example.'

Charlotte's eyebrows rose and she grinned.

'What fun! I'd certainly like to take a look at what you've got although I can't promise anything as I leave publishing decisions to my MD these days. Is it complete?'

'Nearly, could probably finish it in a week or two.'

Charlotte nodded.

'That's fine, if you email me what you've done I'll have a read through and let you know what I think. It'll be good to use the old grey cells again as my own writing is on a go-slow at the moment.' She sighed.

'Perhaps it'll offer inspiration for your own book, Charlotte, and it sounds such an interesting local find. A real toiler of the sea to compete with Hugo's imagined version!' Jeanne said, her eyes shining.

'Now that's quite a hook, thanks, Jeanne.'

Annabel had to think for a minute before she understood. The famous French novelist Victor Hugo had lived in exile in Guernsey in the late nineteenth century and wrote a number of books there, including his homage to the island he came to love, *The Toilers of The Sea*, about a fisherman's battle with a mystical sea creature.

'What a great comparison but I wouldn't rate Daniel's literary powers as anywhere close to Hugo's, though he's a good storyteller.' Annabel laughed.

Charlotte waved a hand.

'Story is much more important to modern readers, particularly if it's real-life. Now, anyone want more coffee?' Three hands went up and she collected the mugs before returning to the kitchen. Jeanne moved closer to Annabel, saying, 'I'm so envious of you finding this chap's memoir, though I'm surprised his family didn't think of making it public.'

She had to think quickly for a suitable reply.

'It was buried under a load of old papers and photo albums in the shed so it's possible no-one knew it existed. He died suddenly in his forties and probably hadn't mentioned it to anyone.'

'Ah, I see. What a lucky find, then. Did you know anything about this Daniel before you found his memoir?'

'There was an old oil painting of him in the main bedroom which Colette and I moved to the shed as I felt the eyes were staring at me. But I was intrigued by him and while there looked for photos and found the family albums, photos of ships and the… memoir.' She risked a glance at Colette who nodded.

'Fascinating stuff. Perhaps we have another writer in our midst,' Jeanne said, with a grin.

Annabel shook her head.

'No, I'll stick to painting. In fact I've recently finished my own portrait of Daniel which might make a good cover for a book. I definitely prefer pictures to words. And I'm about to start my painting of your lovely cottage, Jeanne,' she whispered, not sure if Jeanne had told anyone.

Jeanne nodded, whispering, 'Great, thanks.'

'Here we are, girls, more caffeine. And some of Colette's delicious cakes to go with it.'

'Ooh, scrummy.'

'They look delish!'

Settled down with mugs of coffee and plates of cake, the women lapsed into a convivial silence, broken only by the licking of fingers. Annabel had allowed her thoughts to wander to the upcoming meeting with Richard and came to a decision.

'I was in Herm recently and met a man who writes children's books under the pen name P E Newton, real name Richard Naftel, a Guern living in London. Do either of you know him?' She looked from Charlotte to Jeanne.

'Not exactly. I met his wife at my publisher's party a few months ago, she's one of the editors. Lovely woman who mentioned she was married to a Guern. We got chatting and she told me about their kids and how they'd all just returned from a fab safari in Africa and how she and Richard were going on a cruise this autumn on their own, celebrating their twentieth wedding anniversary. Must admit, I was jealous. Dropped a few hints to Nick, but not sure he registered. Anyway, what did you think of the husband? I understand he's terribly successful.'

For a moment her world stood still. Wife. Anniversary. Fab holiday. Cruise. So much for being divorced and missing his kids...

'Annabel? You okay?' Colette touched her arm, her eyes full of sympathy.

She took a deep breath.

'Yes, yes a bit of a headache that's all. Sorry, Jeanne. You were asking about Richard. A bit full of himself but he was kind enough to give Emilia a signed copy of his latest book, which has made her very popular at school.' She managed a tight smile before excusing herself to go to the loo. Hurt, anger and humiliation battled within her as she brushed away the threatening tears. How dare he! How bloody dare he!

Chapter 21

Colette dropped her off at Seagull Cottage on the way to work, saying she would catch up later. Annabel walked with leaden feet inside and poured a glass of water before collapsing onto the sofa as the tears finally flowed freely. She cried until it hurt to breathe. After wiping her hot, wet face she took a gulp of water and began to breathe more slowly as her chest eased. Bastard! And how could she have let herself be taken in by such a snake? Was she so desperate for male attention she didn't question anything he told her? It was humiliating. At least she hadn't slept with him! If Emilia hadn't been nearly run over then… Oh, God, she would have; was ready for it. Shame mingled with the anger as she took another, swallow of water. A small voice of reason reminded her she should eat some lunch to feel better. Accepting the voice was right she went to the kitchen and rustled up some beans on toast. Good old comfort food. It did the trick as afterwards she felt calmer and ready to start Jeanne's commission.

A couple of hours later Annabel was pleased with the result so far, a pencilled sketch to set out the layout of cottage and garden, and collected her daughter feeling quite relaxed in spite of Richard. They enjoyed some time on the beach before a light shower drove them back to the cottage, laughing in the rain. Once Emilia was in bed Annabel made her way to the studio for another evening with Daniel. She found herself smiling as she entered and saw him perched by the telescope, a welcoming smile on his lips. Her stomach flipped. He really was so damn good looking, what a pity he wasn't the real man instead of that snake Richard…

'Good evening, *bella mia*, and have you had a good day?'

'Well, some of it was good and it concerns you.' His eyes widened and before he could say anything, she went on, 'I saw my publisher friend today and she's agreed to read what I've typed up so far and get back to me. She was definitely intrigued by the idea of the memoir but it's not her decision alone.' Annabel paused as, unbidden, she relived learning of Richard's perfidy. Quickly shaking her head as if to erase the memory, she went on, 'It sounds promising so I think the sooner we finish the better.'

'That's wonderful, Bella, wonderful. I wish I could kiss you!'

I wish you could, she thought, gazing at his bright blue eyes, twinkling even more than usual.

He blew her an extravagant kiss, accompanied by a bow and her eyes pricked as tears threatened.

'Hey, what's the matter, Bella? Have I upset you?'

She shook her head, afraid to speak. Daniel came close, as if to offer a hug and she could feel the warmth flowing around her. But shouldn't a ghost's body be cold? A soft breath of air caressed her cheek and the tears broke through.

'Bella, Bella, what has happened? Please don't cry, I can't bear to see you upset. It's that man, isn't it? The man you've been seeing?'

She caught a glimpse of his face through teary eyes and the twinkling smile was replaced by an angry red scowl.

'Yes,' she whispered, reaching for a tissue to wipe her eyes and blow her nose.

'What's he done to upset you like this?' He stayed close, as if forming a protective shield around her.

Drawing in a deep breath, she said, 'He… he's married.'

'What! The scoundrel. If I was alive, I'd willingly thrash him to within an inch of his life.' Daniel strode around the room flailing his arms about like a boxer going into the ring for a fight. She could only watch in amazement at such a display of heroic manhood from one who, technically, was no longer a man. Oh, if only he was a real, flesh and blood man she'd feel safe in his arms and no longer at risk from predators like Richard. The very thought made her gasp. I've fallen for him, haven't I? How stupid is that? Lost in her thoughts she didn't immediately notice Daniel stop shadow boxing and come back to her side. It was only when a finger tried to catch an errant tear she registered his nearness.

'*Bella mia*, were you in love with this man? Had you become… close?' His voice was gentle causing her insides to melt.

'I think I was falling for him, but we weren't lovers, if that's what you mean. I had a lucky escape there, I guess.' The image of Emilia flying through the air outside the cottage flashed into her mind. Perhaps not exactly lucky…

He nodded. 'I'm glad. I didn't trust him and thought he was a coward. Someone much better will turn up, I'm sure. In the meantime,' he said, with a broad grin, 'you'll simply have to make do with me for male companionship.'

'Yes, I'll do my best, thanks, Daniel. I was due to meet him for a coffee tomorrow morning at The Boathouse in Town, but I won't go. Let him stew.'

'Good for you. He deserves a bloody nose but being stood up might teach him a lesson.' He rubbed his hands together, saying, 'Shall we get on with my memoir now? If you're feeling better?'

'Yes, I'm okay. Where were we?'

Annabel tossed and turned that night, disturbed by images of Daniel and Richard fighting with, of all things, swords and dressed like the pirates in old movies. Weird dreams followed through the night until she was woken by Emilia shaking her and saying she would be late for school. Groggy and bleary-eyed, she showered and dressed on auto-pilot and was downstairs with enough time to give Emilia her breakfast and check she had everything for school.

'Are you all right, Mummy? You don't look very well,' Emilia said as she spooned cereal down her throat at double speed.

'I'm fine, sweetheart, just had a bad night. Now, hurry up and let's go.' As she grabbed her keys her phone pinged with a text.

From Colette –'How are you?'

She quickly replied 'Am OK, thanks. Not meeting R.'

Colette's reply was 'Good for you. Talk later x'

Feeling a little more human, Annabel ushered her daughter to the car and arrived at the school gates with five minutes to spare. Not in the mood to chat to the other mums huddled around the gates she drove straight back home and made a strong mug of coffee. An empty day lay ahead of her and revived by the coffee, she hoovered and dusted the downstairs before going up to her studio to carry on with Jeanne's painting. It took her a few minutes to concentrate aware Richard would shortly be arriving at the café, and tried to stop looking at her watch. A few deep breaths and she picked up her brush and began to lose herself in the process as time receded.

Half an hour later her phone rang, making her jump. Glancing at the screen she saw it was Richard and it was ten forty-five. Ignoring it she carried on painting and again when it buzzed at eleven. Muttering under her breath she switched it off. Right, now she could forget him. Peace of mind restored, she continued painting for another couple of hours and put down her brush, smiling at her progress. Stretching to ease the muscles in her shoulders she then rinsed the brushes before switching her phone on. Several missed calls from Richard. Serve him right, she thought, heading downstairs to make some lunch.

Annabel was about to heat a carton of soup when her phone rang. Richard. For a moment she hesitated – to answer or not. But he'd be back on Herm so it wasn't as if he could turn up and cause a scene.

'Hi, Richard—'

'Annabel, I don't know why you stood me up, but I've… I've had an accident.' His voice was anguished, devoid of his usual self-confidence.

'Oh, what happened?'

'I… I was stepping onto the ferry and tripped. Felt like I was pushed though no-one was near me. I landed badly and it turns out I've broken my right arm. I'm in the hospital and I've had it plastered and they've said I can leave now.' She heard him draw a breath. 'Please could you pick me up and drive me to White Rock for the next ferry?' The pleading in his voice was palpable.

'I'm sorry about your arm, Richard, but no, I won't pick you up. Perhaps you should call your *wife*.' She was about to switch off when he broke in.

'I'm sorry I lied to you, Annabel, very sorry. But I really fell for you and never wanted to hurt you—'

She clicked off the phone, shocked by how much her hand was shaking.

Her next thought was – Daniel!

'Are you here, Daniel? I need to talk to you, *now*.'

She stood with her back to the hob where she had been about to heat the soup before the phone rang, looking for any sign of her nefarious housemate.

'Look, I know what you've been up to, Daniel, and I'm not going to bite your head off, but we do need to talk and *now*.'

A faint movement near the door to the hall alerted her to his arrival and slowly his form materialised. He stayed by the door, arms crossed with a faint smile hovering around his mouth.

'Okay, what happened and why did you do it?' She crossed her own arms, keeping her expression neutral.

He spread his hands palms upwards.

'It was only a gentle shove. I didn't intend for him to break his bloney arm, just take a fall to serve him right for being a cad. Take him down a peg or two. Sort of thing which happened all the time at sea when a sailor did the dirty on someone.' He grinned. 'Mind you, I wasn't sorry to hear him yell when he landed on the deck. You should have seen him! Blaming the crew, the boat, anyone but himself for being a bit clumsy. Caused quite a commotion, he did, threatening to sue them until the ferry captain pointed out he must have missed the step as no-one else was near him. Anyway they soon called an ambulance and he went off still making a fuss.' He shook his head. 'What you ever saw in such a pillock I don't know.'

Annabel wondered the same thing but there was no way she would admit it to Daniel.

'He was quite charming when I met him and… quite a gentleman. He actually had the nerve to ring me to pick him up from the hospital which is how I learnt what you'd been up to.' She tried a stern glare but couldn't keep it up and burst out laughing.

Daniel looked nonplussed.

'Hey, why are you laughing? I thought you were angry with me.'

Controlling her laughter she replied, 'To be honest I should be, but actually I'm grateful. Richard got what he deserved so thank you. Though please don't do anything like it again. I'm a grown woman, I can look after myself.'

Daniel grinned and rushed towards her, offering his version of a hug.

'Oh, *bella mia*, I wish I could kiss you!'

I wish you could, too, she thought, gazing into his eyes as her body responded to his oh-so-near touch. Groaning inwardly, she imagined herself being swept up into his arms and carried up to her bed, then… Nothing. Nothing could or would happen. He was a ghost, for God's sake, not a man.

'What's the matter, Bella? Are you ill? Your face is sort of twisted. Are you in pain?' The tenderness in his eyes nearly undid her. But she couldn't admit to her feelings for him. It might even scare him off and that was the last thing she wanted. Even if he couldn't be her lover she needed him to be there for her. Offering her his love and protection. Though perhaps not going around knocking people down steps and breaking their arms.

Annabel took a long, deep breath before shaking her

head.

'No, I'm fine, thanks. Honestly. It's been stressful and I haven't eaten since breakfast so my blood sugar level's low making me light-headed. You go off to wherever you go during the day and I'll have some lunch. See you tonight, yes?'

Daniel looked doubtful at first, then after a quick, 'See you tonight,' disappeared.

Chapter 22

Later that afternoon Colette popped round with Rosie bearing wine and cake.

'Right, tell me everything while the girls play in the garden. I've brought suitable refreshment for us and they're allowed some cake.'

Annabel found juice for the girls and cut them slices of cake before they trotted into the garden for their picnic. Their mothers settled themselves by the back door with glasses of wine and plates of cake.

'Santé! Right, tell me all.'

Annabel obliged, including the part Daniel played in Richard's comeuppance. At that point Colette burst out laughing and Annabel joined in. It was a few moments before either could speak again

'Hurray for Daniel. What a hero, eh!' Colette shook her head dabbing at the tears round her eyes. 'I'd love to have been there to see Richard take a tumble – thanks to a ghost! What a pity we can't tell anyone, it'd make a wonderful after-dinner story.'

Annabel nodded, still grinning.

'I know, but it has to be our secret otherwise I might end up with a well-meaning ghost buster trying to rid the cottage of an evil presence! This is scrumptious, Colette. Thanks again for bringing it and the wine. Just what I needed after this morning.' She chewed her lip. 'It's silly thinking about it now, but I was actually scared Richard would turn up demanding to know why I hadn't met him. I... I'm not good at confrontation.'

Colette patted her arm. 'Hey, it's not silly. As a famous author he might well've been furious at having been stood up by a mere nobody. I'd guess he probably has a big ego and I think you had a lucky escape even if he had been divorced.'

'Hmm, perhaps. I do know one thing, I'm giving up on men now. They see single mums as easy pickings, ready to believe anything they're told when they turn on the charm. From now on I'm focusing on my daughter, my art and our home. I don't need a man in my life to be happy.' She picked up her glass and took a long swallow, not entirely sure how much she meant it.

The following few days were uneventful. During the day Annabel made progress with her painting, no longer distracted by thoughts of Richard and where their relationship might lead. The evenings were spent with Daniel as he continued to dictate his stories with a sense of an ease between them. Neither referred to Richard and Daniel's apposite revenge on her behalf but she experienced an inner glow whenever she thought of it. He was good company, easing her occasional pangs of loneliness and his stories continued to keep her enthralled and occasionally scandalised.

At the end of the week Charlotte rang and Annabel's mouth was dry as she waited to hear the verdict.

'I love it! It's so male, so full of life and so absolutely of its time and I found it difficult to put down. And what a wonderful dry sense of humour! I wish I could have met this man Daniel, don't you? A real swashbuckler type we associate with pirates in the old movies, don't you think?'

Annabel's heart was thumping fast as she registered Charlotte's excitement.

'Why, yes, he does sound a lot like an old-fashioned movie star, I guess. And I'm glad you like it.'

'I certainly do and I also think it may have the makings of a film, too, but it's too soon to go down that route yet. How long will it be before you've finished transcribing?'

A film! Her head began to spin.

'Another week should do it. I'll try and spend more time on it now I know you're interested.'

'Good, but don't panic. You'll need an agent before it can be offered to a publisher, even my own firm. It's the way the system works, I'm afraid. I'll talk to my own agent and see if they would be interested in seeing the finished manuscript.' There was a pause. 'I don't suppose there are any illustrations or photos we could use? Always helps with a memoir.'

'Yes, I found photos of a couple of his ships and a photo of Daniel himself as a young man and I've painted his portrait from it. He... he was pretty good-looking, actually.' She found herself flushing and glad Charlotte couldn't see her.

'Wonderful! I look forward to seeing them. Look, I'd better dash, have loads to do before I collect James. Speak soon, bye.'

She clicked off her phone, continuing to stare at the screen while the thoughts whirled through her brain. Charlotte loved it. Maybe a film. Need an agent... then reality kicked in and she told herself this might happen, but was far from guaranteed. Although it was a wonderful gesture from Daniel, it might be better not to get too carried away and work hard at building up her career as an artist. Something she had more control over, for a start, and genuine support from the lovely Laura. If her income became more consistent and at a higher level than now, she might be able to obtain a mortgage to buy the cottage without royalties from the book. The thought made her smile. To succeed on her own merits would be much more rewarding than making money from someone else's endeavours. About to carry on with her painting she realised it was time to collect Emilia and went downstairs humming one of Ed Sheeran's latest hits, "Thinking Out Loud". Life was good.

Once Emilia was tucked up in bed that evening Annabel went up to her studio looking forward to sharing the good news with Daniel. She carried a glass of wine in anticipation of a long session.

'Hi, Daniel, are you here? Hope so as I've some good news to share.' She took a sip of wine and opened up the laptop. Moments later she smiled as he materialised in his favourite position by the telescope.

'Evening, Annabella, and what's this about good news?'

She told him about Charlotte's phone call and his eyes lit up.

'Wonderful!' He made the gesture of rubbing his hands together. 'And you said it would be finished in about a week? Well, I've quite a lot left to say yet so we can try, though it might mean working longer each evening.' He winked and she found herself blushing.

'Charlotte did say not to worry if it's not finished then, but I find it helps to work to a deadline. Since you're now the Captain of the SS *Baltic*, I thought there might be less to tell.' She lowered her gaze. 'Was I wrong? Sorry if I presumed—'

Daniel grinned.

'You'd be surprised what stories I still have to tell. Life was different, yes, but not entirely without, shall we say, incidents. I'll need to change a few names but otherwise,' he waved his hands, 'it's business as usual. And I've decided not to include my wartime experiences after all and simply make reference to my joining the Royal Navy as an officer in submarines. What do you think?'

'Sounds a good idea. I'm sure you have stories from that time but perhaps this book isn't the right place for them. Too much death and horror.'

'My thoughts exactly. So, where were we?' He burst out laughing, saying, 'Ah, yes the filthy rich and very old American widow who wouldn't leave me alone…'

The next week passed in a blur of looking after Emilia, painting and typing Daniel's memoirs which proved almost as risqué as his earlier exploits. Annabel began to wonder at his stamina or was it all figments of his imagination? She certainly wasn't going to ask him and as a deceased author there would be no way of checking the truth. When Daniel finally declared he had no more to say, Annabel didn't know whether to be pleased or disappointed.

'Oh, right. Are you sure? We're absolutely at the end?'

Her body was leaden as she realised how much she'd enjoyed spending so many hours with him, her handsome ghost. There would be no reason to, now.

He moved closer and once more she wished to feel his arms around her and his mouth on hers.

'I'm sure. But this doesn't mean we can't carry on spending time together, does it? We can still meet for a chat as friends would, can't we?' His eyes bored into hers and the lead weight lightened.

'Yes, I guess so, although I could spend the extra time building my portfolio for my exhibition.'

He nodded.

'Ah, yes you could. But surely you've heard of the saying, "All work and no play makes Jack a dull boy". You don't want to become dull, surely?' His eyes twinkled and she had to laugh.

'Okay, you win. But I'll have to spend some of my evenings painting when there's enough light and I'd be happy to see you at other times.'

'Wonderful! Spending time with you has been life – or should it be death – changing for me.' He stopped smiling. 'My life, my existence has been lonely for nearly seventy years although I did spend some time with my family, as I told you. But it became limited as they grew older and infirm and until you came along I hadn't had any conversation for years.' He began pacing around as he spoke and her heart ached for him. 'For some reason I have no way of moving on to wherever I'm meant to be and am chained to this half-life, half-death existence. In the few months you've been here I've felt more alive, more involved in the world I left far too soon and unwillingly.' He stopped and faced her, and she saw the pain reflected in his eyes. 'I know this can't last indefinitely and it shouldn't, for both our sakes, but while it does I value our time together and I hope I may be helping you as you're helping me.'

She couldn't stop the tears falling down her cheeks.

Chapter 23

The following morning Annabel emailed the final part of Daniel's memoir, together with scanned copies of his photos and the portrait. It was a bittersweet moment. In spite of them both agreeing they could continue to spend time together, it wouldn't be the same, she thought. She knew a great deal about him and his life and it would be difficult to discuss what was happening in the world with someone who had left it seventy years ago. Daniel didn't know as much about her, of course, but what would she be happy to share? Probably only her early years in Guernsey. In an attempt to shake off her low mood she went out for a long walk around the surrounding lanes taking photos of unusual buildings or colourful plants and flowers. It worked and she was fizzing with ideas for more paintings by the time she returned home. June was only around the corner and the more she could paint the better. In the meantime she was putting the finishing touches to Jeanne's commission and planned to deliver it within the week.

A couple of days later Charlotte phoned.

'I loved those last stories from Daniel's time on the cruise liner. He had such a wonderful way of describing what went on among the rich and famous on-board. What a storyteller!' Annabel grinned. She was right there.

'Great. Does this mean you'll talk to your agent about it?'

'I already have and she's intrigued by the premise and wants me to forward the finished manuscript, which I can now do. Oh, and she'd like to have sight of the original writings as well.'

Bloody hell. What do I do now? They don't exist!

'They're in pretty poor condition having been in a shed for over seventy years.'

'I can imagine, but as you've been able to decipher them they must be legible and she's asked to see them at some point as proof of provenance. Anyway, all looks encouraging and I'll keep you posted. Speak later.'

With panic rising by the minute, Annabel sent Colette a text asking her to ring when she was free. She then made a cup of coffee and went into the garden, hoping for inspiration with regard to the "original writings". Thoughts such as accidentally setting fire to some old notebooks – where from? – to soaking same old notebooks in water to make them unreadable to "being lost in the post" wandered in and out of her mind. Nothing came close to being viable and it began to look as if the idea of publication was doomed before it got off the ground. It had been naïve of them not to realise a potential publisher would want to see the "memoir". She could hardly blame Daniel as if he had lived he would have written it himself. Even the faint sound of the sea lapping on the beach, together with the accompanying cries of the seagulls, failed to lift her despondency. Her artist's eye was finally caught by a brightly coloured butterfly landing on a nearby thistle plant and she sat mesmerised by its beauty. She had always loved butterflies as they had been a part of the life of growers like her parents. As a small child she had thought them magical, ethereal creatures of infinite colours. This one now was a peacock, a mix of orange-red, blue and black. It seemed to cast a spell on her as all her earlier despair disappeared and as she went back inside she was filled with hope.

Colette called later that afternoon and Annabel brought her up to speed.

'Oh that's a bummer. How on earth are you going to say it was actually dictated to you by a ghost?'

'Exactly. I can't and I can't magic up an unwritten

memoir. I'm really hoping you might think of something, Colette, as you know Charlotte and what she might believe.'

There was silence for a moment and Annabel could imagine her friend screwing up her face as she tried to think.

'Look, daft as it may seem, I think you have to tell the truth—' Annabel tried to interrupt. 'Wait a minute, bear with me. I don't mean come out with it straight away. I do believe Charlotte is open-minded about things like ghosts, she's mentioned her family home was haunted, but apart from that, a couple of our mutual friends have had experiences of ghosts here in Guernsey. What we need to do is talk to them, explain about Daniel and perhaps suggest they come round to yours to see him. Make them believe in him.'

Annabel chewed her lip as she considered the idea.

'In theory it might work, but in reality not everyone can see or hear him, including you. So there's no guarantee your friends might.'

'True, but it's worth a shot. One of them is Jeanne and the other is an old friend of hers called Natalie, who bought a cottage near Rocquaine only to find a resident ghost and other weird goings on. Had to call in a vicar to get rid of him. And Natalie's mentioned a friend of hers who's also had to deal with a ghost. So you see, there's a chance someone will see Daniel and he can tell them about dictating his story to you.'

'Blimey, I didn't realise Guernsey was so haunted. I wonder if Daniel's met any other ghosts here. He's never mentioned any.' She was finding it hard to take in, but why would Daniel be the only ghost on the island? Were they all wandering invisibly among them, like he did? Now that was a scary thought!

'He may have, but what's important is do you want me to contact Jeanne and Natalie and explain the situation? Jeanne already knows about the book and seemed fascinated by it so I'm sure she'll want to help.'

'Yes, do ask them. We've got to try something or this book might not get published.'

'Right-oh, I'll let you know when I've spoken to them. In the meantime try not to worry as I'm sure it'll work out.'

Annabel wished she had her friend's confidence but at least they were doing something. She went to find Emilia who was watching television to tell her supper would be ready in fifteen minutes. Too engrossed in the programme she merely nodded. Wondering if she'd had the same reaction if she had said supper was cancelled, Annabel returned to the kitchen to finish cooking the spaghetti bolognese she'd started before Colette's call.

Once Emilia was settled in her room, Annabel went up to the studio hoping to talk to Daniel. Now the book was finished they had not arranged to meet but she hoped he'd be around after admitting he enjoyed her company.

'Hi, Daniel, it's me. I'd really like to talk if you're around. It's important.' She sat down at her desk and waited. Time dragged and she was about to give up when a slight breeze announced his arrival. Within seconds she saw him materialise near the telescope.

'Good evening, Bella, sorry for keeping you waiting but I was on the beach watching some fishing boats going out for the evening. A wonderful sight and it brought back so many memories.' His wistful look touched her heart.

'That's okay, but I'm puzzled. How did you hear me if you were on the beach?'

He shrugged. 'I don't know how it works, but I can hear you call my name wherever I am. We seem to have a stronger than normal connection as it didn't happen with my family. Now, what's happened? You said it was important.'

She told him about the phone call from Charlotte and before he had a chance to comment, went on to tell him about Colette's idea to meet the women who had experience of local ghosts.

'Right, let me see if I've understood correctly. The agent who could find a publisher wants to see my original writings to prove it's my work and I'm real, or was. Right?' She nodded. 'And as they don't exist your nice neighbour has suggested people who have seen other ghosts could come and meet me here to prove I do exist, though dead, as a ghost. Which might be enough to make a publisher happy to publish. Right?' His face was screwed up in concentration and she couldn't blame him. It sounded farcical.

'More or less. At the moment there's nothing to show I haven't made it all up and no publisher wants to get caught publishing a fantasist.' She took a breath. 'How would *you* feel about a couple of women coming here and trying to see you, talk to you? You've told me not everyone can see you so it's a long shot, isn't it?'

Daniel did his usual pacing as he digested her words.

'You're right I can't guarantee what would happen, but as they're more sensitive with open minds, there's a good chance they might see me. For my part, I'm happy to try as it seems otherwise my book will not be published. Correct?'

She nodded.

''Fraid so. But look, Daniel, much as I appreciate what you're trying to do for me it wouldn't be the end of the world if your book wasn't published. I hope to be earning more money from my art in the months ahead and might be able to get a mortgage on this cottage from my own income. Although, naturally, I'd love to see your book out there, gaining rave reviews,' she said, with a broad smile, in an effort to lift his woebegone expression.

He inclined his head, smiling slightly.

'Thank you, Bella, I've enjoyed sharing my adventures with you and wanted the book to give you the security you deserve. We won't give up yet.'

The following morning Colette rang to say she had spoken to Jeanne and Natalie who were happy to help in any way they could and both suggested a woman called Lucy who they knew and had also had ghostly experiences. Natalie said she would ring her and ask if she'll come with them. Annabel thanked Colette and finished the call more positive about the outcome. Three women, eh! All these ghosts in Guernsey and they seem to only appear for women. Wondering why that was she went up to the studio for a few hours of painting, pushing any thought of Daniel's memoir to the back of her mind.

The painting for Jeanne was finished and waiting for a protective varnish before being delivered. Her collection for the upcoming exhibition was starting to grow now and she continually found herself inspired by the natural beauty of her surroundings. The contrast to her old home in Manchester couldn't have been greater, she thought, caught up in the delight of her latest project, an old run-down cottage covered in a mass of varying foliage in a mix of colours which had cried out to be captured on canvas. The day seemed to pass quickly and before she realised it was time to fetch Emilia. Determined not to let her spend more time in front of the television, Annabel suggested a short drive to L'Ancresse Bay and its vast sandy beach for a change. May was proving to be a warm, sunny month and mother and daughter wanted to make the most of it. It seemed other mums had the same idea and they caught up with Emilia's friends from school, the children including her bestie Jennie formed a group playing in the sand while the mums settled down to chat. For Annabel it was a chance to relax in a more normal environment after the stresses of the past few days. Jennie's mum, Wendy, was easy to talk to and they enjoyed a pleasant hour before the group began to break up.

As they packed up, Wendy said, 'I understand you're an artist. Emilia's been telling Jennie how brilliant you are and you've got an exhibition coming up which will make you famous.'

She laughed.

'It's true I'm an artist with an upcoming exhibition, but the rest is my daughter's wishful thinking. She dearly wants us to buy the cottage we're renting and thinks if I'm famous we'll also be rich enough to do it.'

'It's lovely she believes in you and I wish you well with

your exhibition. We can only afford prints ourselves, but I do love to see paintings on the walls. Makes a house a home, doesn't it?' she said, smiling.

Annabel agreed.

Wendy, looking thoughtful went on, 'I don't wish to alarm you, but I've heard your cottage is haunted by a sea captain's ghost. Perhaps not the best place to buy.'

'Yes, so I'd heard but as I'm not afraid of ghosts it's not a problem. We're very happy in the cottage, regardless of whether or not it's haunted.'

Wendy's eyes grew round.

'Well, you know what it's like in Guernsey, probably an old wives' tale. I admit I've never met anyone who's actually seen him, so I'm sure you've nothing to worry about.' Calling to Jennie to hurry up she gave Annabel a quick smile and hurried to her car. Annabel wondered what Wendy's reaction would be if she knew the truth, that she had spent many hours over the past weeks typing up Daniel's adventures as a seaman and gradually falling in love with him. And, not forgetting, he was the one who had saved Emilia from being knocked down by a speeding car as unknowingly witnessed by Wendy. Probably best she never found out.

Chapter 24

The following morning Colette popped round to see Annabel bearing good news.

'I've heard back from Natalie who said Lucy is happy to join in with trying to contact Daniel. Have you explained to him what's happening?'

'Yep, and he's up for it so we can go ahead and arrange a time. It will need to be when Emilia's in bed – or, better still I'll see if she can have a sleepover at her friend Jennie's. The girls have talked about it so shouldn't be a problem. It'll be a Friday or Saturday night if we can get everyone to agree a date.'

'Good idea. I'll sound them out and get back to you. And while I'm here would you like some cake? It really needs eating by tomorrow, so...' She grinned, handing over a cake tin.

'Would be a shame to waste it, wouldn't it?'

Annabel concentrated on her painting for the rest of the day, glad there was something to take her mind off Daniel's memoir and whether or not it would end up published. Just before she went to collect Emilia she received a text from Colette confirming the girls could meet up on Friday evening. She found Wendy at the school gates and asked about a sleepover the coming Friday as she had been invited to see friends. Wendy agreed leaving the two girls jumping up and down with excitement. Annabel knew Wendy wasn't likely to ask for it to be reciprocated thanks to the supposed presence of a ghost in the cottage. Being fair, she probably would have been wary of sending Emilia to a haunted house herself.

Quickly sending a text confirming Friday to Colette, she bundled Emilia into the car in time to miss a sudden shower. When they arrived at Seagull Cottage the rain had stopped but it was too wet to go to the beach. On a whim Annabel suggested they make flapjacks and it wasn't long before the appetizing smell of baking filled the kitchen.

'Can we take some to Colette and Rosie, Mummy, to thank her for all the lovely cakes she brings us?'

'If they turn out alright, yes. We can't give her burnt offerings, can we?'

This set Emilia off into a fit of the giggles so infectious Annabel started laughing. The ping of the oven timer broke through the laughter and Annabel cautiously pulled out the tray of perfectly golden flapjacks. They high-fived their success and left them to cool while Emilia went off to watch television. Annabel made a cup of tea and sat quietly in the kitchen, smiling at how normal life seemed in that moment compared to even six months ago. Her daughter had never seemed to laugh or want to join in doing things with her, simply disappearing to her room after school, her nose in a book. And she couldn't remember the last time Emilia went to a friend's for a sleepover.

'Hi Colette, we come bearing gifts, even though it does feel like taking coals to Newcastle,' Annabel said, as Emilia, blushing, handed over a box of flapjacks.

Colette smiled. 'I never say no to an offer of homemade bakes, thank you. Have you got time to come in?'

'Sorry, no but just to say I've made the arrangements for Friday if you could let everyone know.'

'Will do, and thanks again.'

'Is it Colette you're seeing on Friday, Mummy? I had wondered if it was Richard,' Emilia said as they walked home.

'Yes and some ladies I haven't met yet. I won't be seeing Richard again, sweetheart, he's gone back to London.' She wasn't sure if it was true but thought it likely and a better explanation than the truth.

'I see. He was quite nice to me, but I'm glad it wasn't serious between you. He was a bit odd, I thought.'

Out of the mouth of babes…

Later that evening Annabel met Daniel in the studio.

'Ah, Bella, you look different tonight. More relaxed, less tense. Has anything happened?' He stood close by, studying her so intently she found herself flushing.

'Nothing in particular, simply pleased to see how much happier Emilia is since we arrived and we did some baking this afternoon.'

'Yes, I could smell it. Delicious. It took me back to when my mother used to bake, mainly bread and gâche. Nothing fancy in those days, but she was a fine cook and did her best with what she could afford. And my aunt was a good cook, as well.' His gaze went off into the distance and she knew for the moment he was somewhere else. Then he turned to face her again and smiled. 'Nowadays people don't cook as much from scratch, do they? And you can even get meals delivered. I've seen vans going round houses delivering hot food.' He shook his head. 'Are people too lazy to cook now?'

'It's not laziness, at least not all of the time. I have time to cook as I work from home, but nowadays most women work fulltime and might be too tired to cook when they get home and it can be a treat to have food made for you and delivered to your door. But not every day, no-one does that.'

'Life is very different now and I'm not sure I'd like to be alive at this time. You have lots of weird gadgets and everything happens so fast, you have no time to think.'

'You're right there, the pace of life is much faster than in your day, but it's what we're used to. And I do love all my gadgets!' she grinned.

'I have to admit that computer is impressive. I might have wanted one of those if they'd been invented back then. Which reminds me, any news on when I'll have the pleasure of meeting those lovely ladies?' His eyes twinkled and she laughed.

'Honestly, Daniel, you're incorrigible. Two of the ladies are married and one is engaged and even if they do see you nothing can happen, as you well know. And you must promise to behave, no playing tricks and no bad language, please. They're here on Friday evening and I've arranged for my daughter to be at a friend's for the night just in case she wakes up.'

'Good idea, I wouldn't want little Emilia to be frightened, such a sweet child. She's a credit to you, Bella, you're a good mother even if you're not much of a cook,' he said, grinning.

'Hey! I'm sure I'm better than you ever were.'

'No doubt. I hardly ever cooked a meal in my life. It was only when I returned here after the war that I lived alone and had to try and cook. Fortunately for me a neighbour took pity on me and cooked my meals in her home and I would pay her; otherwise I'd have probably starved.'

'Huh, and you have the nerve to criticise me. Right, I'm going down to watch some television so I'll say goodnight.'

'Goodnight, Bella.' He gave a slight bow and disappeared.

On Friday morning Annabel dropped a very excited Emilia off at school clutching a backpack for the overnight stay. Wendy, smiling broadly, took it from her while mother and daughter shared a goodbye hug.

'Be a good girl, sweetheart, but most of all enjoy yourself and I'll collect you at lunchtime unless Wendy phones earlier to say she's had enough of you.' Emilia grinned and after a quick kiss ran into school clutching Jennie's hand. Annabel had a chat with Wendy before getting in the car, suddenly overcome with sadness. It was years since they had spent a night apart and although it was an adventure for Emilia the prospect left her feeling empty. It was something she would have to get used to, she knew, as her daughter grew more independent.

Once home Annabel made a mug of coffee in an effort

to cheer herself up but as she headed to the studio the thought of what lay ahead that evening brought on feelings of panic. What if no-one except her could see Daniel? Would that mean the end of the book? Such thoughts caused her body to feel leaden and she had to work hard to bring herself to paint. The previous day Laura had been in touch to see how she was getting on and reminded her she would need all the paintings by the end of the following week to give time for framing and arranging the appropriate display. Although this was fine by her, it meant the current painting would be the last one to be included. The basic drawing was complete and all that was needed was to choose the colour scheme and she was ready to go.

Prompt at eight o'clock Colette arrived with Jeanne, Natalie and Lucy or as they jokingly described themselves, the Ghost-Busters. They introduced themselves as Annabel served coffee in the kitchen. The first was Natalie, a slim fair haired woman about her own age.

'Hi, Annabel, good to meet you. I moved into a renovated old farmhouse which, unfortunately for me, came with the ghost of a bitter old man who'd owned it years before and later died elsewhere. I didn't see him until later on but heard him and he'd move things. Quite scary, actually. And I had bad dreams when I was sort of taken over by his late wife who'd been abused by him. It took a vicar to sort it out eventually and it's been wonderful since. And I ended up marrying the woman's son who lived next door!' She smiled.

'Wow! I'm glad you've had a happy outcome. My ghost is lovely although he did try to dissuade me from renting the cottage.' She turned to Lucy, a woman in her thirties with large brown eyes and short brown hair.

'Hi, Lucy, would you like to tell me your story?'

Lucy's smile was shy, but it lit up her face.

'Mine is a bit different as I was haunted by a woman who turned out to not only be my ancestor but probably me in a previous life. Two hundred years ago.'

'Double wow! Can you tell us a bit more?'

Lucy was happy to oblige and everyone was silent as she recounted her tale, including reliving part of the life of her ancestor, Mary.

'I don't think anyone can top that experience, Lucy, and I think you're very brave. I hope life's treating you better now,' said Annabel, giving her a hug.

'Oh, yes, thanks. I'm engaged to a wonderful man and we're expecting a baby.' Lucy blushed.

There were calls of 'congratulations' and hugs all round and then Annabel realised they hadn't heard from Jeanne who, when asked said her story wasn't exactly about a ghost but about a strange cold room in the cottage she inherited which turned out to have a baby's body buried under the floorboards.

'I don't know about my ghost's memoirs, but all your stories would make fascinating books.'

Jeanne nodded.

'Lucy and I are thinking about it. So watch this space!'

After the ensuing chatter died down, Annabel said it was probably time to tell Daniel they were ready for him and in the silence said, 'Okay, Daniel, please come in.' She had already arranged with him to stay upstairs until called. She didn't want him listening in to any conversations or making a sudden appearance.

The women sat quietly around the centre island as Annabel heard the whoosh of air announcing his arrival. Slowly, he appeared near the back door, standing tall and with a huge grin on his face.

'Good evening, ladies. Welcome to my cottage.' He gave a quick salute.

Gasps and 'oohs' greeted his appearance and Annabel looked round to note that only Colette hadn't responded and was looking bemused at the others' response.

Natalie was the first to speak.

'Good evening, Daniel. I, for one, am happy to see you with my own eyes. Annabel has told us quite a bit about you and your fascinating life at sea.'

He stroked his beard, looking pleased with himself, Annabel thought. Relieved they could see him she could only hope it wouldn't make him more unbearable than before.

The others all chimed in with questions and within moments a steady conversation had sprung up between Daniel and the three women, including laughter when they attempted to touch him. Annabel moved to stand by Colette, giving her a hug.

'It's okay, I know you wanted to see him, but he told me most people can't. I think these girls are more sensitive thanks to their previous experience with ghosts, which is what we hoped for, wasn't it?'

She nodded, smiling faintly. 'Yes, you're right and I am pleased, honestly, it's just after hearing all the others' experiences I was feeling the odd one out and hoped to make up for it now.' She sighed. 'It's weird hearing only one side of the conversations and he seems to have them under some kind of spell.'

'You're right. He's putting on all his considerable charm and why not? The poor guy's been dead for so long and admitted how lonely he is so this,' she waved her arm to encircle the girls crowding round Daniel, 'is such a tonic for him, really lifting him up.'

Colette bit her lip. 'I hadn't thought of it like that and it must have been awful for him. He deserves some fun, doesn't he?'

She agreed, watching how he seemed to come more alive as he answered their questions, his eyes sparkling with pleasure.

It was a good half an hour later before the conversations slowed and she noticed how Daniel seemed to be tiring, his body becoming a little fuzzy.

'I think it's time to finish, girls, as Daniel uses a great deal of energy when he materialises and I think you've worn him out, but in a good way, right, Daniel?'

He managed a slight bow.

'Yes, Bella, it's been a wonderful experience for me to meet your friends and I hope you meeting me will pave the way for my book to be published.' He saluted. 'Goodnight, ladies, including the lovely Colette who cannot see me but I can see her.' He blew a kiss in Colette's direction which drew a cheer from the others. Then he was gone.

Chapter 25

Annabel stretched her limbs under the duvet as she remembered it was Saturday and she could have a lie-in. It was odd not to have Emilia rushing in and jumping on the bed as usual but at the same time she appreciated the early morning time to herself. It also meant she had time to mull over the events of the previous evening after Daniel had taken his leave. Initially there had been a kind of stunned silence, broken only when Annabel had said, 'Well, ladies, what do you think?'

'I found it an amazing experience, surreal even. I didn't dream I was chatting to a man who died seventy years ago but seemed as real as you and me, did I?' said Jeanne, regarding her friends with a puzzled expression.

'If it was a dream we were all in it,' Natalie replied, 'and I'm so pleased to be a part of it. After my own unpleasant experience of ghosts I was unsure what to expect but Daniel was a revelation. Friendly, intelligent and, boy, what a handsome man!' She turned to a smiling Annabel and added, 'I'd be jealous if I wasn't married to a gorgeous man of my own.'

'It has been difficult at times as it's a bit like being stalked in your own home, but he's slowly learning to respect my space and we're getting on a lot better now.'

Colette heaved a sigh.

'You all seem to have fallen for this ghost and I didn't even get to see him. It's so not fair!'

The others quickly moved to give her a hug, telling her how Daniel had called her lovely. At this she perked up a bit, particularly when Annabel offered to open a bottle of wine and they all said yes. Once it was poured she asked Lucy what her thoughts were.

'Well Daniel's definitely not a figment of anyone's imagination,' she chuckled, 'as others have said he appears solid, real and altogether fascinating. I look forward to reading his memoir and learning more about him. And you seem to have got yourself an intriguing house guest, Annabel.'

'That's one way of putting it!' Annabel replied, sipping her wine. 'The big question is, how do I get the book published without any writings?' She looked around the room, eyebrows raised in question.

'I think you need to convince Charlotte now. We can all confirm Daniel's no figment of your imagination and he did live here and did become a sea captain. It would be good for her to see him for herself if they're both up for it and then she has to persuade the agent the memoir is genuine without the usual provenance. Tricky, but not impossible,' said Jeanne, looking at the others for endorsement. Natalie and Lucy nodded in agreement.

Annabel heaved a sigh of relief. Perhaps it would all work out after all.

The optimism was still there the next morning and Annabel finally sprang out of bed and into the shower focusing on picking up her daughter later and planning how to spend the afternoon with her. At the end of the evening Annabel had produced Jeanne's painting and she had been so pleased with it she had been speechless for a few moments. Recovering her voice, she said she would take it round to show Charlotte, who might want to commission her own painting and while there she would update her on the real story behind Daniel and his memoir. Annabel was both pleased with the success of her first commission and that Charlotte would soon be aware of Daniel the ghost. It was simply a question of waiting for a phone call from Charlotte if and when she managed to digest the almost unbelievable story.

She took her time over breakfast, finding it oddly

enjoyable to eat without constant demands or questions from a little person. She was on her second cup of coffee when the post arrived with a soft thud through the letterbox. As her post was usually limited to bills or unwanted circulars she didn't immediately fetch it, savouring instead the aroma of coffee and the quiet. When she did pick it up she was surprised to find an expensive-looking white envelope postmarked Manchester. It was typed so not from her mother-in-law. Intrigued she opened it to see it was from a firm of solicitors and the penny dropped. Of course, Cynthia had mentioned a trust fund for Emilia, and with everything else which had been going on, she had forgotten about it.

Annabel sat down to read the letter attached to some form of legal agreement. Cynthia's solicitor apologised for the delay, saying it had taken longer than expected to set up a trust fund for Emilia, but it had now been formalised using a Guernsey Trust Company and would remain under Cynthia's control until Emilia reached eighteen. Her eyes glazed over at some of the legal jargon and she skimmed down the pages until she saw the sum of fifty thousand pounds mentioned. Wow! Fifty thousand! Annabel blinked. Yes, she had read it correctly. In eight years' time her little girl would have access to a lot of money. Part of her couldn't help thinking it would have been more useful now, helping her to buy a house maybe, but it was clear Cynthia's real aim was to ensure her beloved granddaughter benefited rather than the daughter-in-law who had allowed her son to die. Annabel knew it was most definitely not what Clive meant when he asked his mother to help them but... she sighed, it would give Emilia a head start in life and for that she was grateful. Telling herself she would write to Cynthia later to thank her, she cleared away in the kitchen and went upstairs to finish getting ready. Time to collect her precious daughter, she thought, with a grin.

It had become cloudy by the time Annabel left the cottage and worried it might rain later she suggested to Emilia they go to Oatlands, a few minutes' drive away. They had been there previously and enjoyed the choice of activities both inside and out and they could also have lunch there and make a full afternoon of it. After the events of the past few days Annabel wanted to be busy and distracted and this was ideal. A delighted Emilia agreed and the first activity was mini-golf and as they played Emilia told her how much she had enjoyed her stay at Jennie's and they had been allowed to stay up watching videos while eating popcorn. Annabel listened with a contented smile on her face, glad her daughter was enjoying her new life as much as she was.

The afternoon sped by, including go-cart racing for Emilia and shopping in the craft shop for Annabel after an enjoyable lunch. They arrived home happy and relaxed and soon after supper a yawning Emilia declared she was ready for bed.

'Right, sweetheart, you need to make up for the lack of sleep last night.' She smiled, giving her a cuddle. 'I'm glad you enjoyed staying at Jennie's and I for one had fun this afternoon.'

'I did too and you're the best mummy in the world,' Emilia said, planting a big kiss on her cheek before going upstairs.

Annabel sat for a few moments in silence warmed by her daughter's words. In reflective mood she hunted out a letter-pad, hardly used these days thanks to emails, and wrote a letter to Cynthia acknowledging receipt of the solicitor's letter and expressing her thanks on Emilia's behalf. She finished by saying how she was looking forward to seeing her and Deirdre in September. Then it was time for a glass of wine before going up to see if Daniel was around. He would be dying to know how the previous evening had concluded, she thought, and bound to want to see her.

In fact he was pacing around the studio when she arrived and rushed towards her, his arms flailing, crying, 'I've been waiting ages! What kept you? Emilia went to bed hours ago.'

'Hey, calm down. I do have a life you know, things to do, letters to write and Emilia went up earlier than usual so I'm not late.' She sat down, willing herself to not react to his temper.

Daniel stood still, appeared to take deep breaths, but did a ghost need to, she thought idly, as he began to smile.

'Sorry, I do forget sometimes you have a life beyond this room and me. One of the curses of being a ghost is you become totally self-absorbed. Selfish. Could you please tell me what happened after I left last night?'

She said how they had all been impressed with him and his obvious genuineness and it had been decided Charlotte, the publisher, should meet him if possible.

'Charlotte hasn't had any direct experience with a ghost so we're not sure if she will be able to see you, but it'd help enormously if she did. Her agent's reading your memoir now.'

'Right. I'm happy to give it a go, especially if she's as attractive as those other friends of yours,' he said, winking.

'Honestly! This is serious, Daniel, a lot hinges on persuading the agent of your memoir being genuine without any actual writings. And as it happens, Charlotte is gorgeous but don't overdo the flirting or she may change her mind about publishing.'

'I promise to be on my best behaviour.'

On Monday afternoon Jeanne rang.

'I've just got home from seeing Charlotte,' she said, sounding slightly breathless. 'It was a bit unnerving, trying to explain how we went round to meet Daniel, your live-in ghost who's been dictating his memoir to you over the past weeks. By the look on Charlotte's face I think she thought I'd been out on the razz. Took a while to persuade her I was serious, and that was only after she'd phoned Natalie for confirmation.'

'Oh, God, I'm sorry, Jeanne. Perhaps I should have gone round—'

'No worries, it probably came better from me as we've

known each other longer. She was aware some of us had had experiences of ghosts and seems to be open to the idea of them. I think it was simply a shock hearing about Daniel and the book. To be honest, I think she was a bit hurt not to have been included in the recce the other night, which I can understand. Anyway, bottom line is she would like to come round and meet him if she's able to.' Annabel heard her muffled voice talking to someone else. 'Sorry about that, the gardener wanted to know something. Where was I? Ah, yes, Charlotte coming round. I think she'll be gutted if she can't see him as I think her curiosity has been well and truly roused.'

'I'm sure. Daniel's up for it, he does love meeting beautiful women, as he says. Shall I phone Charlotte to arrange a time?'

'Yes, please. I'll be agog to hear how it goes. In fact we all will. Best of luck. Oh, and she loved my beautiful painting so you may get another commission soon.'

Annabel immediately rang Charlotte, apologising firstly for the lack of truthfulness about the origins of the memoir before asking when she would be free to come round. Charlotte, noticeably cool at first, seemed to thaw and they agreed on the following evening at eight thirty, giving time for Emilia to be asleep. Relieved to be a step forward on the complicated path towards publication, she turned her attention to the final touches on her latest painting before collecting Emilia from school.

The following evening Annabel found it hard to relax as it neared Emilia's bedtime. She busied herself in the kitchen, cleaning worktops which were already spotless and mopping a floor only cleaned that morning. She jumped at the slightest noise and barely listened when Emilia was telling her something about school.

'Mummy, are you okay? You look far away and I'm not sure you've heard me, have you?'

Annabel, turning to face her said, 'I'm sorry, sweetheart,

you're right I was miles away and should have been listening. Can you tell me again, please?'

Emilia explained there was to be a class trip to Lihou island the following week and pupils needed to take a packed lunch and a waterproof. 'It's all here in this letter and you have to sign to say I can go.' She held out the letter looking hopeful.

Annabel glanced through it and smiled.

'Of course you can go and you'll have a lovely time. I went there when I was about your age and you just have to make sure you leave before the tide comes up over the breakwater or you'll be marooned for the night.'

'Ooh, that sounds exciting. Might be fun to get stuck there,' she grinned.

'When you're older the schools organise residential trips with lots of activities so it's best to wait until then. Let me sign this and you can put it in your bag for tomorrow and now, young lady, it's time for bed.' She handed Emilia the signed form who gave her a big hug before going upstairs.

There was half an hour before Charlotte was due and Annabel was still nervous but had calmed down somewhat after talking to her daughter, who meant more to her than whether or not a book might be published. She had agreed with Daniel she would go straight up to the studio with Charlotte and he would arrive once they were there.

At eight thirty the doorbell rang and she went to welcome Charlotte, not quite sure how it would go after her earlier deception.

'Hi, Annabel, lovely to see you and this fab cottage I've heard so much about,' Charlotte said, giving her a hug.

'Thanks, come in. It's quite small but it's fine for the two of us.'

'From what I hear that should be three, not two,' Charlotte said, grinning.

She found herself flushing.

'Yes, I guess so. I'm so sorry about—'

Charlotte raised her hand.

'Look, Jeanne explained it all to me and I can appreciate your predicament. God only knows how I would have handled the same situation,' she said, laughing.

'Thanks. Would you like a coffee or tea before we go to my studio? It's where I paint and also the only room Daniel's allowed in, officially. Although he does have a habit of popping up elsewhere uninvited.'

'I'm all right, thanks. Shall we go up? I do hope to see this Daniel but I'm also nervous as well as worried I won't be able to.'

Annabel led the way upstairs, treading softly by Emilia's bedroom and hesitating for any sign she was awake. All was quiet so she continued up to the studio floor and opened the door. It was empty. Charlotte followed her in, exclaiming over the telescope.

'It's a beauty, isn't it? My proudest possession.' The deep voice seemed to come from nowhere, until he appeared next to the telescope, his eyes on Charlotte.

She gasped, 'Hello, Daniel. I… I can see you. Wow. I've read your memoir and want to say it's an incredible story.'

He gave her one of his bows as Annabel stood back, quietly relieved Charlotte could see him after all.

Charlotte, seeming to gain more confidence, began asking him questions about some of the incidents he described in his memoir and it wasn't long before a proper repartee took off. They were quite a contrast, Annabel thought, smiling inwardly; the English aristocrat and the Guernsey swashbuckler as he called himself.

'And did you never think of settling down with a woman and having a family, Daniel?'

Daniel glanced towards Annabel before replying. 'I did play with the thought, particularly after I became captain of the transatlantic liner and met many beautiful women. But,' he shrugged, 'I left it too late and war broke out and I joined the Royal Navy. Perhaps it's just as well I didn't marry as it would have been a true sorrow to leave a wife and perhaps children behind so soon. There was no-one to mourn me except my sister.' The sadness in his voice echoed around the tiny room and Annabel felt her eyes water.

'Oh, how sad, Daniel. I do feel for you,' sniffed Charlotte, retrieving a tissue from her pocket. 'It's a shame we can't tell the world you're a ghost, stuck between life and death and with such a story to tell. But I'm determined to tell it for you and perhaps then you'll find the peace you seek.'

'I'm touched by your words, Charlotte, and perhaps I'll then be able to move on. However, my main purpose is to help my dear friend Annabel earn enough money to buy my cottage and why I want her to receive the royalties. Do you think the book could sell enough copies to achieve that?'

Charlotte looked surprised and glanced towards Annabel.

'Yes, it was Daniel's idea and why he persuaded me to type it.'

'I see. It might well become a best seller but there's no guarantee it could bring in a healthy income for Annabel.' She paused. 'I assume you have no living relatives, Daniel? Because if you have then they would legally be entitled to any royalties, not Annabel.'

Chapter 26

The silence seemed to stretch on forever. Annabel felt sick. Of course! Why hadn't they thought of that! All of this work and stress might have been for nothing.

Daniel finally spoke.

'In fact I do have a living relative. Matthew Daniel Vaudin, my great-nephew, who inherited this cottage from his mother. He emigrated to Australia years ago and is Annabel's landlord.'

'Oh, that could cause a problem, I'm afraid.' Charlotte frowned, looking from one to the other. 'It's a legal minefield. If you were alive, Daniel, you could transfer the royalties to whomever you wished, but as you're not, then,' she shrugged, 'legally they would belong to Matthew. Except that without you dictating the book to Annabel it wouldn't exist.'

'Could it be published as fiction based on fact?'

'I don't know, Annabel, I'd have to think about it. We don't publish fiction but that may not be a problem. It's more about whether there would be as much interest in a work of fiction. Entirely different ball game.' She shook her head, looking pensive. 'I think we'd better leave it there for the moment but I won't mention our problem to my agent. Let's see what her reaction is to the finished book first. I sent it to her a couple of days ago.'

Daniel bowed his head.

'Whatever comes of it I want to say how much I've enjoyed meeting you and the other ladies and I do hope we may meet again.'

Charlotte smiled and went as if to shake his hand, then laughed.

'It's been a pleasure, Daniel, and I love your memoir. However it's proving to be the most extraordinary submission and the first time I've been face to face with a real ghost writer!' she said, laughing as she left the room.

Daniel looked puzzled and Annabel whispered she would explain later before she went to show Charlotte out. She returned with a glass of wine and sat at her table while Daniel lounged against his telescope.

'Charlotte was laughing because nowadays a number of books, usually published by celebrities, are actually written by someone else who remains anonymous. And,' she chuckled, 'they're known as ghost writers, because no-one knows who they are!'

Daniel burst out laughing.

'No wonder Charlotte could see the funny side of it – I'm a *real* ghost writer publishing *my* book under a false name. Good one!'

A few days later Annabel loaded all the paintings for the upcoming exhibition into her car and drove to the gallery in L'Islet, her stomach knotted with nerves. Would Laura like the new paintings? There was no time to do more so she could only hope she did.

Laura's assistant helped her to carry them through to a backroom while Laura was with a client and together they set them out on long tables. Seeing them arranged like this gave Annabel quite a thrill.

'These are beautiful, Mrs Easton, they're going to look wonderful when framed,' said the young woman, dressed in a smart trouser suit and looking about fifteen, Annabel thought.

'Thank you, that's kind of you to say.'

A minute later Laura came in and the girl left to cover the shop. Laura gave her a hug before standing back to focus on the paintings spread on the tables like a brilliant tapestry of colour.

'Annabel, *mo chara*, these are stunning! Even the ones

I've seen in photos are so much more vivid and I can see in your new ones how you're reflecting the beauty of the island.' She clapped her hands. 'Ooh, this is exciting. I just know your exhibition will be a success, my friend, and I can't wait to show everyone your beautiful work.'

'Thanks, Laura, I… I'm glad you like them.' She was giddy with relief and could only hope that Laura's faith in her would prove warranted. With the future of Daniel's book looking uncertain to say the least, she needed to start earning a decent living from her art.

'Like? I love them. I don't think you appreciate what an incredible artist you are and I'll be advertising your exhibition not only here, but in Jersey as well. But to start with we have to look at your prices for each piece. Will you allow me to guide you? We don't want you undervaluing yourself, do we?' she said, tilting her head.

It took what seemed forever to go round each one, with Laura noting each work with its title and price and Annabel simply agreed with her, hardly believing the sums involved but trusting in Laura's experience. Eventually they came to the last one which was lying face down.

'What's this?'

'I brought it along but it's not for sale. It's a portrait of a sea captain to show I offer portrait commissions.' She turned it over and there was Daniel smiling at her. She blinked. A trick of the light.

'But this is marvellous, Annabel. Did you do it from life or a photo?' Laura studied it, a smile on her face.

Ah, a bit of a tricky one.

'From a photo and an old portrait. The subject died years ago. A member of the family.'

'You surprise me, you've managed to capture so much life, the essence of the man, as if he's there in front of you.' She turned to face her. 'It's a shame it's not for sale, but I understand why it isn't. I'd be happy to hang it as an example of your portraiture and I'd be surprised if you don't earn some commissions from it.'

'Thank you, I appreciate that.'

After that there was paperwork to be sorted and Laura asked her to provide a short bio and a photo for publicity and promotional material. Promising to provide both later that day, they parted with another hug and Annabel floated back to the car. Thinking this called for a treat, she went to Colette's restaurant for coffee and cake and her friend joined her for a few minutes. Colette was happy to hear how well it went with Laura and said she was rooting for her and would happily display posters advertising the exhibition when they were available. By the time she got home Annabel was punch-drunk on the genuine goodwill being showered on her. It wasn't until she looked in the fridge for something for lunch she remembered she had forgotten to do the weekly shop that morning and had to nip round to the local Co-op for supplies.

Annabel continued to go out sketching and began new paintings. Her online sales ticked along but as they were mainly prints the income only just covered the rent. For any new paintings she planned to raise her prices in line with Laura's suggestions and would charge more for the prints as well. Knowing she could no longer rely on a future income from Daniel's book acted as motivation to upscale her art business. Charlotte had pointed out even if the book was to be published it could be two or three years before publication. The good news was Charlotte phoned to say her agent was keen to take it on but Charlotte had told her there was a 'technical issue' to resolve first.

'I wish I could fathom a way round this royalties issue, Annabel. It makes perfect sense for you to receive them. Have you had any ideas?'

'Daniel did point out to me that we're using a pseudonym and not his real name, so could this by-pass any living relative? It might not be obvious who the real author is.'

'I'm not sure but we need to see if any real names are mentioned in the memoir. Do you know if there are? Family in particular.'

'I don't think so, but I'll check with Daniel. What about provenance? We're stuck on that one.'

Charlotte's laugh rang down the phone.

'You could say so! As the publisher I could sign an affidavit to say I've seen proof of provenance as indeed I have, the author himself. So, as long as my agent doesn't disagree and submits to my firm we might be okay. I'll chat to my MD and give him the heads up before he sees the manuscript. In the meantime let me know about the names, please.'

That evening Annabel went up to the studio and called out to Daniel.

Seconds later he arrived in a whoosh of air, smiling broadly.

'*Bella mia,* it's so good to see you again. I've missed you.'

'Well, I've been busy and there wasn't much to say until today when Charlotte phoned. Do you remember if you've used real names in your memoir, especially when mentioning your family?'

He frowned.

'I only ever used first names of anyone I sailed with, didn't I? And I think the same with my family, such as it was. Can you check on your computer?'

'Yes, I was going to do that and if there are any full names we could change them. We might avoid having your relative claim the royalties if it can't be proved it was your memoir. We changed your name to Daniel Gregg, didn't we?'

'Yes, that's right. Clever girl. Shall we start checking now or are you too busy?' he said, grinning.

'Okay, okay might as well make a start,' she said, chuckling.

Over the next few nights they checked the whole memoir and only found a couple of names which needed changing and Annabel sent the revised document to Charlotte. She then sent it to the agent for forwarding to the MD. The waiting game began and Annabel focused on her painting.

A week before the opening of her exhibition Annabel received a phone call from the letting agent, Jon Emery.

'Morning, Mrs Easton, how are you?'

'Fine thanks, Jon. Is there a problem? I haven't missed paying the rent, have I?'

'No problem, you're good.' There was a pause. 'I thought I'd better let you know the owner, Mr Vaudin, is arriving in Guernsey in a couple of weeks, apparently he's attending some sort of marine conference here and has asked if he can come and see the cottage at some point.'

Her stomach twisted. He was the last person she needed turning up when they were trying to finalise a book deal without his knowledge.

'Not a problem if he gives me plenty of notice. Is he checking I haven't trashed the place?' she said, trying to make light of it.

'Of course it will be a time to suit yourself, Mrs Easton, and we've assured him you're an excellent tenant. He... he's told us he's planning to sell the cottage when your tenancy expires, in nine months' time.'

Chapter 27

It was like being punched in the gut. Her legs turned to jelly and she had to sit down. 'No,' she wailed, her head in her hands as she rocked back and forth in the chair. It was so unfair! He had no right to sell the cottage! It was her home! But an insistent voice of reason answered, yes, he did. At that moment, she found herself hating Clive for leaving her in such a financial mess, forcing her to rent a home for them both and leaving her at the mercy of a landlord's whims. It would take at least two years of selling her paintings at top prices to save up the thousands of pounds needed for a deposit. And it would need at least that time to provide a good track record of income for a mortgage. It didn't sound as if the horrible Mr Vaudin would be inclined to wait so long.

'Oh, Daniel, please help me. I need you,' she called out to the empty studio.

'I'm here, *bella mia*, what's happened?' His deep, loving voice answered.

She looked up to see him only inches away, his face etched with concern. Taking a deep breath, she told him of the agent's phone call and the imminent visit of his great-nephew.

His eyes widened in shock and he struck one hand with a fist as if spoiling for a fight and paced up and down the room.

'The bastard! He clears off without a by-your-leave to the other side of the world, leaving his poor mother to fend alone, and then on a whim decides he wants to sell the family home. I won't stand for it. I'll make his life miserable. I'll scare off potential buyers. See if he likes an angry ghost showing what he can do.' He stopped and glared at her, his face suffused with anger.

Annabel could only stare, feeling both grateful for his righteous indignation but wary of his anger and where it might lead.

'I appreciate you're angry, Daniel, and I don't blame you. I'm angry and upset as well as I was hoping this lovely cottage could be a long-term home for me and Emilia.' She drew in a deep breath. 'However, if I remember correctly, you said your nephew didn't seem to be aware of you when he lived here so he's not likely to be scared of anything you do. And even potential buyers might not notice your presence. Colette doesn't see you and yet she wants to.'

'Hmm. Watch this.' He picked up her laptop and pretended to throw it across the room.

'Oh. Of course, you lifted up Emilia before the car could hit her. So you could do the same with objects, like a poltergeist.' She watched with bated breath as he then carefully replaced the laptop on the table.

He shrugged. 'I don't know anything about poltergeists, but I do know I can throw things around if I wished. And could make quite a mess,' he said. Seeing her look horrified, he added, 'Naturally I wouldn't throw your stuff around, Bella, only the old things left by my niece. And only then if I had to. I promise I will not let that... that whippersnapper sell this cottage, except to you when you can afford to buy it.'

'I hope it won't come to that, Daniel, though I appreciate your support.' She twiddled a paintbrush, while thinking. 'It's possible the man has a family to support and needs the money.'

'As far as I know he wasn't married. Doris would've told me if he had, he was the apple of her eye. Though he could have married recently, o'course.'

'I guess we'll find out at some point. Not that it'll make any difference, he has the legal right to sell no matter what we think. At least I'll have nine months before I have to leave.' Her voice wobbled as she said 'leave' and tears threatened. Daniel came as close as he could and she felt the warmth surround her and then a soft feather-light touch on her cheek.

'Oh, Daniel, I'll miss you if I have to leave. Will you be able to move with me?'

'I don't think so. Although I can travel around the island, I seem to be pulled back here, to where I died. But don't give up yet, Bella, anything could change.'

For a couple of days Annabel went around in a bit of a daze, finding it hard not to think about leaving Seagull Cottage. Fortunately for her peace of mind, Laura arranged for interviews on the local radio and in the *Guernsey Evening Press* which kept her mentally and physically occupied. Then she was provided with a quantity of posters advertising the exhibition and went around various businesses handing them out. The first to be visited was Colette's and she was happy to put a couple in the café windows as well as smaller flyers on the tables. As Annabel went round the island she was overwhelmed by the support she received and excitement began to kick in and push out any thoughts of Matthew Vaudin. This was her moment to shine and show everyone what she was passionate about – her art. Her new-found friends all promised to come to the private viewing before the official opening and Laura had invited a number of her regular clients to attend the viewing, to be celebrated with drinks and canapés.

The viewing was on a Friday and Colette volunteered to have Emilia round for a sleep over, with Jonathan in charge while she attended the viewing. Little Rosie rushed around in excitement when told her big friend was coming to stay and Annabel could only be grateful for everyone's help. All she needed now was a smart outfit befitting the occasion of her first major solo exhibition, the one in Manchester having been a shared event, and two days before the big event she went into Town searching for every woman's dream buy; beautiful, flattering and not costing the earth. Laura had recommended a couple of boutiques to try and it was in the second one she found what she wanted. An emerald green silk trouser suit which flowed over her slim frame and complemented her fair hair and blue eyes. As she saw her reflection in the mirror her face lit up in a huge smile. You're looking pretty good, girl, she thought, twisting round to see the full effect. Laura had counselled her that to be a successful artist she needed to look the part, especially when hosting her own exhibition.

Friday arrived and promised to be a lovely early summer's day. A few fluffy clouds floated in an otherwise blue sky and it was warm enough for Annabel's new outfit. After dropping off an excited Emilia at school, she drove on to the gallery to see how her paintings looked. Her daughter would have liked to attend the viewing but it was adults only so Annabel promised to take her round on Saturday when it might be quieter.

'Good morning, Annabel. Anxious to see what we've done with your gorgeous paintings, no doubt?' Laura's broad smile and twinkling eyes were reassuring and she smiled back.

'I have been feeling nervous, I admit, but I'm sure you've done a wonderful job.' She gazed around the downstairs gallery where other artists were on display and wondered if she would merit a permanent display after the two-week exhibition.

'You'll be pleased to know I've had a grand response to my RSVPs and there will be about fifty guests coming this evening, which is unusual for an unknown artist. And there will be photographers from the local newspaper and a glossy magazine to bring us in more publicity.' She started to lead the way upstairs as she spoke and Annabel followed, her stomach full of fluttering butterflies. At the top of the stairs she stood transfixed at the sight of the beautifully framed paintings covering the walls, creating a dazzling display of colour and light.

'Oh my God! It's… it's wonderful! Thank you.'

Laura beamed.

'My dear girl, I have only hung your pictures on the walls, it's you who have created such beauty and I must thank *you* for that. Come, let's go round together and do let me know if you need to change anything. There's still time for minor adjustments.'

Each painting had its own typed label with a title and brief description and the paintings were hung at different levels and in groups of similar themes and Annabel did not want to change a thing. To her eyes it was perfect and brought a lump to her throat. As they approached the end she gasped, 'Oh!' Daniel's portrait had been allotted more space and its own overhead light, increasing the realistic effect of the portrait as his eyes seemed to follow her.

Laura grinned.

'Doesn't he look marvellous? He draws you to him, doesn't he? It's incredible what you achieved with an old photo, Annabel. For sure, you'll be gaining commissions from anyone wanting a portrait.'

'Thanks. I'll need your advice on what to charge, though.' Her eyes were glued to him, his enigmatic smile and deep blue eyes making her heart thump so loud she wondered if Laura could hear it and moved away slightly.

'Right, I think it's time for a cup of coffee, don't you? Let's go down and have a chat about what's likely to happen tonight.'

Restless after the visit to the gallery, Annabel went for a walk at Bordeaux, not wanting to think about the evening ahead. In spite of Laura's enthusiasm, she worried the viewing would be a flop and no-one would buy her paintings. In spite of her misgivings she took a sketchbook with her and instead of drawing the view she drew a quick sketch of a woman and child building a sandcastle. It was rare for her to include people but after Laura's comments about Daniel's portrait she decided to have a go. As she was putting finishing touches to the sketch her head down in concentration, she didn't notice the woman had moved and was startled to hear a voice say, 'May I see what you've drawn? It seems to be me and my son.'

'Of course. I hope you don't mind, it was such a lovely image of you both.' Embarrassed, she wondered if she should have asked her permission.

The young woman, in her twenties she guessed, studied the sketch intently before, with a smile, she replied, 'Of course I don't mind, it's lovely, thank you. No-one's ever drawn me before and it's so much nicer than a photo.'

She looked pensive, as if wondering what to say and Annabel said, without thinking, 'Would you like it? I was planning to use it in a painting, but if you like it, it's yours.'

Her eyes widened as Annabel tore out the page and held it out to her.

'Surely you normally charge for drawings? I'm not sure I could afford it. You're obviously a proper artist, not an amateur.'

Smiling, she nodded. 'Yes, I do sell my artwork but this was simply a quick sketch for fun, so please accept it as a gift. If you want to see more of my work I have an exhibition at the gallery in L'Islet starting tomorrow, no pressure to buy.'

'Thank you, you've made my day,' she glanced at the signature, '*Annabel De La Mare.* And you're local, great. I'm Beth and so pleased to have met you, Annabel, and I'll pop into the gallery and spread the word, for sure.' With that, she nodded goodbye as her little boy pulled at her free hand, saying he wanted an ice cream.

Annabel was left grinning broadly. Although it was a shame she no longer had the sketch for a painting, it felt good to have made another mum happy and it confirmed Laura was right about people keen to have their portraits painted. Another time she would have to charge the going rate, which according to Laura was a great deal more than she had imagined.

Before she left the beach she quickly re-drew the little group while it was fresh in her mind, sketching Beth and her son as they stood waiting for an ice cream at the kiosk. Then it was time to pick up Emilia and prepare for the evening ahead. All she could do was pray the viewing was a success and she was on the path to fame and fortune. Whatever.

Chapter 28

After depositing Emilia at Colette's Annabel took a taxi to the gallery arriving twenty minutes before the opening time of six o'clock. She had made an extra effort with her hair, part up-do to look more sophisticated and used more make-up than normal and had been told how beautiful she looked by her daughter. Feeling reassured she entered the gallery to find it was buzzing with waiters and waitresses stacking glasses, bottles of wine and soft drinks on one table and others laying out plates of canapés on another. She stood for a moment wondering what to do and then Laura appeared and gave her a big hug.

'The star of the evening! And don't you just look grand! That green brings out the blue of your eyes and I love how you've done your hair. You're looking the part, so you are. Come, we'll have a quiet drink in the office while the girls and boys do their stuff.'

Once in the office Laura poured them both a glass of chilled champagne before saying, 'Sláinte!'

'Sláinte!' Annabel repeated, assuming it was the Irish for Santé, or cheers.

'You have nothing to worry about, *mo chara*, all you need to do is enjoy yourself. People will want to talk to you, of course, but you can keep it short and sweet and if someone becomes a nuisance simply give me the nod and I'll rescue you. I'll never be far away, never fear.' She went on to describe the order of events, starting with Laura giving a brief introduction of her and her work as guests were given a drink and then all would go upstairs to view the paintings. Laura planned to introduce her to some of the guests and there would be the photographers to smile for. Annabel hoped her friends would be early arrivals, wanting their moral support. She guessed Laura would have to circulate and the thought of standing there on her own was scary.

At six the door was opened and guests began arriving, to be greeted by Laura before being offered drinks by the waiting staff. Annabel hung back, with a fixed smile, as she scanned the incomers for friendly faces. She spotted Charlotte, with the others right behind, chatting to Laura, before they all came over to her offering smiles and hugs.

'You have a super turnout compared to some I've been to, Annabel, and I don't think I've ever heard Laura talk as passionately about a new artist before,' Charlotte said, giving her a hug. Annabel felt her shoulders ease at the welcome words. Perhaps the evening would be a success after all.

Minutes later, Laura began shepherding the guests upstairs before taking Annabel's arm and following behind. The sight of the crowd gathered in front of her paintings made her want to rush downstairs and hide, but Laura kept a firm grip on her arm, whispering, 'Don't panic, remember everyone is here because they're keen to see your lovely pictures and not simply to enjoy free bubbly and snacks. We'll give them time to browse before I introduce you to some of them and then pose for the photos. It'll be fun, I promise.' She gave her a dazzling smile and Annabel couldn't help smiling in return. Butterflies were still in full flight in her stomach but she was able to stand back and watch as the guests circled round the room giving her work their full attention. It reminded her of being at uni when the tutors turned up to examine the students' work set out on display in the art room. At that time her work was considered to be of a good standard though not inspirational. Over the years since she had honed her craft and found her unique style in the process. Fingers crossed her style would appeal to these art lovers.

'Right, let's do some introductions,' Laura said, squeezing her arm.

An hour later Annabel was tucking into a delicious canapé, washed down with a fresh glass of champagne, and feeling as if she had just come through a stiff job interview. Everyone Laura had introduced her to had been lovely, but it had been intense and afterwards she could barely remember her own name let alone those of the guests. It had been hard smiling for the various photographers and made her wonder how on earth models managed day after day. But Laura had declared her to be an unqualified hit and had finally given her permission to sneak downstairs for sustenance and some peace and quiet while she did the sales chat upstairs. It wasn't long before her friends found her to offer their congratulations.

Charlotte was first.

'What a wonderful collection! I found it so difficult to choose my favourite so in the end I bought two and I think they'll be marvellous in the conservatory.'

'Why, thanks, Charlotte, you didn't need to, you know—'

'Of course I didn't need to but I wanted to because I love your work and think you're very talented. And I expect to make a huge profit when you're famous!' she said, laughing.

'I also bought one of your amazing beach scenes as although I've quite a collection of art in my home, none are local and I particularly love your use of colour,' said Natalie, giving her a hug. Jeanne reiterated how much she adored the painting of her home and that Nick had said he'd loved it. Then Tessa and Colette chipped in to say they wanted to buy signed prints and Annabel said Laura was organising Limited Edition prints once the exhibition was finished. Overwhelmed by their support, she found herself moist-eyed as they declared they had to leave when Laura came looking for her.

'Ready to come back upstairs? The guests are beginning to leave and you can see which paintings have sold. I hope you'll be as pleased as I am,' Laura said, with a grin.

As they returned upstairs they passed those leaving, all ready to shake her hand and wish her well. With less people milling round Annabel was able to see her paintings more clearly and was shocked to see the number of red stickers, depicting sales. Her eyes widened as she wandered round, noting only an occasional non-stickered painting.

'I can't believe it! Are so many really sold?'

'For sure. To be honest, even I hadn't expected to sell as many the first night but…' she shrugged, 'people loved your fresh approach, the almost ethereal quality of your paintings and, although we had raised your prices, they were still lower than my clients are used to paying. From now on, you'll be able to charge more for any new work.' Laura beamed and Annabel felt happy tears filling her eyes.

'Thank you. I… I couldn't have done this without you.' She gave Laura a hug.

'I'm pleased to be the one who launched you, my dear girl. Oh, and I could have sold your Captain ten times over tonight and at twice the price of other paintings. Definitely one for prints and several people said they'd be interested in personal portraits. I think you'll have a busy year ahead, *mo chara.*' Laura went off to chat to the few remaining guests and Annabel found herself drawn towards Daniel's portrait at the far end of the room. She couldn't help grinning like the proverbial Cheshire cat as she stood there, glowing with the success of the evening.

Suddenly a deep voice in her ear said, 'Well done, *bella mia*, well done. And so many people loved my portrait I almost materialised.' Startled, she looked round quickly, but no-one was near.

'Honestly, Daniel, I wish you wouldn't do that. You could have scared people away and ruined my evening.'

'Nonsense, I made sure you were alone and I promise I've behaved myself all evening. It was impossible to resist being here to share your triumph. And what a triumph it's been! You must have made pots of money already—'

'Shush!' she whispered, 'someone's coming.' She heard the familiar whoosh of air as he left and turned to find one of the guests approaching with their hand outstretched as they said goodbye. Annabel smiled and managed to say goodbye calmly while feeling anything but. He really was the limit, taking such risks, she thought, as she made her way back to where Laura was standing, deep in conversation with a slightly older and extremely attractive man.

'Annabel, come and say hello to my husband, Gerry. He's come to take me out for supper at Colette's restaurant and I've suggested you join us, if you're free.'

'Hi, Annabel, it's good to meet you. Laura's been telling me all about your paintings and what a successful viewing it's been. Please do join us for supper.' They shook hands and his smile was so warm she decided to accept the invitation after wondering if Laura had twisted his arm.

'I'd love to join you, thank you.'

'Good,' Laura said. 'Let me scoop up the stragglers and then close up. Our table's already booked so no panic.' She went off to steer the few stragglers down stairs and Gerry chatted to Annabel as they too made their way down to where the waiting staff were packing up the remnants of the canapés, probably due to be eaten by them later that evening, she thought, suddenly realising she was hungry and would enjoy a proper meal herself.

They were soon on their way to the restaurant at the Bridge and Annabel relaxed in the luxurious comfort offered by Gerry's car, which she thought might be a Jaguar. She amused herself by wondering if she would be able to afford such a vehicle herself one day if she was truly on the verge of success as everyone had implied. Would be nice, she thought, breathing in the smell of the leather upholstery, though buying her own home was definitely the first priority.

It was a beautiful sunny evening and when they arrived at the restaurant Annabel could see through the windows that it was almost full. It was good to see her friend's business doing well, particularly as it was where Laura had first spotted her work.

'Hope you're hungry as I'm aiming at the full three courses,' said a smiling Laura as she pushed open the door. A loud cheer erupted from a large table at one side and Annabel blinked. How on earth?

Laura laughed.

'Surprise! Your friends are waiting for you and I don't know what we'd have done if you'd said no. Come on in and join the party.'

She was laughing herself as she arrived at the table to be greeted by the Gang, as she thought of them. Colette, Charlotte, Tess, Jeanne and Natalie all stood up and raised their glasses as she was ushered to a seat between Colette and Laura with Gerry taking a seat the other side of his wife.

'We did debate whether or not to let Gerry join us, being the sole man, but we thought he deserved to be here as he's part owner of the gallery.' Laura grinned and nodded towards him, already chatting easily to Charlotte. 'I think he'll enjoy having so many ladies to himself for once.'

Annabel agreed, happiness fizzing within every cell of her being as she gazed around at everyone who had shown her so much support and wanted to celebrate this special occasion with her. She couldn't remember when she had been as happy. Surreptitiously she brushed away a tear as she sipped yet more champagne.

Chapter 29

Annabel woke the following morning, dry-mouthed and with a thumping headache. Through blurry eyes she noted the time was after ten and for a moment panicked. Emilia! Then she remembered she had slept over at Colette's and wasn't due to be collected until later, as requested by Rosie. Rubbing her eyes she padded downstairs to grab a glass of water before making a cup of tea. She was sipping the tea in the kitchen when her phone rang.

'Mrs Easton, it's Jon Emery from the agency. Is this a good time to talk? You don't sound too well.'

She coughed to clear her throat and her stomach clenched at what she knew was coming.

'It's okay, Jon, I overslept, that's all.'

'Sorry to disturb you then but I've had a call from Mr Vaudin who arrived in Guernsey yesterday and wants to see the cottage as soon as it can be arranged.' There was a pause and she sipped more tea, trying to calm herself. 'Would Monday be convenient for you? Say eleven o'clock?'

No it bloney wouldn't, she thought, no time would be convenient as far as she was concerned. Taking a deep breath she replied, 'Yes, suppose so. I hope he won't take long as I've lots to do.'

'I understand he wants a quick look to remind himself what the cottage looks like now as he hasn't seen it for over twenty years.' Another pause. 'I happened to see the *Press* this morning, Mrs Easton, and there's a great article all about your preview evening at the gallery yesterday. Seems to have been quite a success and I'm pleased for you.'

'Why, thank you, Jon. I'd better get a copy of the paper.

Were there photos?'

'Yes, including a good one of you with some guests.'

'Right. Will you be coming round with Mr Vaudin on Monday?'

'No, hardly necessary as he's the owner. Goodbye for now, Mrs Easton.'

'Goodbye.'

Annoyed, she paced the kitchen drinking her tea and muttering out loud about the 'insufferable man' who was spoiling everything by turning up wanting to take her home from her just as she was enjoying public acclaim as an artist. If it hadn't been one of her best mugs she would have thrown it against the wall.

'Hey, Bella, what's the matter? I thought you'd be happy this morning.'

Startled, she turned round to see Daniel with his arms spread open as if to give her a hug. She moved towards him and felt his warmth encircling her as she told him about the phone call.

'That bloody nephew of mine! Doesn't waste any time, does he? I'll give him a piece of my mind when I see him.'

'Hmm, but remember he can't see or hear you, unless something's changed since he left here.' Thinking it would be great if the younger man could see his uncle's ghost, she pictured an angry Daniel berating his nephew as he marched around the room in full-on fierce sea captain mode. It made her smile, briefly.

'Surely there's something I could do to make him change his mind? I need to think about it. Damn and blast the lad!' He stomped around the kitchen, his face creased in thought as Annabel stood by feeling helpless.

'Do I tell him about the book? Explain you dictated it to me as it's the only way I could have known about your sailing days.'

Daniel paused his turn around the kitchen.

'If you did that then he could lay claim to the royalties if it's published. We're trying to avoid that.'

'I know, but it might act as a sweetener to him and encourage him to let me stay until I can afford to buy. I'm seeing Laura this afternoon to find out how much I've earned so far. She might be able to give me a rough idea of my potential earnings from my art over the coming years and I'm hoping it will be enough to get a mortgage, without relying on the book royalties.'

'It would stick in my craw to let my nephew claim the royalties instead of you. Without you there'd be no book, you did all the work.' He came closer and "hugged" her. 'I'd sooner the book wasn't published than he get the money.'

'Thanks, Daniel, I appreciate that. We'll have to think about it, but now I must dash as I'm due to pick up Emilia shortly. See you later.' He nodded and disappeared and she shot upstairs for a shower, her mind whirling. How on earth was she going to deal with Matthew Vaudin? Should she tell him about his uncle, the ghost? And the book they wrote together? Her good mood from the previous evening had completely evaporated. The only comfort was the apparent success of her exhibition and the boost to her income. Something to be very thankful for, if nothing else.

She was greeted at Colette's by an excited Emilia, crying, 'Mummy, Mummy, you're in the paper! I said you'd be famous.' Giving her daughter a kiss she glanced over to Colette who was trying to hang on to an equally excited Rosie before Jonathan arrived to take over.

'Morning, Superstar. What's it feel like to be famous, eh?' Colette grinned at her.

'Like a hangover. But it was a fab night wasn't it? Thanks so much, Jonathan, for having Emilia, it was great to finish off with the meal.'

'No problem, only too glad to help and,' he pointed to the morning's newspaper on the worktop, 'it looks like it was a big success.'

'Sit down and have some coffee and cake and have a look at the *Press* while the girls go and play outside for a bit.'

Annabel needed no bidding, anxious as she was to read

what had been written about her and the exhibition. Wow! She had made the front page! Then she reminded herself Guernsey wasn't exactly a hotbed of news stories. Nearly half the front page was taken up with a full colour photo of her and Laura and a group of guests gathered in front of her paintings. She was impressed and glad she had chosen such a colourful outfit. The accompanying article more or less followed the text on the handouts, covering a brief bio of herself and how Laura had "discovered" her through a display in a local restaurant. It also quoted responses from some of the guests declaring how they found the work "refreshing" and "imaginative". There was even a reference to Daniel's portrait which had been "much admired for its realism". She snorted with laughter at the quote wondering what they would have thought if they had known it was the portrait of a ghost.

'Good article, isn't it?' Colette said, setting down their coffees and two slices of cake. 'You should be very proud, girl. Great photo and great write-up.' She gave her a quick hug.

'Thanks, it went better than I could have hoped. All the credit must go to Laura, though, she did a brilliant job all round.'

'True, she did, but your paintings were the star of the show and don't forget that.'

'I guess.' She sipped her coffee, looking thoughtful. 'I owe you one, too, Colette, and I'd like you to choose an unsold painting for yourself as a thank you.'

Colette's mouth dropped.

'Are you sure? That's very generous of you. Perhaps a print—'

She shook her head.

'No, if it wasn't for you I might never have been "discovered" by Laura, so please choose an original.' She laughed, 'Assuming there's something left that you like. If not I'll paint you another.'

Flinging her arms around her and nearly knocking over

the coffee in the process, Colette said, 'I loved all of them so I'm sure I'll find something, thank you.'

'Good, then come with me and Emilia this afternoon and make your choice. You'll have to leave it on show with the others until the end of the exhibition, like everyone else, but it's only for two weeks.'

'I think I can wait that long,' she said. 'I'll ask Jonathan if he wants to be involved in the choice or if he'll leave it to me. Usually anything to do with the house he lets me decide. Typical man.' Laughing, she went off to find him in the garden with the girls and Annabel, smiling at her friend's pleasure, tucked in to the cake and finished her coffee.

A couple of hours later Annabel drove Emilia and Colette to the gallery in L'Islet.

'Wow, Mummy, there's lots of people here. Are they all wanting to buy your paintings?'

She looked round, noting there were a few inspecting the artwork on display downstairs, while more were heading upstairs to her exhibition.

'Not everyone, sweetheart, some are just window-shopping I expect, wanting to see what all the fuss is about. I—'

'Annabel! Over here!' Turning she saw Laura waving from the back of the room and caught up with her, Emilia and Colette in tow.

'Have you seen the *Press*?' Annabel nodded. 'Well, it seems to have brought out the masses as there's been a steady stream of people the last two hours. It's been grand.' She was beaming as she gave all of them a hug.

'Well, I do hope you haven't sold everything as I want Colette to choose a painting as a gift from me.'

Laura chuckled.

'Not quite, but for sure there's been a lot of interest. You'd better go up now, Colette, and perhaps take Emilia while I have a talk with her mammy.'

The two of them left and Laura drew Annabel into her

office and closed the door.

'There now, that's better. Sit down and would you like a drink? Tea, coffee, bubbly?' she said, grinning.

'I'm good, thanks.' She coughed, before asking, 'Have you had a chance to tot up my sales?' Her palms were moist as she waited to hear the fateful figure.

For answer, Laura picked up a sheet of neatly typed figures and passed it to her. All paintings sold were listed, more than half of those she had provided for the exhibition. At the bottom was the total, less the fifty per cent agreed commission. She blinked.

'Blimey! I… don't know what to say. It's more than I could have hoped for.' And a big chunk towards a deposit on the cottage, she thought.

'And me. Art's such a personal choice and even though I loved your work, it didn't mean others would and all exhibitions of an unknown artist are a gamble. Fortunately,' she said, with a laugh, 'the gamble paid off. For us both. And I'm sure it won't be long before all your work will have the little red stickers on them. In fact, I have a couple of clients from Jersey who couldn't make the preview who are coming over this afternoon. Oh, and here are the details of those who want to commission portraits.' She handed her a list of three names with contact information.

'Thanks,' she croaked, her throat dry.

'I think you need a drink. Tea? If you're driving?'

She nodded.

Laura brought them both tea and they continued to chat for a few minutes while they drank. They discussed Limited Edition prints and which would be the best paintings to start with and then went on to talk about the possibility of printing blank cards for all occasions.

'Your paintings lend themselves to such a variety of options allowing you to appeal to all pockets. I'd be happy to recommend excellent printers when you're ready.'

Annabel's mind was buzzing when Colette returned with Emilia, announcing she had made her choice of a painting. Laura made a note of it and then the three of them left, nipping into the nearby supermarket for some food shopping before going home.

Arriving back at the cottage seemed like an anti-climax to Annabel. The build-up to the exhibition had been so intense and all-consuming and now, well, now she wasn't sure where she was. On the brink of a new and exciting phase in her career as an artist, for sure, but... But would she still have a home in a few months' time? The thought ate away at her as she unloaded the groceries and tried to answer her daughter's questions about the opening night. Naturally, Emilia was excited for her and was convinced she was on the way to fame and fortune as in the movies and she couldn't burst her bubble and say there was a way to go yet. And they may lose the home they both loved. Once the shopping was packed away Annabel suggested they went to the beach, mainly as a way to clear her still aching head but also as a distraction for them both. Minutes later they had collected the beach rug, buckets and spades and a Frisbee and were looking for a place to set up camp. There were other families on the beach and as it was low tide they managed to find a sandy stretch with damp sand perfect for castle building. Determined to give Emilia all her attention after their time apart, she used all her creative energy to produce a particularly fine, large sandcastle with a moat and decorated by pebbles and shells collected by her daughter. Emilia clapped her hands.

'Wow, Mummy, it's awesome. The best yet. Can you take a photo, please before it's washed away?'

'Of course and I'll print them out so you can take them to school. When I was a little girl we used to have sandcastle competitions in the summer and I always wanted to win one, but I never did. The trick is to always use damp sand as we've done now.'

Emilia threw her arms around her, saying, 'You're the cleverest mummy in the whole wide world and I love you to the moon and back.'

'Oh, sweetheart, thank you and I love too. You're the best daughter a mother could have.' They stayed locked in an embrace for a few minutes and Annabel felt tears pricking her eyelids. Okay, a roof over your head and money in your pocket were important, but nothing beats sharing cuddles with your child.

Chapter 30

'So, how did it go at the gallery today?'

The question greeted Annabel as she arrived in her studio that evening and found Daniel with his eye glued to the telescope making the most of the late sunset.

'And good evening to you, too, Daniel.' She set a small glass of wine on the table, ascribing to the view that a hair of the dog might help her lingering hangover. After sitting down she frowned as he continued to keep his back turned to her. The man has no manners, she thought. 'It went well as Laura's buzzing with ideas about increasing my income and I've already earned a good chunk towards a deposit in spite of the fifty per cent commission to the gallery.'

He swung round and stared at her.

'What? They've taken half what you earned? That's daylight robbery, that is. Thieving bastards, that's what they are. And I thought that Laura woman seemed so nice.' He flung his arms up and began pacing.

'Hey, calm down. It's the standard rate for galleries and they take a big risk showcasing a nobody like me. And I've still earned more in one evening than I did over the past how many years. And, by the way, if we do get your book published any publisher's going to make much more than fifty per cent of any sales. What's much more important is how do I deal with your nephew when he comes round on Monday?' She took a gulp of wine as she felt her shoulder muscles tensing already.

Daniel stroked his beard looking, unusually for him, lost for words. After a few moments of stroking then scratching his head, he said, 'I've been thinking about it since you told me and, much as I hate to admit it, I'm not sure what either of us can do. He's not going to take any notice of me if he can't see or hear me and as far as he's concerned you're simply someone renting his property. And it wouldn't be his property if I hadn't gone and blasted well died before I'd changed me will leaving it to a seaman's charity like I planned.'

'Ah, but if that had happened, Daniel, I wouldn't be able to rent it now and you might have gone off to wherever you're meant to have gone. And we'd never have met.'

He grinned.

'Maybe something good's come of it then, Bella. I would have hated not having met you.'

'I would certainly have missed you, too.'

Their eyes met and unbidden she felt the spark of attraction sizzle in her body. Groaning inwardly at the sheer stupidity of such a reaction, she forced herself to look away. God help me, fancy falling in love with a ghost! I must be mad…

'Bella,' his voice was soft and she looked up to see such tenderness in his expression she had to take a deep breath to calm herself.

'Yes?'

'We both know we have feelings for each other, feelings which can only lead to unhappiness for us both. I should leave and allow you to find the happiness you deserve.' She shook her head. 'But I don't want to leave until I know you're secure and have, perhaps, found love again.' He reached to offer a feather-like stroke on her face, and she trembled inside. 'I'll let you decide what to say to my nephew to persuade him to sell the cottage to you when you're ready. Even if this means telling him about me and *our* book. If he has any decency he'd share the royalties with you, anyway.'

She nodded, unable to speak.

By Monday morning Annabel was as nervous as she'd been the day of the preview and kept herself busy cleaning and tidying the cottage. It wouldn't hurt to create a good impression, she told herself, flicking away invisible dust in the sitting room. Old cottages never looked totally clean, too many nooks and crannies and uneven surfaces, not like the all-gleaming concrete and glass visions she'd seen on television shows. Give her a cosy cottage anytime, spiders included. Certainly Seagull Cottage had proved to be a perfect home for her and Emilia and she couldn't bear the thought of losing it to some arrogant Guern-cum-Aussie who thought he could swan in and ask her to leave whenever he liked. By now feelings of righteous anger made her feel hot and faint and she had to drink some cold water and take a few deep breaths. She was also worried Daniel might turn up and create havoc with his nephew, though he had promised he wouldn't. It was time to let go her anger and go for the charm offensive. He was only a man, after all. Smile sweetly and just be *nice*. What could go wrong?

Dead on eleven o'clock the doorbell rang.

Annabel, taking deep breaths and with a fixed smile, opened the door, screamed and promptly shut it again.

A few seconds later the doorbell rang again.

Feeling faint and wondering what on earth to say, she opened the door again, to stare into the face she had come to know so well. Daniel's face. Or rather Daniel with stubble rather than a full beard and wearing a casual shirt and jeans.

This Daniel was frowning.

'Mrs Easton? I'm Matt Vaudin, I believe you were expecting me. Is there something wrong?'

'Um, no, I... I thought I saw a rat on the path behind you. Sorry, come in.' She moved away, her heart beating fast and shock freezing her brain. A rat? What was she thinking? Leading the way to the kitchen she would have given anything to be able to swoon into a chair like young ladies of old.

'You have a rat problem? I should speak to the agent.'

'No, that's the first one I've seen. Or thought I saw.' She cleared her throat. 'Would you like a coffee before you look round?'

'I'm good thanks.' He stared around at the kitchen and she tried to study him without being obvious. The likeness to Daniel was incredible. Same dark, curly hair, deep blue eyes and the set jaw partly hidden under the designer stubble. Tall, too, and well-muscled, obviously kept fit. But then he was from Australia and everyone lived outdoors there, thanks to the sunnier climate.

'It's so different to what I remember and so small. But at least the kitchen's a big improvement.'

'I didn't see it before, but I love the kitchen. Modern but cosy.'

'Hmm. If you like cosy. Can I see the other rooms, please?' She found it hard to be nice, he was so brusque and unfriendly. Arrogant like his great-uncle. She wondered if Daniel would be looking on and if so what he'd think. He hadn't been overly impressed with him beforehand.

'Of course, let's start with the sitting room.'

She took him through all the rooms, only receiving the occasional nod until they arrived in the studio.

'Why, that's my great-uncle's telescope,' he said, going straight towards it. 'I'm surprised it's still here after all these years.'

'Yes, he loves it.' The words were out before she could stop them.

He spun round, mouth open wide.

'What do you mean, "he loves it"? He's been dead for over seventy years.'

'I know but he sort of lives here. He's a ghost, and he was here when you lived here with your mother. She could see him and they talked together, just like I do.'

'Are you mad? A ghost? There's no such thing as ghosts—' His tanned face darkened just as he appeared to be shoved off the telescope by an invisible force, which then materialised into Daniel.

Annabel watched as if in a daze as Daniel, his face red with anger, pushed his nephew toward the window, saying, 'Don't believe in ghosts, do you? Well, I could throw you out of this window if I chose, boy. Now show some respect to Annabel here, or I might just do that.'

She wasn't sure if Matt heard him until his face paled.

'Who are you? Are you real?'

Daniel laughed. 'Well, I'm a real ghost, though I have no real body. You never saw me when you were a boy, but I was here. And, by God, you look very like me, except for that poor excuse for a beard.'

Matt seemed to be having an inner struggle as he moved away from the window and clung onto the telescope. He looked at Annabel and then back at Daniel.

'I… I did see you a couple of times but I didn't believe what I'd seen. Mum told me about you and that you talked to each other but I didn't want to believe her. I couldn't wait to get away—'

'Aye, and you broke your mother's heart, leaving her to go swanning off to the other side of the world. The life went out of her and she lived like a hermit from then on. Should be ashamed of yourself for what you did.' Daniel glared at him, his fists clenched by his side and Annabel was only glad he wouldn't be able to hit his nephew.

'I admit I'm not proud of leaving Mum like that, but I wasn't much more than a boy and thought more of myself and what I wanted. If I could go back in time I'd behave differently.'

Annabel saw a flash of sadness in his eyes and for a moment felt sorry for him. Then, remembering he wanted to sell her home, she changed her mind.

'Easy to say that now, Matt, but it won't help your mother none, will it? And I'll tell you now, you were the last person I would have wanted to inherit my house as you don't deserve it.'

His nephew flinched as Daniel's anger seemed to rise by the minute and Annabel panicked that her chances of getting Matt to change his mind were dwindling with each attack from his uncle.

'Perhaps I should leave—'

'Yes, this is a family matter.'

'No, Annabel has been like family to me since she moved in and knows more about me and our family than you do. And I don't want you to kick her out of my house, do y'er hear? If things had been different you wouldn't have inherited the cottage; it was supposed to go to a sailor's charity when I died. Wasn't expecting to die so soon, that's the problem,' Daniel growled, his fists still clenched.

'I can hardly be blamed for your early death, Uncle, I wasn't even born then. But I can see why you're upset with me, from what you've said about my mother, you've every right to be.' He looked from Daniel to Annabel and managed a half-smile.

'When I came here this morning I thought I was just giving due notice to a tenant that I wasn't planning on renewing their lease. I certainly never expected to be at the receiving end of a tongue-lashing from my long-dead great-uncle. Am I dreaming or is this for real?'

For the first time since his arrival she smiled.

'Oh, it's for real. And if you get the chance to know him better, you'll find the captain's a bit of a softy underneath the bluster.'

Daniel looked hurt.

'My dear Annabel, I've a right to be angry with my nephew, both for how he behaved in the past and for how he's planning to behave now. By kicking you out of *my* cottage.'

'Please, Uncle, Mrs Easton, it looks like we need a reset. I agree I may have behaved badly in the past, but I thought I was acting totally within my rights with the lease on the cottage. Could we agree to call a halt now as I have another meeting to attend and then I could come back tomorrow morning if that's okay? Give us all time to think things through. I, for one, am badly in need of doing just that.' He waved his arms in a conciliatory gesture and Daniel, huffing and puffing said yes and then Annabel nodded her agreement.

She escorted Matt down the stairs experiencing a mix of emotions. Shock from seeing how alike the two men were and then how they reacted to each other and also a small flicker of hope that maybe she and the nephew could come to an agreement over the cottage. Otherwise why suggest another meeting?

As they reached the front door he turned to her and, grinning, said, 'There wasn't a rat was there?'

'No.'

Chapter 31

'Well, that went well, didn't it, Daniel?' Annabel found him staring out of the studio window, his shoulders slumped.

He turned to face her, his expression as glum as she'd ever seen. Her heart sank. How would she cope with a depressed Daniel? A bossy, arrogant one was preferable.

'I... I didn't expect him to be so like me. Not just in looks, it's obvious we're related, but he was so sure of himself, at first anyway. You know, Bella, it was like seeing myself as I was. Alive, full of energy, wanting to make my mark on the world. Which I did, before that blasted war interfered with my plans. With everyone's plans. Nothing was the same again after. My damned leg meant I had to give up my career in the Merchant Navy and what else was I good for, eh?' He stamped around the floor, shaking his head.

She wanted to comfort him, hated to see his pain. It hadn't occurred to her what it would be like for him to see the physical embodiment of himself, not having known what his nephew looked like. But now she knew and understood.

'I'm so sorry, Daniel, it must have been a shock. It was for me, too, but obviously far worse for you. But he isn't you and never could be. You've done some remarkable things in your time, things to be proud of and you must hold onto your achievements. And if we do get the book published, the whole world will know of them.'

He came to a halt and smiled at her.

'My wonderful Bella, thank you for your kind words. It does help, believe me, although I can't help feeling sad at the moment. It will pass, I'm sure. I've had many years to feel sad about my life – and death – but I've had to carry on.' He came close and she could feel his energy encircling her. 'But it's you who is important now and I'm sorry if I've messed up your chance of buying this cottage. I... was too hasty with my nephew.'

'You were a bit but it's positive he's offered to return so as long as you stay calm and let me do the talking, it might work out. Now, I need to get out of here and do some sketching to take my mind off you both. See you later.'

Two hours later she was feeling calmer having had a productive time with her sketchbook. Whether or not it was as a result of the decidedly weird stand-off between Daniel and Matt she wasn't sure, but her imagination had been fired up. It had been a shame to stop but it was time to collect Emilia. Keen to enjoy as much time as possible outside, Annabel suggested a picnic on the beach and with the longer, warmer days they were able to spend a few hours there, both enjoying some paddling as well as throwing the Frisbee. Emilia's flushed cheeks and sparkling eyes once again confirmed Annabel's decision to return to Guernsey to be the right one. All she could hope for now was to be able to keep the cottage they both loved.

The following morning Matt returned as agreed, at eleven o'clock.

'Good morning, Mrs Easton. Do you promise not to scream at me today?' he said, with a grin and a hint of Aussie twang peeping through.

She smiled back, saying, 'As long as you promise to listen to what your uncle and I have to say.'

'Fair dinkum, if you let me explain why I'm here,' he said, nodding.

Not sure if he was being sarcastic she escorted him upstairs to the studio where Daniel was waiting.

The two men – or rather one man and a ghost – nodded to each other in silent greeting. Annabel had brought up two chairs for them and they formed a circle round her worktable. Strictly speaking Daniel didn't need a chair but she had pointed out it looked better if they were all seated on a level.

'Mr Vaudin, perhaps you'd like to start.' She looked towards him.

'Please, call me Matt, Mr Vaudin makes me sound ancient.'

'I'm the ancient one around here, lad, sadly,' his uncle muttered.

'Yes, okay, Matt. Please tell us why you're here and want to sell the cottage.'

He shifted on the chair, looking uncomfortable.

'The truth is I'm considering an offer for a job here as the harbour master and thought I could sell the cottage and buy something more… suitable.'

'Oh.' It was all she could say.

'You're coming back? After all these years? Why? Something go wrong for you out there, has it?' Daniel glared at his nephew.

'Not that it's any of your business—'

'O'course it's my business. I'm your great-uncle, dammit! We're family, ain't we? And this is – or was – my cottage which I built with my own two hands and I have a right to know what's caused you to come back and want to sell it.' Daniel's face was suffused with anger and if he'd been alive Annabel would have been worried about his blood pressure.

'Okay, Uncle, you win. If you must know I split up with my wife about a year ago and things haven't gone too well for me since. We sold our house and I had to leave my job and move to another town and, well, it's not been great.' He sat twisting his hands, eyes cast down.

'But why did you have to leave your job because your marriage ended? Had you been playing around at work?'

He looked up and shook his head.

'No, but my wife was having an affair with my boss and there was no way I could stay. They got married as soon as we divorced.'

'Ah, I see. Sorry to hear that, lad. So why didn't you

come back here when your mother died?'

Annabel hated to admit it but she was beginning to feel sorry for the man.

'I'd enjoyed living in Australia, had a good life and had made friends so it seemed right to stay.' He looked Daniel in the eye and said, 'Remember we never had much money when I was growing up, Uncle, and my memories of Guernsey weren't great, thanks to Dad leaving us as he did. I'd worked hard to make a success of my life over there and thought I could make it work again.'

'So what's changed your mind?'

'An old friend from school got in touch out of the blue and we swapped stories of what we'd been up to over the years, the usual stuff. He sounded so happy and content, married to a local girl and with a good job in finance. They enjoyed travelling around Europe and reckoned they had a good work, life balance.' He paused, biting his lips. 'It made me realise I'd not been as happy as I thought even before the split with my wife. I worked sixty hours a week and although we lived on the coast, barely had time to enjoy time at the beach or socialise and we rarely went on holiday away from Australia. Couldn't afford it.'

'Sounds like a case of the grass isn't always greener after all,' Daniel said, in a "I told you so" tone of voice.

'I guess. Though I don't regret emigrating as I did enjoy my earlier years there when I was, you might be surprised to hear, in the Merchant Navy, becoming an officer on ships plying between Australia and New Zealand.'

Annabel gasped. 'So you're a Captain, Matt!'

He shook his head.

'Not quite. When I married I was a First Lieutenant but stopped sailing and took a shore-based job. I ended up as a harbour master in Victoria.'

'Well I'll be damned! I hadn't seen you as navy material, lad, and your mother never really said what you were up to.'

Matt looked sheepish.

'To be honest, that's my fault. I didn't exactly keep in

touch with Mum, as I wanted to draw a line under my past. Never even told her I was married as I knew she wanted me to have kids. As it happens, my wife didn't want them, so...' He shrugged. 'I hadn't planned to go to sea even though I studied marine engineering at uni and the idea took root when I arrived in Australia.'

For a moment there was silence as Annabel and Daniel digested his nephew's story. The bottom line, as far as she was concerned, was he had decided to return after the promise of a job and a fresh start in Guernsey. Which would impact her stay in the cottage. It dawned on her that she had only seen Matt as the enemy who wanted her home and not as a man who might have good reasons for wanting it; someone, who like her, had experienced loss and wanted a fresh start. She watched him as the two men started talking about their respective lives at sea and realised more strongly how similar they were, in looks and in mannerisms. In real age they were close, she thought, with the nephew about the same age as the uncle who died at forty-five. She was warming to the nephew who was as attractive as his uncle, but her priority remained her own security.

'So what d'yer think, Bella, eh?'

'Sorry, Daniel, I wasn't listening. Think about what?' Two sets of almost identical eyes were trained on her.

'My memoir, of course. I was telling my nephew you've helped me type up my book and we're hoping to get it published. And I want you to get all the royalties, not him, mind.' He shot a dark look at his nephew.

'It's true, then, Mrs Easton? My uncle's... ghost dictated a whole book to you from memory?' He looked anything but convinced and she could hardly blame him. It didn't sound at all believable.

'Please, call me Annabel. Yes, it's true and my publisher friend is very keen to publish but was worried about you, as next of kin, trying to claim the royalties.' She took a deep breath before adding, 'You see, Daniel wants me to buy this cottage because my daughter and I love it here and don't want to move. The royalties might eventually help me financially, but in the meantime I'm a professional artist with a very successful exhibition here in Guernsey selling my paintings, so I'm financially independent. I'm hoping to earn enough to get a mortgage within a year or two, if you could wait that long. Please.'

Chapter 32

Matt blinked, looking bemused. As well he might, she thought, it was so surreal.

'I see, or I think I do. It seems you're a single mum with a variable income wanting to save up to buy the cottage and might be glad of the royalties from an as yet unpublished book, written by my ghostly great-uncle. Correct?'

'Now, listen here, lad, don't you get uppity with Annabel,' his uncle growled. 'She's a lovely Guernsey lass who was widowed not long ago in England, left with little money and returned here so her daughter could grow up on this special island just like she did. She's a wonderful artist and I'm sure she'll do well living here.' He turned to face her, his expression so full of love she felt tears in her eyes. 'But most importantly Annabel has been a good friend to me once she got used to me being around,' he said, chuckling. 'It was tricky at first and I upset her a few times, but she still offered to help me with my memoir and spent many hours typing it for me on her computer so the least I could do was try to make sure she got paid for it. And remember, without her, this book of mine wouldn't exist.'

Then, before anyone could reply, Daniel's figure began to dissolve.

'Daniel, are you alright? Are you still here?' Annabel cried.

'I'm here but I've used up too much energy to stay visible. Feeling rather tired, so it might be best if I go and leave you two to talk.' She heard the whoosh as he left and turned to see Matt shaking his head in bewilderment.

'If it wasn't for you, Annabel, I'd think I was going mad.

My… my uncle seems so real one minute and then the next – poof! Off he disappears into thin air.' He rubbed his chin then fixed her with the eyes eerily reminiscent of those of his great-uncle. 'First off, I'm sorry to hear about your late husband and the situation you find yourself in. I can only imagine how hard it's been for you.'

'Thank you.'

'My uncle seems to be very fond of you, if ghosts have feelings. My mother spoke of him warmly and I… I did see him a couple of times but didn't want to admit it. Mum stopped saying anything after a while.' He smiled, a smile so similar to Daniel's it made her gulp. 'The agent told me the cottage was difficult to rent because of a ghost and I pooh-poohed it. Apparently even he was scared to come round. Did the ghost, my uncle, try to scare you away?'

She laughed. 'He sure did, but I was determined to take the cottage not only because I fell in love with it, but because it was all I could afford. I'm not what I'd call brave, but somehow I wasn't scared of him and we came to a kind of arrangement which has worked well for most of the time. Later he started telling me of his adventures and how he'd wanted to publish his memoir and it all snowballed from there.'

'How did you convince a publisher to take on a memoir you couldn't possibly have written?'

'Ah, well we invited her to come and meet Daniel and fortunately she was able to see him – as not everyone does. It's being submitted to her MD now and we hope to have a decision soon. Although as it can take years for a book to get published there won't be any royalties for ages.' She went on to tell him how initially friends were invited round to see Daniel before inviting the publisher, Charlotte, and how everyone enjoyed themselves, especially Daniel.

He stood up and stretching, suggested they walked in the garden. On the way downstairs she proffered coffee which he accepted and a few minutes later she brought out two mugs while he was nosing around the shed.

'Thanks. Did you find anything interesting in the shed?'

'Yes, quite a few old family photos which will be useful for the book. And you, of course, as it's your family history. They're in my study if you want to see them.'

'Not just now, thanks. Shall we sit down over there?' He nodded towards the little bistro table and chairs near the back door. Once settled, Matt said, 'I never used to care about family history and stuff, but now my family's gone and I'm alone again, it seems more important. I wish I'd let Mum tell me more about our family before I left, but I was ashamed about what my father had done to us and didn't want to know anything connected to him.' He looked wistful as he sipped his coffee and again she began to feel sorry for him and told herself not to be so daft. He owned this lovely cottage, had a good job lined up and wouldn't be single long with his good looks.

'You can always ask Daniel, if you two can stay on speaking terms.' She smirked. 'His memory is fantastic and he's hung around this cottage since he died so must have seen everything you'd want to know.'

He grinned back at her.

'Might just do that. He's quite a character, isn't he? And I think you've been very brave to live here with a ghost. Must have been scary at times.'

'There have been moments, yes, but he also saved my daughter's life, for which I will be eternally grateful.' She went on to describe what happened when Emilia nearly got run over by a fast car on the bend.

Matt's eyes widened in shock.

'Wow! That must have been as scary as hell! Good ol' Uncle Daniel, eh! And no-one realised what had happened?'

'No, it really looked as if she'd been lifted by the drag of the car, it all happened so fast, you see. I still get the shakes whenever I think about it,' she said with a shiver.

'He's really something, isn't he? I'll definitely have to work on building up a relationship with him while I can.'

'So, when do you plan to move here?' She tried to sound

nonchalant but her voice began to wobble.

He scratched his head.

'I haven't yet accepted the job, but if I do then I would start in September. The plan was to rent somewhere until—'

'The cottage was sold.' She couldn't stop the note of bitterness in her voice.

'Hey, Annabel, please. I said the plan *was* not is. After meeting you and… my ghost of an uncle, I'm not so sure. Daniel's made his feelings clear with regard to you and the cottage and I do see where he's coming from.' He stared down at his feet, looking lost in thought. Annabel began to think there might be hope after all. As he looked up, he grinned. 'I don't know what I'll do now, if I'm honest. But I'd like to give you the chance to buy the cottage if I can. I understand it won't be soon, but I do have funds from selling my house so,' he shrugged, 'I might be able to work something out. Is that okay?'

She had to restrain herself from hugging him. After all he was her landlord not a friend.

'Oh, Matt, thanks so much. It's very kind of you and I'll do my best to buy as soon as I can.' She cleared her throat. 'What do you want to do about Daniel's book?'

'As my uncle said, without you there'd be no book so I think you should receive the royalties if and when it's published.' He smiled and with a tilt of his head, asked, 'Any chance I could read it now? I'd love to find out what my uncle got up to in his sailing days.'

She felt the smile spreading across her face with another urge to hug him.

'That's generous of you, Matt, and I'm sure Daniel will be pleased. I'd be happy to email you a copy as it is now and I've no doubt you'll find it illuminating.'

A gruff voice butted in. 'I *am* pleased you've seen sense, Matt, and I'm beginning to think you're not such a bad 'un as I thought.'

They both looked around but no-one was there. At least no-one visible.

'Have you been listening to us, Daniel? What have I said about giving me privacy? And how long have you been here?' Annabel fumed. How dare he!

Matt's face was thunderous.

'Uncle, Annabel's right, your behaviour's appalling and you should leave now.'

'Alright, alright perhaps I shouldn't have listened in but I was only here for a few minutes. I'll go.' A whoosh of air signalled his departure and Annabel let out a sigh of relief.

'He really is the limit, Matt. I can only hope he manages to find the way to move on to wherever he's meant to be before he drives me nuts.' She sighed as she knew she'd miss him if he went and she would forever be grateful to him for saving Emilia. But he did keep crossing a line.

'Are you okay now? It's lucky for him he doesn't have a physical body or I'd have been tempted to punch him.' His fists were clenched as if ready for a fight.

'I'm fine, thanks. I should be used to his behaviour by now, I suppose, and I don't think he'll change. He's spent the past seventy years acting as if he still owns the place and I suspect his sister and your mother didn't argue with him.'

Matt grinned.

'I agree, but he's met his match with you, hasn't he? And good on you for standing up for yourself.' He started pacing around the little patio, hands thrust in his pockets and she caught him staring at the shed. 'This might sound daft, although let's face it, the whole situation's bloney weird, but I'm wondering if Daniel had to hang on here until someone helped him with his memoir.' Turning round he went on, 'You said it was very important to him, he had looked into publishing it when he was alive, but didn't get the chance to write it. Perhaps if the book's now published he'll have set out to do what he wanted and can move on. What d'yer think?'

His deep blue eyes locked onto hers and a frisson of electricity shot through her. She swallowed hard. What on earth?

'Could be, I guess. Hard to know when you're dealing with a ghost. He probably doesn't know himself what's keeping him here. I'll talk to Charlotte the publisher and see what the state of play is and if they're going to publish explain you've agreed to waive any rights to the royalties and I'll be named as the editor or something.'

'Good. Right, guess I'd better get going, I've taken up enough of your time. Should we exchange numbers to save going through the agent? I'm here for a couple of weeks at least if you'd keep me updated on the publisher?'

After swapping their phone numbers and email addresses Matt looked as if he was about to say something and she waited, unsure if she should speak first.

'Thanks again, Matt, for being so… so generous about the royalties and for giving me a chance to buy the cottage. If you take the job we could stay in touch.'

'I'd like that very much. And I hope you'd see me as a friend rather than your landlord.' He smiled, causing his eyes to crinkle at the edges and she felt the frisson of attraction again.

'Yes, fine by me.'

Chapter 33

Flustered after the impact Matt seemed to have on her, Annabel found it hard to concentrate on her latest painting and decided to ring Charlotte instead.

'Hi, Annabel, good to hear from you. How's the exhibition going? I loved the piece in the *Press* and thought you looked totally the successful artist in the photo.'

'Thanks, it's going well and I've sold loads. Laura's buzzing with ideas for me so all good. I actually wanted to ask you about Daniel's book as I have some news on that front...' She went on to tell her about Matt meeting his uncle and his agreement about the royalties.

'Wow, that's brilliant and it's the honourable decision since you sort of wrote it anyway. I was talking to my MD last week and he's finished it, thought it a great read and is happy for us to publish it after editing. Which won't be too heavy-handed given how pretty much anything goes these days. You'll be part of the editing process of course, but I'd suggest you don't tell Daniel,' she said, laughing.

'I won't, for sure. And I'm so pleased you're going ahead. What happens now?'

They went on to discuss the contract arrangements which would be handled by the agent and once everything was signed an editor would be in touch.

'We're pencilling in the publication for late next year and in the meantime we can offer a modest advance which will need to be earned out before you receive royalties.' She mentioned a figure which sounded fine to Annabel as any extra income would help a potential mortgage application. After ending the call she turned back to her painting, motivated once more.

The next few days were an oasis of calm after the events of the previous week and Annabel established a routine of sketching in the morning and then painting until Emilia finished school. She popped round to Colette's early one evening and filled her in about Matt and his meetings with Daniel.

Annabel watched her friend's face display disbelief, amazement and pleasure as she heard what had transpired.

'Blimey! Wish I could have been there to see it. Sounds totally surreal, which is what it is – a ghost meeting his look-alike great-nephew.' She shook her head then grinned. 'Is this Matt as gorgeous as Daniel looks in his portrait? Any chance…?' She raised her eyebrows.

'Honestly, Colette, give a girl a chance!' She found herself flushing as she thought of Matt with his piercing blue eyes and dark, curly hair. Yes, she had to admit he was as gorgeous as Daniel, with the benefit of being alive, not dead. 'He's good looking, yes, and I do find him attractive but I hardly know the guy and he might not take the job and just return to Australia. End of.'

'Hmm. Well, if he does take the job then I'm sure he'll be making regular checks on his cottage so you'll soon get to know each other better, won't you?' She paused to top up their empty wine glasses before saying, 'The fact he's giving you a chance to buy the cottage and to receive the book royalties says he's a good bloke who, I reckon, fancies you.' Smirking, she carried on, 'Quite frankly I'd be very surprised if he doesn't take the job.'

Annabel had to admit it was what she was hoping for as well.

Later that week her phone rang and Matt's name came up. Taking a calming breath she answered, 'Hi, Matt, how are you?'

'All good thanks and I wanted you to know I've

accepted the harbour job and start in September.'

'That's great news and I hope it all works out well for you. So, what happens now? Back to Australia?' He was going to stay! Grinning broadly, she was glad he couldn't see her reaction, as it might give him the wrong idea.

'Not yet, I have to line up a place to rent before I leave.' There was a pause before he went on, 'How'd you fancy joining me for a celebratory drink or perhaps even a meal? If you can't get a babysitter we could make it at lunchtime?'

Unprepared she hesitated. Going out for the evening would be a rare treat, but... Perhaps better to go with lunch with no issues of babysitting.

'I'd like that and lunchtime would work better for me.'

'Terrific. How about tomorrow? Do you like Thai food?'

'I haven't eaten any but willing to try if it's similar to Chinese.'

'Great, because I found a Thai café with outside seating and stunning views over the harbour in Town which I'm sure you'll like. Shall I pick you up at twelve?'

'Sounds perfect. See you tomorrow.' Switching off her phone, she couldn't help smiling. Okay, they were just friends meeting for a celebratory lunch. No big deal. But it was nice to be asked.

Later that evening she climbed up to the studio as usual and found Daniel waiting. They had continued their meetings even after the book was finished, finding things to talk about particularly after Matt's arrival.

'Evening, Bella, how was your day?' He was polishing the telescope with a soft duster she had left there for him. It didn't really need cleaning but he seemed to take pleasure from the process. She would have been even happier if he'd offered to dust the house but that was never going to happen, was it?

'Good, thanks. Matt phoned to say he'd taken the job, starting in September.'

'Has he, indeed? I wonder what helped him make up his

mind, eh?' he said, with a chuckle.

Annabel felt the heat rise in her neck and turned away to look for something, anything on the table.

'How should I know? It means you two can spend more time together once he's back permanently. But before he returns to Oz he has to find somewhere to rent.'

'It's lucky this cottage isn't available then,' he said, with a sly smile. 'But I'm glad he's coming back all the same. Our family's been here for generations, y'know and we should have more locals living here rather than importing people for the better jobs.' He moved nearer to her and reached out his hand to rest weightlessly on hers. 'You like him, don't you, *bella mia*?' His voice was soft, like a caress.

She looked up into his eyes, lined from squinting into many suns at sea, and full of love for her.

'Yes, I do. I wanted to hate him, threatening to take my home from me as he did. Then,' she sighed, 'he turned out to be a decent guy who'd like us to be friends and is taking me out to lunch tomorrow.'

Daniel's eyes widened, matching his broad smile.

'I knew it! He fancies you and why wouldn't he, eh? He's not my great-nephew for nothing and not just in looks either.'

Annabel wasn't sure how to take it. On the one hand Daniel had made it clear how fond he was of her and on the other he seemed delighted at the prospect of her and Matt becoming an item. And she wasn't sure if it was what she wanted anyway. It was too soon after the disaster with Richard. She couldn't risk giving her heart to anyone as quickly again.

'Does this mean you'd be happy if Matt and I became a couple? After all you've said about him?'

He waved his hand dismissively.

'That's before I met him properly and you weren't keen either, were you? Look, I care about you, Bella, and if I was alive I'd fight any man for your hand, but I'm... a... a ghost and can't be a proper partner for you. We both know that. Your happiness is paramount to me and if it's possible Matt could make you happy then I'd be pleased for you.' He blinked and she caught a brief wave of sadness wash over him before his smile returned. Annabel's eyes were moist at the thought of their possible separation, even though it was inevitable under the unusual if not bizarre circumstances.

'It's far too soon to tell if we'll end up as a couple, more likely we'll just remain friends. But I appreciate how painful it might be for you if we did.' Taking a steadying breath, she went on, 'I'm wondering if it's time for you to consider moving on, Daniel. Your wonderful memoir is completed and will be published at some point and… and,' she paused, 'there's nothing to keep you here now. I'll make sure there's a note in the book to say you died accidentally from a fall so you'll no longer be considered to have died by suicide. That's what you wanted, isn't it?'

He nodded.

'You're right, *bella mia*. I hadn't realised it until now, but I must have been waiting for something all these years and I hated the thought everyone thought I had killed myself in a fit of depression.' He punched his hands and she saw his eyes flash in anger. 'I was never someone to do that and I wasn't ready to die, far too young. And I was looking forward to writing my memoir, had even bought the notebooks ready to be filled.' He moved restlessly round the studio, running his hands through his hair and muttering under his breath. Annabel stayed quiet thinking it best for him to work it out for himself. She had planted the seed but only he could follow through. Or could he? Would he need help to move on, like from a vicar? She remembered something Natalie had said about calling on a vicar to force a ghost to leave her cottage. Daniel didn't seem to be religious but perhaps it would be worth a try.

At last he came to a standstill, his brow deeply furrowed.

'I don't know what I'm supposed to do, Bella. How do I move on? Over the years I've tried a number of times to leave but I seem tied to the cottage, probably for the reasons you've suggested. Can you help me?'

'Would you allow me to talk to a vicar who helped my friend Natalie? You met her the other week and she'd had a ghost in her home.'

His face cleared, even managing a smile.

'Of course I remember Natalie and she told me about her ghost, a nasty man when he was alive and dead. She didn't mention a vicar but if it helped her and him then I'm happy to try. What do I have to lose, eh?'

Chapter 34

Annabel woke on Friday morning to find a clear blue sky and the sun burning off an early mist over the sea. The tang of salty air floated through the window of her bedroom, making her smile. She chose a knee-length sundress instead of the usual shorts and T-shirt as she anticipated the lunch with Matt. Another reason for her good mood was the upshot of her phone call with Natalie the previous evening. Apparently a long retired vicar, a Mr Ayres, had helped her ghost on his way and she was happy to give Annabel his phone number.

'He's nearly eighty and though he likes to keep busy, has to pace himself. Just mention me and I'm sure he'll help if he can.'

After returning from the school run she phoned the vicar.

'John Ayres speaking.'

'Good morning, I'm Annabel Easton, a friend of Natalie Cross…' She gave him a short version of Daniel's story and his desire to move on and could he help.

There was a long pause and for a while she wondered if he was still there or was possibly deaf.

'Mr Ayres?'

'I'm still here, I was simply taken aback. It's been a long time since anyone asked for help with a ghost.' He chuckled. 'I was beginning to think I might have cleared the island by now. But obviously not. I'm willing to do what I can, but my energy isn't what it was when I helped Natalie. It should be easier if your ghost is keen to move on, many aren't, sadly.'

'Brilliant, I really appreciate your help, Mr Ayres. I'll get back to you soon with a suitable time. Do you have any days you're not free? My ghost is around during the day if it helps.'

'That must be awkward for you although from what you've told me you two seem to have a good relationship.' She heard a soft chuckle down the line and grinned. This vicar sounded just what they needed. 'I am free most days except Sundays when I assist at the services at St Saviours Church.'

'Great, I'll be in touch. Thank you.'

Annabel popped to the studio and called out for Daniel, who can't have been far as he appeared in seconds. She explained about the vicar and he seemed ready to go ahead but she sensed the sadness behind his agreement. It would be a bittersweet moment for both of them when the time came but it had to happen.

Matt arrived promptly at twelve, greeting her with a peck on the cheek.

'I like your dress, you look very summery.' He gave her an admiring glance and she sensed goosebumps on her arms. She fought hard not to think of the disaster that was Richard and how the nearly-relationship had ended. It wouldn't be like that with Matt. They were only friends and he was off back to Australia soon so…

The intimacy of the car appeared to intimidate any personal chat and they restricted themselves to the safe subject of the weather; considered not too bad in Guernsey but couldn't compete with Australia.

'Was it the better climate which drew you to emigrate?'

'Partly, I suppose. I simply found the island far too small and insular, with everyone seeming to know your business, which I hated. Looking back I think I saw it through a kid's eyes and wasn't grown up enough to see you can choose privacy in a small environment if you want to. And it's amazing how many Guerns I bumped into in Melbourne.'

'My parents emigrated to Perth when they retired as my mum's brother had been there for years. Sadly my uncle died recently but Mum and Dad are well settled there now with other family around. Although actually they're on a world cruise at the moment as my uncle left them some money. He was one of those expats who "did good" as they say.'

'You've never been out there to see them?'

'No, it was too… difficult when my husband was alive and even more so now. Perhaps in the future.'

'Mm.'

They were pulling onto the Albert Pier to park the car and conversation stopped while Matt kept an eye open for a space. Once found, it was only a short walk up to Cornet Street and the entrance to The Terrace Garden Café.

'My, this is different,' Annabel exclaimed as they went outside to the exotic terrace embellished with fountains and statues proclaiming its Eastern provenance. She was drawn towards an empty table near the perimeter fencing partly shaded by a palm tree. 'What a view! Fancy not knowing about this place.' She gazed out over the harbour, busy with visiting yachts, bobbing gently against the pontoons, and then further out towards Castle Cornet and beyond still to Herm and the less visible island of Sark. Magical.

'Great, isn't it? Will be handy for lunch when I'm working in the harbour office over there,' he pointed towards the piers where the ferries arrived and departed. 'I'll collect a menu for food when I fetch the drinks. What would you like?'

'Half a lager, please.'

She sighed in contentment, allowing the sun to caress her face, glad she'd slavered on sun cream that morning with the rise in temperature. Gazing around she noticed the tables were filling up, mostly by locals on their lunch break judging by their clothes and with a few tourists looking around in amazement at the setting and the view.

'Here you are,' he set down two lagers and menus before taking a seat opposite. 'Hope you find something you like and I can recommend the Pad Pak and Pad Thai if you prefer non-spicy. Or you can play safe with English choices,' he said grinning.

'It wouldn't be right to play safe, would it? I'm game to try something new though perhaps not too spicy. I'm warm enough as it is,' she said, feeling the perspiration on her neck.

They scanned the menus and both settled on the Pad Thai with chicken and Matt went back to the counter to order. He came back a few minutes later with the buzzer which would announce it was ready for collection.

'Right, what have you been up to?'

She told him about her deep conversation with Daniel and the subsequent call with the vicar.

'I'm impressed. You've obviously made a real connection with Daniel for him to open up like that and to agree about the vicar.' He sipped his lager, looking thoughtful. 'You can't help feeling sorry for the old devil, can you? Who'd want to be left hanging around your own home for over seventy years and not be a part of the life around you? Bloody frustrating, I'd think.' He shook his head, his expression serious.

'I've always felt sorry for him, which he appreciated. I now have to come up with a time for Mr Ayres to do whatever he does to help him move on to wherever he's supposed to be.' She bit her lip, already aware of an inner ache at losing Daniel. Clearing her throat, she went on, 'Would you want to be there when… when it happens? If it's okay with Daniel?'

'Sure, I think I should be. I need to make amends for not being there for my mum, and it'll be a bit like a death, won't it?'

She nodded.

'Okay, so I'll try and arrange it before you leave. Have you got a date yet?'

He was about to answer when the buzzer announced their food was ready and, with an apologetic grin, he went off to collect it. She was left hoping he wouldn't be returning to Oz too soon as she wanted to get to know him better. He soon reappeared bearing a tray with their food and Annabel noticed the admiring glances from other women and the less friendly looks aimed at her when he reached their table. Even though he wasn't her boyfriend it made her smile and sit up straighter.

'Okay, here we go. And if you hate it I'll happily order you something else.'

'I'm sure it'll be fine, thanks.' And it was.

'Mm, I love it, thanks for suggesting it. Do you eat a lot of oriental food back home?'

'Yes, we're not all about throwing prawns on the barbie, you know.' He laughed and she joined in, lightening the mood after the previous conversation. They went on to discuss favourite foods and cooking. It turned out he was more of a cook than her.

'I've always found it relaxing after a day at work although more often than not it's something quick as it's late when I get home. Which reminds me you asked when I'm going back.' His eyes locked onto hers and she held her breath. 'I may have found a place to rent, but, to be honest I don't have anything to rush back for. Having left my job it's just sorting out the rented apartment I've been living in.' Reaching out to touch her hand he said, 'I'd like to know you better before I leave, but it's up to you. How do you feel about us seeing each other over the next couple of weeks? To see how it goes.' His touch produced a tingling sensation in her body like static electricity.

'Yes, I'd like that. But I must tell you I'm in no rush to enter a serious relationship and would want to take things slowly. Become good friends first. If that's okay with you?'

He nodded. 'Suits me too. I guess we're both right to be cautious. There'll be plenty of time to see how it works when I'm back in September. In the meantime I'd like to suggest a personal guided tour of your best-selling art exhibition.'

'No problem.' She thought for a moment before adding, 'If we're going to see each other, I think it'd be a good idea for you to meet my daughter, Emilia, don't you?'

'Absolutely, if you think she's ready after losing her father not too long ago.'

'Clive wasn't the greatest father or husband during the last couple of years before he died so Emilia sadly hasn't the best memories of him.' She frowned as old memories flashed in. 'She's even hinted she'd like me to meet someone but I haven't been ready so I don't think there'll be a problem if you're okay with the idea.' She looked him in the eye, afraid to see any hesitation.

'Annabel, I'd love to meet your daughter. As I told you, my ex-wife didn't want kids but I would have loved them. Tell you what, why don't we all go to the art gallery tomorrow morning and then out to lunch after?'

'Sounds perfect. Emilia's already been but I'm sure she won't mind going again. She seems to think I'm some sort of superstar artist now and after telling everyone at school about me I've been invited by the head to give a talk to year six,' she said, flushing.

'Good one, Emilia! Sounds like you two have a pretty close relationship,' he said, tilting his head.

'We do and it's why I was keen to return here rather than stay in Manchester. I wanted her to enjoy the kind of childhood I had growing up here.' She went on to tell him about her parents and how she eventually ended up in Manchester with Clive. He listened carefully, made appropriate comments and then told her a little more about his own childhood. They had desserts, another lager and then coffee before reluctantly agreeing it was time to leave. Annabel, flushed from the combination of sun, alcohol and her sexy lunch date, was content to be driven back to the cottage where they shared pecks on the cheek. She remained buoyed up by the thought of seeing him again and getting to know him better. All she had to do now was hope Emilia was as happy to learn about her new "friend" as she had suggested.

Chapter 35

'Hi, sweetheart, how was school?'

Emilia looked excited as she took her hand, passing her a letter from school. A quick glance told her it was about an upcoming trip to Herm.

'Please can I go, Mummy? We have to have parent's permission as we're staying overnight in tents where you used to go with your parents. It'll be such fun.' Big eyes pleaded with her to say yes and she didn't hesitate.

'Of course you can go as I wouldn't want to spoil your fun, would I?' She grinned, pleased to see her daughter looking happy.

Emilia beamed and started skipping along beside her as she chatted about her day. Annabel, to her shame, was only half listening as she wondered if the trip, set for two weeks' time over a weekend, would allow her to spend more time with Matt. Emilia would be away from the Friday night until Sunday lunchtime and her body tingled with part suppressed excitement at the possibilities presented by her absence. It might be too soon, but…

'Sweetheart, I've met the man who owns our cottage, which is where he grew up. He's really nice and would like to go with us to the gallery tomorrow to see my paintings and then take us out to lunch. What do you think?'

Emilia frowned. 'He's not going to make us leave the cottage is he? I don't want to go, I love it.'

'Oh, no, sweetheart, he isn't, in fact he's happy for me to buy it one day when I can afford to.'

The frown turned into a big smile. 'He must be a very nice man then and I'd very much like to meet him. But where does he live now?'

'He moved to Australia many years ago but is coming back to live here soon and will rent another house to live in.'

'That doesn't sound very sensible, does it, if he already owns the cottage. If I were him I'd ask us to leave.' The smile disappeared.

'He was thinking of doing that but I explained how much we love our home and he's now happy for us to stay and he's found somewhere else to live. We've… become friends and he wants me and you, of course, to be happy.' She pulled into the drive and switched off the engine before taking a tentative look at her daughter.

'Oh.' Emilia's eyes grew round. 'Is he your boyfriend, Mummy?'

'No, we're simply friends. Would you mind if he did become my boyfriend?'

Her daughter grinned. 'I'll tell you after I meet him tomorrow.'

Annabel laughed, tussled her daughter's hair and said, 'Fair enough.'

Later that evening Annabel went up to the studio, mentally preparing what she had to say to Daniel. It wouldn't be easy but…

'Good evening, *bella mia,* I thought you'd be paying me a visit tonight. How was lunch with Matt?' Daniel was lounging by the telescope, his arms crossed and an enquiring smile on his face.

'Hi, it was good, thanks. The first time I've tried Thai food and I enjoyed it.'

'You know I didn't mean the food, Bella.' He pursed his lips. 'How are you two getting on? By the look on your face I'd say you're falling for him. And I'd be surprised if it wasn't mutual.'

The heat rose in her neck. Oh dear, was it that obvious?

'We do get on well and he wants to meet Emilia tomorrow so is taking us all out. I really like him, Daniel, but after the disaster with Richard I don't want to rush into anything and he feels the same after his divorce.' She played with her brushes on the table, finding it hard to look him in the eye.

'Hey, Bella,' he said softly, 'don't worry about me. I'm pleased you two are getting closer, I'd hate to think of you on your own after I've… gone.' He moved closer and she could feel the familiar warmth flowing around her. 'You have my blessing, both of you.' She looked up and saw he was smiling, but it didn't quite reach his eyes. 'Have you arranged a time for that vicar to come round?'

'Not yet; I wanted to speak to Matt first and he wants to be here, if it's okay with you.'

He nodded. 'Of course, but isn't he about to return to Australia?'

'Not yet, he has some things to sort out first.' She cleared her throat. 'Mr Ayres has said any day but Sundays, so you choose. He can come during the day when Emilia's at school, which I'd prefer.'

'Then I'll leave it to you to arrange, *bella mia*, and we'll pray whatever this man does will work and I can leave you in peace.' His smile faltered and it was as if she had been punched in the stomach, the pain was so real.

'Goodnight, Daniel,' she muttered and rushed from the room before the tears fell.

The next morning Emilia hovered in the kitchen as the time for Matt's arrival drew near. Annabel saw it as a positive sign and metaphorically crossed her fingers she would like him. And he her. Otherwise any relationship was doomed from the start as she couldn't commit to someone if her daughter was unhappy. When the doorbell rang Emilia rushed ahead to open the door.

'Hello, you must be Matt, I'm Emilia.'

Annabel stood behind her and caught Matt's eye, who, grinning, reached out his hand.

'Hello, Emilia, I'm pleased to meet you and I look

forward to spending time with you both today.'

Emilia shook his hand solemnly, then retreated to stand behind her mother.

Matt greeted Annabel with a light peck on the cheek and asked if they were ready to leave. Grabbing her bag and keys she ushered Emilia outside and they followed him to his car.

'He speaks funny, Mummy, is that how they speak in Australia?' she whispered.

'Yes, though his accent is a mix of Guernsey too. Okay so far?'

'He does seem nice and he's quite good looking, isn't he?' Another whisper.

Annabel nodded and they both fell silent as they reached the car. Matt seemed to sense some awkwardness and kept up a chat with Emilia, sharing how he went to the same school at her age and by the time they had travelled the short road to L'Islet the tension was easing. After parking the car they walked to the gallery and stood outside a moment for Matt to take a look.

'This is new since I left, "The Scully Art Gallery". It looks very professional, doesn't it? And, hey, is that one of your paintings in the window?' He pointed to a large beachscape right in the front.

'Yes it is and all the others are upstairs in the exhibition gallery.' She paused. 'Do you like it?'

'I love it and can't wait to see the rest, come on, let's go in.' Smiling, he stood back to let her go in with Emilia and followed behind. As they entered they were immediately greeted by a smiling Laura.

'Annabel! What a lovely surprise, and Emilia too.' Hugs and kisses were exchanged before Annabel was able to introduce Matt as 'her landlord and friend'. Laura appeared shocked as she shook his hand. Turning to Annabel she said, 'Isn't he the image of the Captain upstairs?'

'Yes, he's the great-nephew of Captain Daniel, the original owner of my cottage. Matt's been in Australia but is coming back to live here soon.'

'Well, it's grand to meet you, Matt, and if you like art you've come to the right place. We always have a great selection on display and Annabel's have been particularly popular.' Turning back to her she said, 'Can you spare a few minutes to chat when you've shown your friend round?' accompanied by an almost imperceptible wink. She nodded and, taking Emilia's hand, led the way upstairs with Matt behind them. As they passed visitors coming down smiles and greetings were exchanged. Annabel guessed they knew she was the artist as her face was plastered all over the posters advertising the exhibition.

As they arrived at the top, Matt whispered, 'What's it feel like to be famous?'

She tutted, waving her arm dismissively.

'Well I think you're famous, Mummy, and I bet these people here think so too. Ooh, I can see more red stickers!' Emilia rushed off to see how many more paintings had sold.

'Well, aren't you going to show me round?' Matt waited, his eyebrows raised.

She led him to the beginning of the display, trying to avoid the inquisitive looks of other visitors and letting him choose the pace.

'Are you interested in art? Or are you simply being polite?'

'I didn't use to be, but over the past few years I've begun visiting galleries and buying an occasional print from local artists.' He studied the painting in front of them, one of her abstract beach scenes saying, 'I recognise Bordeaux and love the figures and how you've created such movement in the scene. You're actually pretty good, aren't you? No wonder your paintings are selling so well.' He turned to smile at her and a warm tingling spread through her body.

'Why, thank you, kind sir. Lavish praise from such an expert as yourself.' She tried to keep a straight face but failed and they both laughed. 'Come on, we're holding up potential buyers here,' she said moving away. They continued their tour with Matt complimenting particular paintings and it gave

Annabel a thrill to see the additional red stickers.

Emilia came back, looking flushed and held her hand, whispering, 'There's not many pictures unsold, Mummy, and I heard people saying how wonderful your paintings are. I wanted to tell them you're my mummy, but thought it might look as if I were boasting, so I didn't.'

'Good girl, it's not nice to boast but it's okay to feel proud of something we've achieved.' They carried on round the room until they had reached the end and Matt drew to a sudden stop.

'Daniel! Well, I'll be damned. It's brilliant, Annabel, and honestly it could be me with a bushier beard. How on earth did you paint…' he stopped, as she shook her head, indicating Emilia.

'I found an old photo of him in the shed but there's also an oil painting his sister commissioned from the photo after he died, so I used them together with some artistic licence.'

'Ah, I see, is that his ship in the background?' She nodded, again indicating her daughter, who, fortunately, was looking bored and edging towards the stairs.

'You go on down, sweetheart, we'll be down in a minute.' Emilia ran off, leaving Annabel to breathe a sigh of relief.

'I'm sorry, I'd forgotten your daughter knew nothing about Daniel. It must be so hard trying to keep such a secret.'

'It is and she doesn't know about the book either, and this picture will be on the cover, though I won't need to explain anything for a while yet. Let's go down, shall we?'

Once downstairs, Matt took charge of Emilia while Annabel sought out Laura.

'Hi, you wanted to chat?'

'Yes,' Laura said, smiling broadly. 'As you probably noticed, there are few paintings not yet sold and with only a week to go, there might be none by the end. So, we need to talk about prints. I've had a couple made from the scanned originals before they were framed for you to see the quality.' She opened a large folder on the desk and took out prints of two of her paintings.

Annabel studied them closely.

'They're brilliant. The colours, tone and depth are spot on. I'd be happy to put my name to them, for sure.'

'Good, so…' she went on to discuss costings, selling prices and print runs so that some prints would be available as soon as the exhibition closed. Annabel had half a dozen new paintings which would be available to show downstairs with other artists' work and she agreed to keep up a steady flow of work as necessary. After finishing the discussion, she was about to leave the office when Laura, giving her a hug, said, 'And whatever you do, hang on to the great-nephew. He's gorgeous – bound to be good for your artistic inspiration!'

Floating on a cloud of positivity, all she could do was grin and went off to find Matt and Emilia.

'You look as if you've won the lottery,' he said.

'In a way I have, with Laura as my agent my artistic career is now flying.'

'Which is great news, but now we have to think about food and this young lady,' he said, pretending to tickle Emilia, 'says she's starving and could we go to Colette's restaurant, please.'

She noted her daughter grinning and how relaxed she was with him, and sighed with relief. 'Yes, let's go there. It's at the Bridge, so not far. Colette's my lovely neighbour who, by the way, befriended your mother and her husband was her doctor.' As they walked to the car she explained how it was through Colette that she met Laura and was offered the exhibition. In less than ten minutes they had parked at the Bridge and were entering the restaurant.

Once seated at a table Matt commented on the menu.

'This takes me back, it looks like traditional local and French dishes, similar to those my mother cooked.'

'There's a story behind it. Jeanne, who's married to Colette's brother, found old recipes in her grandmother's house, a mix of Guernsey and old French and wrote a book which made a bestseller list. Colette, a young chef then, helped Jeanne check out the recipes and was so taken with the results she vowed to open her own restaurant one day and feature the most popular dishes and it's been a great success. And,' she pointed to the walls, 'she offered to display my artwork and will now focus on prints.' She smiled, adding, 'Guernsey connections in action.'

He laughed. 'Love it! And I admire how quickly you've settled back here and formed your own connections. I hope I'll be able to do the same when I'm back permanently.'

Emilia, who had been engrossed in the menu, looked up, saying, 'Don't worry, Matt, as Mummy's so famous I'm sure she'll help you make lots of friends.'

Matt caught Annabel's eye and they both struggled to keep a straight face.

'Thanks, Emilia, I'll make sure to ask her help when I move back. Right, are we ready to order?'

Lunch segued into a trip to the beach at L'Ancresse where they bought a ball from the kiosk to provide some exercise. At one point Annabel took a breather and watched Matt and Emilia kicking the ball around accompanied by much laughter. It warmed her heart to see how much Emilia was at ease with him and how effortlessly he connected with her. He was so different to his great-uncle, much more relaxed and at ease with people, she thought. It occurred to her she had been seeing Matt as a version of Daniel, due to their strong physical similarity. But they were very different characters and she had lots to learn about him before she could commit to a relationship. And it would be the same for him.

Chapter 36

After the trip to the beach Matt drove them back to the cottage and after a little hug from Emilia and a bigger hug from Annabel, he left, saying he would call later. Once they were in the kitchen Annabel poured each of them a glass of water and said, 'Okay, sweetheart, what's the verdict?'

Scrunching up her face Emilia seemed to be giving the question serious attention and for a moment Annabel was worried. Then, with a huge grin, her daughter said, 'I think Matt's super cool, Mummy, and I can tell by the way he looks at you he thinks you're pretty cool, too. So you two should get married.'

Annabel choked on her water. It took a few gasps and coughs before she could answer.

'Hey, not so fast. We've only just met, it takes time to get to know someone properly and then, perhaps, fall in love,' she said, blowing her nose.

Emilia shrugged.

'Grown-ups make such a big fuss about this "being in love" thing. Isn't it more important to be good friends?'

'Most people start off as good friends before they start loving each other, so in a way you're right, sweetheart. But married people do need to love each other to be happy together.' Taking a sip of water she went on, 'For now, I'm just asking if *you* like Matt and if you're okay with me going out with him.'

'Yes, I do like him. Happy now?' She splayed her hands.

Annabel smiled.

'Thank you, yes. Now off you go and watch some television while I concentrate on supper.'

Once Emilia was in bed Annabel phoned Mr Ayres and they agreed for him to come round the following Thursday morning at ten o'clock. With leaden feet and heart she then went upstairs to the studio, calling softly for Daniel.

A few moments later a whoosh of air proclaimed his arrival and he slowly materialised. Seeing her expression he came towards her, saying, 'What's happened? Is Emilia okay?'

Shaking her head, she said, 'My daughter's fine. It's… it's been arranged for Thursday morning. The vicar.' Tears threatened to escape down her cheeks and she hastily brushed them away.

'Ah. I see. D-Day, Daniel's Departure Day.' He twisted his lips. 'It's how I began to think of it once you told me about the vicar. Look, Bella, don't be sad. Think of all the extra years I've had to annoy my family and others.' He managed a chuckle. 'It's well past my departure date and I have no complaints. Between us we wrote a book which will be my legacy so I have much to be thankful for.' He "stroked" her cheeks, saying, 'I will be happy to go now I know you won't be alone.' And with that he disappeared.

Matt took them out for lunch on the following day, Sunday, followed by a trip to Oatlands which, he declared, had been transformed since he left the island. Annabel deliberately pushed him and Emilia to share activities as a test. It appeared to work as by the end of the afternoon anyone observing them would have thought they were father and daughter and she watched them laugh together in a way Emilia hadn't with Clive in the last years of his life. As he dropped them back at the cottage, Matt whispered to her, 'I didn't realise how exhausting it is to be a parent, but it's also a lot of fun.'

'It certainly is. And I think it's fair to say Emilia likes spending time with you, too.' They arranged to meet for coffee only the next day as he had various appointments to attend.

'Moving back is proving more complex than it was to

leave. Paperwork to fill in and officials to meet, I'm beginning to feel like an illegal alien,' he said, laughing.

'Hopefully it'll be worth it.'

'You bet it will,' he replied, winking.

Annabel suggested Matt and Daniel spent time together over the next couple of days giving Daniel a chance to share the family history, but making sure Matt had left by the time Emilia finished school. From what they said, they enjoyed the time together and it made it easier for her to accept Daniel would soon be leaving.

By Wednesday evening Annabel was emotionally torn. Spending time with Matt had been fun and she could see a relationship might work in time. But she now had to face saying goodbye to Daniel who had played such a large part in her life over the last few months. She had come to love him, a ghost, yes, but also so much more. At times he had seemed so real she had momentarily forgotten he was ephemeral, liable to disappear in a second. She had come to know his hopes, his dreams, his regrets as if he still breathed, still lived. His life had been cut cruelly short and yet, not quite. She was in the sitting room, nursing a large glass of wine, knowing she couldn't face Daniel on this, his last night. It seemed to her like the condemned man's last night before execution even though he had already died. And tomorrow would herald, she hoped, a peaceful transition to another world where Daniel would be welcomed by those who had gone before. His mother, sister, niece. Dabbing at her eyes, she raised her glass, whispering, 'To you, Daniel, my lovely friend, may you finally rest in peace.'

The sun was shining through the gap in the curtains as Annabel woke on Thursday, a little groggily after the two glasses of wine she had drunk the night before. Blinking the sleep from her eyes, she slowly pulled back the curtains to a sight which normally made her heart lift with joy. Not today. The sea was sparkling as if covered with a layer of diamonds and was as smooth as glass, a sight to lift any sailor's heart. Except perhaps one. A sailor who would never sail again. She bit her lip, telling herself it was what he wanted and had waited for long enough.

If Emilia noticed she was more subdued than normal, she never said, chatting away on the drive to school and giving her a cheery wave as she went through the gates. Annabel exchanged greetings with other mums on auto-pilot before driving home. She was surprised to see Colette waiting by the front door. Then she remembered she had phoned her the previous night, a little emotional, to tell her about Daniel and the vicar's imminent visit.

'I've just dropped Rosie off at nursery and you sounded so upset last night I thought I'd better check in on you. How're feeling?' Colette gave her a hug, then moved back to look more closely. 'Not great, by the look of you. I've brought cake and strong coffee,' she held up a flask and a tin.

'Thanks, you're a star. Come in.' Going through to the kitchen she collected two mugs and plates and Colette poured the coffee and set out the cake. Annabel swallowed some coffee before saying, 'Thanks, I needed that. Overdid the vino last night.'

'I guessed as much and no wonder. I've never even met your Daniel, but he sounds quite a guy, I mean ghost and I'll miss him on your behalf.' There was silence for a few moments while they ate their cake and then Colette asked, 'How's it going with Matt?'

Annabel perked up a little as she brought her friend up to date with how well they were getting on, including Emilia. 'He's coming later as he wants to be here when, you know, the vicar does his stuff.'

'Oh, Annabel, I do hope it works out for you, he sounds a great guy.' She stood up, swallowed the last of her coffee and said, 'I'll get out of your hair before he or the vicar arrives. Catch up later, okay? And phone if you need to talk.'

Hugging, Annabel said, 'Thanks again for coming round and I promise to phone if I can't cope.'

Cheered by Colette's visit, she tidied up the kitchen and then went to her room to brush her hair and freshen her make-up. She determined to put on her best face, as much for Daniel as for herself. Back downstairs she went into the garden, taking deep lungfuls of fresh air as she walked. The salty air was invigorating and all her senses were on full alert within minutes as she waited for Matt to arrive. She reminded herself he represented a possible future – her future – while Daniel symbolised the past and she would always cherish his memory.

She was near the front gate when Matt arrived and she gave him a wave as he pulled into the drive and she experienced the familiar warm fuzzy feeling as he smiled in return.

'Hi, how're you doing?' he said as they moved towards each other for a hug.

She finally drew away, saying, 'Okay, thanks. Shall we go in? Mr Ayres won't be long, a friend's giving him a lift.' They walked arm in arm into the cottage, unaware of the figure at the attic window.

Chapter 37

They had only been inside a few minutes when they heard a car arrive, a door open and close and then the car leave.

'Good morning, my dear, I'm John Ayres, and you must be Annabel.' An elderly man, with thick white hair, a trim body and a twinkle in his eyes belying his years stood by the door.

'Good morning, please come in.' She led him into the kitchen and introduced him to Matt as Daniel's great-nephew.

'Would you like a tea or coffee, Mr Ayres?'

'No thank you, my dear, perhaps later.' He stood still then moved to the hall and the bottom of the stairs where he appeared to offer a silent prayer. Coming back to the kitchen, he said, 'He died there, I believe,' pointing back to the hall.

'Yes, he did. Would you like me to call him now?'

Mr Ayres smiled, saying, 'No need, he's here already, aren't you, Daniel?'

Annabel watched as the familiar figure began to materialise by the door to the hall and found herself trembling. Matt threw his arm around her, whispering, 'It's okay, I'm here, we're doing this together.' She relaxed into his arms as the trembling eased and saw Daniel smiling at her. She smiled back.

'Ah, Daniel, I'm very pleased to meet you, although not in the best of circumstances, I'm afraid. My name is John Ayres and, with your permission, I will guide you to your rightful place in the kingdom of heaven.'

Daniel bowed. 'I'm pleased to meet you, too, Mr Ayres. I've been too long in this limbo, but are you sure I will go to heaven and not hell? I wasn't always a good Christian, I'm afraid,' he said, rubbing his beard.

'There's no need to worry, Daniel, I have it on, er, good authority that you are awaited in heaven,' Mr Ayres said, smiling broadly. 'Now, are you all ready to say your goodbyes?'

Annabel and Matt moved together towards Daniel and he moved into the room so they were almost touching.

Daniel spoke first.

'I may have only known you for a short time, Bella, but I've come to love and admire you for being a good friend to me in such unusual circumstances,' he said, glancing at Mr Ayres, who nodded, 'and I wish you well in the future and many happy years in this, my home,' he spread his arms out. 'And Matt, I was granted a chance to see you as a child and a grown man and you have my love and best wishes for your future.' His face was filled with sadness as he finished.

Annabel, her eyes moist, cleared her throat before saying, 'I've loved our time together, Daniel, and you'll always have a place in my heart. I owe you so much it's hard to say goodbye, but I must, for your sake. Goodbye and God Bless.' Overcome, she buried her head in Matt's chest.

'Well, Uncle, there's little I can say other than I'm also glad I got the chance to meet you and learn more about you and your life. I wish you peace and a well-earned rest.' Matt's face was solemn.

My Ayres coughed.

'Well said all of you. Now it's time for me to offer the words normally used at a graveside committal, but still appropriate now.' They all bowed their heads as he intoned, 'As Daniel served you faithfully throughout his life, may you give him the fullness of your peace and joy. We give thanks for the life of Daniel, now caught up in your eternal love. We make our prayer in the name of Jesus who is our risen Lord now and forever. Amen.'

Annabel and Matt muttered, 'Amen,' and then looked up.

They watched open-mouthed as Daniel began to spin and was propelled upwards as if caught in a blast of air and then – nothing. He had disappeared.

Mr Ayres made the sign of the cross, mouthing the words, 'God Bless.'

Chapter 38

Once Mr Ayres had left, collected by the friend who had brought him, Annabel and Matt were desperate to get out of the cottage. For Annabel it was as if she had watched a friend die in front of her eyes, helpless to stop it. She had convinced herself it was for the best, especially for Daniel, but… not easy to see. Matt hugged her tight, suggesting they go for a walk on the beach and grab a coffee and she nodded, too numb to speak.

'God that was something else. I don't know what I expected, but there was definitely some powerful energy at work there.' He led her over the road, sat her on a bench and checked she was okay before going to the kiosk for coffee. Annabel hardly registered he'd left before he was back, handing her one of the two large coffees before sitting down. She took a tentative sip, knowing it would be almost scalding.

'Did we do the right thing, Matt? Daniel looked so sad.'

'For sure. Of course he was sad, he loved you. But it must have been a terrible strain all these years and he didn't hesitate at the end, did he? Although I was sad to see the old devil go, I'm glad for him. And what a legacy he's left, eh, his memoir? And all thanks to you,' he said, giving her a hug. They remained lost in their own thoughts sipping at their coffee and staring out to sea. Daniel's sea. Annabel knew she would grieve for some time to come, but she would also hold special memories of her time with him. And, glancing sideways at Matt, she could now face the future with renewed hope and the possibility of love on the island which held her heart.